AF556070

Bloodshed in PUNJAB

Untold Saga of Deceit and Sabotage

Bloodshed in PUNJAB

Untold Saga of Deceit and Sabotage

G.S. Chawla

HAR-ANAND
PUBLICATIONS PVT LTD

Second Edition, 2017

Published by Ashok Gosain and Ashish Gosain for:
HAR-ANAND PUBLICATIONS PVT LTD
E-49/3, Okhla Industrial Area, Phase-II, New Delhi-110020
Tel: 41603490
E-mail: info@haranandbooks.com/haranand@rediffmail.com
Shop online at: www.haranandbooks.com

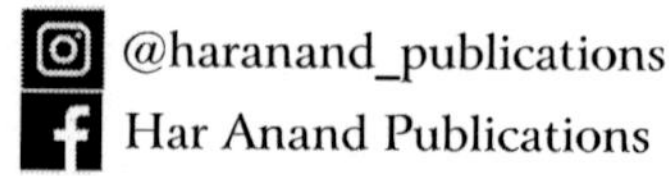
@haranand_publications
Har Anand Publications

Printed in India at Royal Press

Preface

Terrorism is the worst thing happening in the 21st century, which has engulfed most powerful nations of the world today and living has become most insecure. It is not India alone that is the victim of terrorism, though India is the worst sufferer. Most powerful countries like USA, U.K. Russia and France as well as Spain, Iraq, Afghanistan and the breeder of terrorism, Pakistan itself are victims of terrorism. While American CIA and the ISI of Pakistan are mostly responsible for the spread of terrorism and using fundamentalist forces in the world to destroy their enemies and now they themselves are victims of those fundament forces, the ruling powers in other countries are equally responsible for using and encouraging fundamentalist forces for political reasons and ultimately they themselves become victims of these very forces. It is not a secret that CIA of America and Mossad of Israel are the biggest terrorist forces which alone are responsible for the spread of terrorism in Asia and later Americans themselves became victims of those very forces which were created by them. Ruling Politicians never learn any lesson. The fact cannot be denied that CIA with the help of ISI of Pakistan was responsible for creation of "Talibans" to defeat the Soviet Union occupying Afghanistan, and also for the rise of Saudi Terrorist Osama Bin Laden. CIA had wholly funded the Talibans who were trained by the Pakistan Army. The same Talibans and Osama Bin Laden became a terror for Americans and the CIA. Till 2001, when 9/11 terrorist attack took place in New York city, Americans had always ignored India's pleas that Pakistan was the sponsor of terrorism against India. India gave lots of proofs of Pakistan's involvement at official level in cross-border terrorism against India, but every time India sent proof, Americans said it was not enough. It was only after the 9/11 attack that Americans opened their eye. For over 30 years I have been writing that CIA was the biggest terrorist group in the world that trains and sponsors terrorism against other countries. It is only after 9/11 that the CIA stopped sponsoring terrorism against other countries including India. CIA was more responsible than even the ISI for the spread of terrorism.

In India, Congress leadership sponsored and encouraged fundamentalists like Sant Jarnail Singh Bhindranwale and laid the foundation for unrest in the country which CIA and Pakistan's ISI fully exploited resulting in the unfortunate assassination of Indira Gandhi herself at the hands of fundamentalist forces. Rajiv Gandhi was assassinated by the LTTE, as he wanted to stop aid to it the LTTE, terrorist organisation. The Congress has been propping up Bal Thakre's nephew Raj Thakre who has set up a parallel organisation to the Shiv Sena, and is no different from what Jarnail Singh Bhindranwale was doing in Punjab. In Pakistan, the ISI sponsored Jehadi organisations like Lashkre-Toiba, Talibans, Jaishe Mohammad, Harkut-ul-Jehade Islami, Hizbul Mujahideen, Jamait-e-Islami, etc. were the creation of the ISI, which were used by the ISI not only against other countries, especially India but against its own politicians also. Benazir Bhutto was the victim of ISI sponsored terrorism, and as the UN report disclosed then Military Ruler of Pakistan, Musharraf neither provided her full security despite reports of threat to her life nor had thorough investigations into her assassination. Today, the entire world has become insecure and unsafe because of terrorism, for which CIA and ISI are the main culprits. But they will never learn any lesson. India has been a victim of both CIA and ISI plans for over 40 years and both of them have been jointly working to destablise this country. The CIA was as active against India as the ISI till 9/11 in 2001, and it stopped supporting terrorist groups only after the Americans had a taste of terrorism in the 9/11 attack. But Pakistan's ISI further intensified its proxy war against India after 9/11, and encouraged and sponsored terrorist groups in Pakistan for cross-border terrorism against India. For forty years, CIA and Pakistan, both have been trying, to bring unrest in India and they have been concentrating on fundamentalist forces in India for this purpose. In fact, when Reagan Administration came to power in USA in 1981, Indira Gandhi received reports about the CIA's enhanced interests in India to destablise it. Both ISI and the CIA shifted their concentration from Jammu and Kashmir to Punjab where they had planned to use hard-liner Sikhs to raise the slogan of "Khalistan". This is the same strategy, which earlier Pakistan Army Ruler Ayub Khan had tried to use and one of his Minister, Manzoor Qadir was deputed to cultivate with Sikh groups. Later, this task was taken over by Zahoor Illahi, whom Zia ul Haq had entrusted this task. Their thinking was that if they succeed in organising groups of Sikhs by supporting them with financial help and arms to revolt against the Indian establishment, this will weaken India to a great extent as this will have a bearing on the psyche of Sikh soldiers in the army.

The propping up of Sant Jarnail Singh Bhindranwale against the akalis by the Congress leadership, Giani Zail Singh with the approval of Sanjay Gandhi and also setting up of organisations like Dal Khalsa, had given good opportunities to the CIA and ISI to meddle in this situation and take full advantage, which they did. The Congress leadership fell in this trap and ultimately the situation went out of their control. It was a beginning of a new chapter in the history of Punjab which took the state through a terrible period for over two decades. This is the saddest period of the state and the country also.

Many strategic experts have come to the conclusion that even the dreaded terrorist organisation ISIS is the creation of CIA and some European countries to bring unrest in the Middle East and create Sunni-Shia wedge much more deeper, to keep the Middle-East countries fighting among themselves. Even arms and ammunition are supplied to the ISIS by some Western countries as the ISIS has no arms and ammunition factories of its own.

Americans and its CIA have always their own interests in view and they always plan their strategies keeping their own interests in view. Indian leadership may be thinking of having close relations with the USA administration but Americans will always give priority to their own interests than any other country. Americans know how to use Indian leadership whether it is the UPA Government or the BJP-led NDA government; both play into their hands. In fact, after the assassinations first of Indira Gandhi in 1984 and later of Rajiv Gandhi in 1991, no Indian leader is prepared to confront Americans on any issue. From their hearts, they know the capacity of the CIA-Mossad and the American leadership. I have been of definite view that although Indira Gandhi was assassinated by her two Sikh body-guards, and Rajiv Gandhi was assassinated by the LTTE, no Government in India has deeply gone into the motivating spirit of the Assassins. The fact remains, both Indira Gandhi and Rajiv Gandhi had apprehensions of American-CIA plans. Americans had never liked Indira Gandhi, in fact, the entire Gandhi family, and American thinking on Indira Gandhi was visible from the Nixon-Henry Kissinger plans during the 1971 Indo-Pak war, and from the declassified documents of Kissinger-Chou-En lie talks in Bejing, after 10 July 1971, on the Indo-Pak situation, during which Kissinger had told Chou-En lie that: "We are totally opposed to Indian military action against Pakistan. I do not normally see Ambassadors, but I have warned the Indian Ambassador on behalf of the President that if there was an attack by India, we will cut off all economic aid to India. We have told Russians of our view." These declassified documents are an eye-opener, giving definite indication of its slant against India. Indira Gandhi had always suspected Americans' intentions. Rajiv Gandhi had, just a few hours before his assassination, expressed his views and suspicion on CIA plans, in an interview to a foreign lady journalists of *New York Times* travelling with him in his plane.

Barbara Crossette's report in the *New York Times* was revealing. Barbara Crossettee and Mrs Neena Gopal had travelled with Rajiv Gandhi in the same plane and this interview was taken just one or two hours before his assassination. In 2008, the Foreign Correspondents Association in India had celebrated its Golden Jubilee, and a book containing selected writings of foreign correspondents who in the past have been writing from India, and Barbara Crossette's report was a part of the book, released at that time.

Rajiv Gandhi's interview with the two correspondents is very revealing on many issues including Pakistan. When he was asked about how he thought he would get along with Pakistan's new Prime Minister, Nawaz Sharief, who is pushing through economic liberalisation policies that Indian politicians including the Congress party talk about but never put into practice, Gandhi said he had never met Sharief and could not judge what kind of relationship they would have. “But I know who could have solved these problems with us” he said, “Gen. Zia. We were close to finishing agreement on Kashmir, we had the maps and everything ready to sign. And then he was killed.” The article stated that as Prime Minister from 1984 to 1989, Gandhi had a good working relationship with President Mohammad Zia Ul-Haq, who died in an unexplained plane crash in August 1988.

Barbara Crossette’s report discloses: “Gandhi said there was evidence that General Zia had been murdered, but he would not say more. Neena Gopal asked him if he did not think that some outside power had decided to upset the development of better relations with Pakistan. He said he thought that was likely. She asked whether India and Indian leaders might not be targets as India took a larger role in the region. He agreed. He said that danger would not come from the Soviet Union, however, which was too busy with its own problems.

“Are you talking of the CIA again?” Barbara Crossette asked him. Prime Minister Indira Gandhi, his mother, used to say that she feared the American intelligence agency would kill her one day, an apprehension dismissed as paranoia by all but Soviet diplomats in New Delhi,” Gandhi smirked.

Barbara Crossette wrote that in the end, Mrs Gandhi was shot in 1984 by Sikh body guards, four months after she sent troops into the Sikhs’ Holiest shrine, the Golden Temple in Amritsar. Now her son, who had many enemies among disaffected Indians, not the least separatist groups, has followed her into martyrdom, and no one may ever know who was to blame for the crime. In that blinding second of his death, he was walking towards a sea of people, a picture uncannily reminiscent of Mohandas K. Gandhi's last stroll in the garden in New Delhi moments before he was struck by a Hindu fanatic."

But, unfortunately, no Government in India, has gone deep into the conspiracies and causes of the assassinations of both Indira Gandhi and Rajiv Gandhi. Rajiv Gandhi himself had apprehensions about American intentions and a few weeks before his assassination, had told me personally that "We will be able to form the next Government after the Elections, but Americans will not allow it to run." On the basis of my talk with Rajiv Gandhi. I had published a report, "Will the US allow Congress to survive". It was published in the *Pioneer* Lucknow dated 1 May 1991, just 20 days before his assassination, and the same report in the *Lokmat Times* dated, 3 May 1991, under the caption: "Renewing ties with US task for Cong." I had published another report in the *Pioneer,* Lucknow dated 17 May 1991, under the caption: "Rajiv flays US presence in Bangla." Rajiv Gandhi was very friendly with me and he used to talk to me very frankly. He had full trust in me. It was in this background that I published another report in the *Pioneer,* Lucknow dated 30 May 1991, just 9 days after his assassination, under the caption: "Hidden hand" may never be known. In this report, I had said: "The Congress (I) leaders, in general, straightaway talk of CIA's involvement in the conspiracy for the meticulously planned brutal assassination. The same view is shared by some Janta Dal and left parties' leaders. Whichever agency, group or individual is responsible for the killing it has a powerful backing, is the general view.

Politicians talk about the hidden hand but in hushed voices, even the left leaders talk about it ruling out nothing, indicating a scare: Who may be the next target. "This is only one para from that report but there were other factors also mentioned in the report.

The object of writing all this is to show that the CIA-Mossad were the sponsors of terrorism in the world, at different times in different areas where they had deep interests. There was no doubt that the Americans were totally aligned with Pakistan right from its inception and were hell-bent on destablising India. Even the start of militancy in Punjab was the brain-child of the CIA and the Americans were propping up hard-core Sikh ultras settled in USA and Canada and the CIA had played a major role in the rise of militancy in Punjab. Whatever the Indian leaders may be proclaiming, the fact remains that they were all scared of the CIA, whether it was V.P. Singh, Narsimha Rao, or AB Vajpayee. None of them was prepared to take any step that could annoy Americans. They were prepared to go to any extent. Even Manmohan Singh and Narendra Modi followed in their footsteps. The UPA Government was in power for 10 years but nothing concrete was done to go into the conspiracy part of the Rajiv Gandhi's assassination. Even Indians suspected of conspiring were not touched. This is the CIA fear, and nothing else.

A few weeks before the assassination of Rajiv Gandhi, his private secretary, V. George, rang me up one evening around 10 PM conveying that Rajiv Gandhi will have dinner at my place two days later. He said Rajivji has expressed desire that before he starts election tour of U.P., he would like to visit my house for dinner. When I told George that it was too short a notice, he said I should not postpone it as all his engagements had been filled. Next morning George asked me if he could put in the computer as a "Press dinner," I said no. I said you can put it as a private dinner, as there will be no press, no politician and no businessman; there will be some intellectuals only. For the dinner, I invited two Vice-Chancellors, VC of Gurunanak Dev University, Amritsar, Dr. G.S. Randhawa and Zahoor Qasim VC of Jamia Milia, along with their wives, Justice Kuldip Singh and his wife, Dr. S.K. Kackar, who was then Director of the AIIMS, IJS Chhatwal, former Indian High Commissioner to Canada and Dr. L.S. Chawla, from Punjab. I had also invited Jetinder Prasad and his wife, Kanta Prasad, to look after Sonia Gandhi. It was at this dinner that Rajiv Gandhi took me aside and told me: "Do you know there is a dinner today for Adnan Khashoggi, a Saudi billionaire, an arms dealer, who was working for the CIA and Mossad, at the residence of Dr. J.K. Jain, a BJP leader, close to Chander Shekhar and Chandraswamy and he said J.K. Jain had tried his best to persuade him to attend the dinner even for a short-while. But Rajiv Gandhi, as he told me, explained to him that for him G.S. Chawla's dinner was more important, which he cannot cancel. So, he refused to go there.

Khashoggi was in town for a few days. It was Chandra Shekhar's regime, and Chandraswamy, a very close friend of Khashoggi, was running around looking after Khashoggi. It is evident from Rajiv Gandhi's refusal to accept invitation to attend dinner for Khashoggi that he did not want to be in their company and he had a lot of apprehensions.

A former Mossad Agent, Victor Ostrovsky and Claire Hoy, in their book *By Way of Deception,* a devastating insider's portrait of Mossad, have given some details about Khashoggi working for Mossad and how the Mossad had been using him.

There are a lot of details about it in this book including the details how the Mossad has been training the LTTE including the names of trainers and the places where they were trained. Only a few weeks later, the gruesom assassination of Rajiv Gandhi throws a lot of light on the forces behind the assassination. Unfortunately, that no Government has tried to go deep into the conspiracy aspect, may be because of the fear of the biggest terrorist organisations working behind the scenes.

The Country is facing a serious terrorist threat from the terrorist sponsored, trained and financed by the ISI of Pakistan, not now but earlier helped by the CIA also. But Punjab has been relatively quiet for almost two decades. After a lull of a long period, the fundamentalist forces are once again raising their heads and the situation in Punjab is going out of hand day by day and there is a serious apprehension that if not handled adequately, the developments of early 1980s may once again surface; and now it will be very difficult to control. Unfortunately, our ruling politicians and even in the opposition are not thinking on these lines and they are always trying to use the situation and not to solve it, whether it is the Congress party or the Akali leadership. Both belong to the same category and always give preference to their electoral gains rather than national interests. When Amrinder Singh was Chief Minister of Punjab, from 2002 to 2007, he did establish some contacts with some Sikh hard-liners and accommodated them. In 2004, when the Manmohan Singh Government was formed at the Centre, the Congress top leadership at one point of time did think of replacing Amrinder Singh. Amrinder Singh's move to have a resolution from the Punjab Assembly to annul the canal agreement with Haryana and Rajasthan, was his master stroke to save himself as it was a clever move to please the Sikh hard-liners and show them he was following their policy as they were opposed to this water agreement. This had shaken the Central leadership of the Congress, which got worried that if Amrinder Singh was removed, he will become a hero in the eyes of Sikh hard-liners and he was capable of going closer to them. He had already established his sympathies with them by resigning from Lok Sabha in 1984, as protest against the Operation Blue Star, and later joining the Akali Dal and taking oath at the Akal Takhat on 1 May 1994, along with Akali Dal (A) President, Simranjit Singh Mann, Surjit Singh Barnala, Jathedar Jagdev Singh Talwandi and G.S. Tohra, then President of the SGPC, known as "Amritsar Declaration" pledging to work for the creation of a separate Punjabi speaking state where they could enjoy the warmth of independence. In 2015, when the BJP was openly talking of distancing away from the Coalition with Akalis in Punjab, the Chief Minister, Punjab, Parkash Singh Badal, had started cultivating with hard-liners to give them the impression that he was with them. He started writing letters to the Union Home Ministry for transfer of Sikh militant prisoners lodged in jails outside Punjab, on charges of anti-national activities and other serious cases, although they were convicted by courts. Home Ministry did agree on transfer of some but later, on protests from their Punjab unit, they started having second thoughts on this issue. Punjab BJP had made public statements opposing such moves. While the Congress and Akalis have their own agenda, the RSS did not lag behind as it started concentrating on establishing its *shakhas* in rural areas which created doubts in the minds of a large section of Sikhs in Punjab. During the Vajpayee Government, VHP top leadership had tried to create communal tensions between the two communities in the state by declaring that Sikhs were a part of Hindus. When the VHP top leader created this controversy, L.K. Advani enhanced this VHP leader's personal security giving him Z-Plus security. The Akalis were fully aware of the BJP plans to withdraw from the coalition and fight the next Assembly elections independently. But after the BJP's humiliating defeat in Bihar, the BJP cannot afford to leave the coalition with the Akalis. Pakistan's ISI is trying hard to revive the militancy in Punjab and the ISI is pressurising those militants hold-up in Lahore for this purpose. The ISI did try a few years earlier also but could not succeed. Now this is a renewed attempt with much bigger zeal and plans. After Indira Gandhi's assassination, Pakistan's ISI has become emboldened. Both CIA and the ISI had feared Indira Gandhi. Indira Gandhi had given a free hand to the security agencies, and the Defence and Intelligence agencies to deal with the situation firmly with iron hand. If the ISI used to sponsor some terror act, somewhere in India, especially in Punjab, Delhi or its neighbourhood, its reply used to be given within an hour or two, either in Lahore or Karachi or some other important place that had given shivers to General Zia. Even Narsimha Rao was firmer on this than all the Prime Ministers who followed him. The situation became vulnerable from the period of I.K. Gujral who ordered the intelligence agencies to keep off Pakistan. He had his own diplomacy with Pakistan. When A.B. Vajpayee visited Lahore in a bus in April 1999, on his return to India he also asked the Intelligence agencies to keep off Pakistan. During the Vajpayee's regime, maximum and most serious terrorist attacks took place in India, sponsored by the ISI, which included an attack on the Badami Bagh Cantonment in Srinagar on 20 April 2000, Kargil War in 1999 itself, Red Fort attack on 22 December 2000, an attack on Indian Parliament on 13 December 2001, Akshay Dham Temple in Gujrat, on 25 September 2002, attack on Kashmir Assembly, attack on Jammu Cantt residential area, and an attack on a Temple in Jammu. All this happened during the tenure of Vajpayee. Army was alerted on the border with Pakitan for 10 months. But it had no effect and this created an impression in Pakistan that "these dhotiwalas cannot fight," and the ISI further intensified its activities against India. When Manmohan Singh on his first visit to Srinagar, after becoming the Prime Minister announced there itself of "zero tolerance on human rights violations," and followed the Policy of Vajpayee directing the intelligence agencies to keep off Pakistan. In fact, after the two assassinations, first of Indira Gandhi and later of Rajiv Gandhi, every Prime Minister was scared of the CIA as they had seen the fate of two leaders and nobody was prepared to give a free hand either to the armed forces or the intelligence agencies to deal with Pakistan and they all had been looking towards Americans for "guidance." The Narendra Modi Government had given some freedom to the security agencies, but he is equally close to Americans. Americans always watch their own interests vis-á-vis Pakistan and India and despite knowing that all the arms they were supplying to Pakistan and the financial help they were doling out to that country, were being used against India, they have not done anything to stop it. India has repeatedly taken up this matter with the Americans but they did nothing except showing verbal sympathy. Indian leadership will have to understand this. It is doubtful if the present Indian leadership can take any step independent of Americans.

The latest developments in Punjab are a dangerous indication of revival of militancy in Punjab. Neither Congress nor the Akalis will realise this. At the Centre, provocative statements of the BJP's fringe elements and tacit silence of top BJP leadership and the Prime Minister Narendra Modi, are equally very disturbing, which the present ruling class may not be able to visualise. All these are dangerous trends that will lead to serious apprehensions for the future of the country.

Another very serious matter for the country is spread of drugs i n the border state of Punjab. A majority of younger generation has become drug addict. Smuggling of drugs from Pakistan and Afghanistan is through borders of Punjab, Jammu and Kashmir and Rajasthan. Neither the Central Government nor the State government is fighting this menace with all the seriousness it deserves. The 1965 war with Pakistan was not only fought by the Armed forces but by the people of Punjab also, who stood like one person with the armed forces and gave all the assistance the forces needed. In the future wars with Pakistan, Punjab will not be able to give as much support to the armed forces as it gave in 1965. This will be a very big achievement of the ISI. The politicians ruling Punjab and at the Centre are not realising this. This could not have happened without nexus between politicians, smugglers and some security agencies.

Since I had been extensively writing on terrorism, especially from its inception in Punjab, I am writing this book on the suggestions of some good friends who knew how much deep I was in touch with all these developments for almost four decades. Hence this book.

Contents

I

Agreement Sabotaged

Although the developments in Punjab that ultimately led to the *Operation Blue Star* in June 1984 followed by a spurt in terrorism that engulfed Punjab for over a decade, date back to over four decades of political fight between Akalis and the Congress, I would like to begin from an event that has almost been forgotten by both Akalis and the Congress that took place in 1982 and the top congress leadership feels embarrassed to talk about it, and I am personally certain that if the leadership at the centre had not backed out on the understanding with the Akalis to avert any major confrontation, the history of Punjab and the country would have been altogether different. There was every possibility of the Central Government averting any extreme step of *Operation Blue Star*, and the country still would have the benefit of having a leader like Indira Gandhi. This is a tragic story of how the top leaders of the country become victims of the surroundings around them, who, for their own beliefs and political interests, succeed in misguiding and misleading those leaders, putting the security and integrity of the country in danger. This is exactly what happened with Indira Gandhi and later Rajiv Gandhi. Even Sonia Gandhi does not seem to have learnt any lesson from the history. I must say with full emphasis on my command that Indira Gandhi was never anti-Sikh or even anti-Akali. She was a genuine secular leader who respected the Sikh community from her heart.

Same was the case with Rajiv Gandhi. But both were surrounded by such elements that could influence their thinking that these elements could succeed in feeding their minds, in a way, with reports from different corners that these leaders could become victims of these conspirators, whom they trusted immensely.

BHINDRANWALE'S IRON-HANDEDNESS

Without going further on the people who surrounded Indira Gandhi and Rajiv Gandhi, about which I will deal at a later stage, I would come to the point of the event that I am referring to. In 1982, when the situation in Punjab was going out of control, Akali leaders were all in different jails and Jarnail Singh Bhindranwale, who was the creation of the Congress leadership, had become law unto himself. Indira Gandhi decided to involve Sardar Swaran Singh, a highly respected Punjab leader known for his acumen for negotiations—the man who could talk to Z.A. Bhutto for seven rounds of talks on Kashmir in 1963 after Chinese aggression without giving out anything; to talk to Akalis for some settlement on their demands. She was going abroad but she was so worried on Punjab developments that she involved Sardar Swaran Singh to undertake the task of talking to Akalis immediately.

THE AKALI LEADERS

Akali leaders were in different jails—Parkash Singh Badal in Ludhiana jail, Gurcharan Singh Tohra, some others in the Ferozepur jail and some others in some other jails. He used to undertake his meetings with Akali leaders in the jails only around midnight. He had succeeded in bringing them round for talks with the centre. The Akali leaders were released, but there was no progress in the negotiations for any settlement. The Akalis were already carrying on their *Dharam Yudh* morcha from the Golden Temple complex, which had been hijacked by Jarnail Singh Bhindranwale, who had shifted the centre of his activities to the Golden Temple Complex. The Akalis had announced that they would announce their next programme to intensify the agitation on 4 November 1982. Sardar Swaran Singh was pleading with the Central leaders, the Cabinet Committee appointed by Indira Gandhi on Punjab, to somehow avert a situation in which the Akalis announce their next programme. His plea was that according to Sikh traditions, a programme once announced from a Gurdwara stage, will not be withdrawn and Sikhs would go all out to fulfill that vow. Therefore, somehow the Akalis should be persuaded to postpone that announcement but they would have to be given some excuse for that purpose. He had also succeeded in persuading the Akalis not to be very rigid and if there was an opportunity given to them by the Government for that purpose, they should respond positively. On the afternoon of 3 November 1982, the Cabinet Committee on Punjab met in Parliament House, which was also attended by Sardar Swaran Singh, Dr. P. C. Alexander, the then Principal Secretary to Indira Gandhi, who was deeply involved in the negotiations, and P.P. Nayyar, Special Secretary in the Home Ministry who was dealing with Punjab. The Akalis were sitting in the SGPC office in Amritsar. Sardar Swaran Singh was negotiating between the Cabinet Committee and the Akali leaders on the phone. Sardar Swaran Singh had convinced the Akalis that what Bhindranwale was doing, was not in the interest of Sikhs and it was harming the Sikhs. The Akalis agreed to postpone their announcement provided they were given a way out. Sardar Swaran Singh and the Cabinet Committee drafted a statement to be made next morning by the Home Minister, which was approved by the Akalis and they reached an understanding that after this statement was made in Parliament, the Akalis would announce postponement of any further agitation. Everybody, Cabinet Committee, Sardar Swaran Singh and the Akalis felt satisfied over the statement. It was a brief statement in which the Government had stated that the Akali demands were in three categories—religious, political and economic demands. As far as religious demands were concerned, the Government was prepared to accept them. But for political demands, the Government would have to consult some other states also, which were involved in the dispute, like river waters distribution and the issue of Chandigarh, for which the Government would need some time. The Government, according to the draft, appealed to the Akalis not to announce any programme for their agitation and wait for the Government to complete talks with other states also. In the second paragraph of the draft, the Government had praised the role played by the Sikhs in the freedom struggle and in the country as a whole. The meeting was over by about 5.00 p.m. Around 6.00 p.m. I went to the Home Ministry to meet P. P. Nayyar. When I entered his room, he was dictating something to his P. A. and with a smile on his face, indicated me to occupy a seat on the sofa set that was at a distance of about 15 feet. As soon as he finished his dictation, he asked his P. A. to type out both the letters immediately and bring the letters to him. He also indicated me to come and occupy a chair near his office table. I congratulated P. P. Nayyar for the understanding reached with the Akalis. Those days I was working with the *Indian Express.* He sought a promise that I would not publish anything on this. I told him that I would not use this story unless he gave me a clearance. He sent away his driver and told me that I should drop him at his Lodhi Estate House. Those days I was living close to Lodhi Estate in Shahjahan Road government flats. His P. A. typed out the letters in 10 minutes and brought to him those letters. This was a letter from the Home Minister to the Speaker of the Lok Sabha that he would like to make the enclosed statement in the Lok Sabha next day on 4 November. I read the letter and the copy of the statement attached. He asked his P.A. to take the letter to Home Minister's residence for his signatures and then get it delivered to the Speaker. A copy of the letter and the statement was sent to the Prime Minister for her information. When we reached P.P. Nayyar's residence, I pleaded with him that as a fried why was he ruining my best story of the year. I told him that there were other Ministers also present. Moreover, it could be leaked out by the Akalis also from Amritsar. He agreed on my writing that story provided I spoke to one of the Cabinet ministers. I told him that I would speak to Sardar Swaran Singh before I wrote the story. I reached my house and immediately contacted Sardar Swaran Singh and congratulated him on the success he had achieved. He confirmed everything I had already seen and I immediately informed P.P. Nayyar that I had spoken to Sardar Swaran Singh and he had confirmed everything. Nayyar was happy to hear this and said now I could go ahead with my report.

BITTERNESS BETWEEN THE GOVERNMENT AND AKALIS

I wrote a report on the understanding reached between the Centre and Akalis, which appeared as a front-page lead story in Indian Express on 4 November (photocopy of report) I went to Parliament on 4 November and after the question hour; I was waiting for the Home Minister, P.C. Sethi to make his statement sardar Swaran Singh was sitting in the lobby to hear that statement. After the question hour when P.C. Sethi, the then Home Minister, made a statement, it was a different statement that I had read the previous evening. I was surprised over it. After the Home Minister finished reading his statement, I went to the Central Hall of the Parliament to meet Sardar Swaran Singh. He was equally shocked. I asked him, "Sardar Sahib, why, this change in Government's stance?" He was very disappointed and told me that I could quote him. He said, "This is neither the same statement nor the same spirit." He further said, "Now I am going to withdraw from the negotiations." That was the end of the task he had undertaken. The Akalis who were waiting for the Home Minister's statement felt betrayed and announced the boycott of the Asian games that were to start two weeks later, on 19 November 1982. It was this boycott that created more bitterness between the Government and the Akalis as every Sikh, whether he was a senior army officer or a police officer or a High Court judge, coming to Delhi was stopped and humiliated by the Haryana Police under instructions from the then Chief Minister Bhajan Lal.

A few days later, P. P. Nayyar met me and I asked him about the change in the statement. First he avoided talking about it. But later on, on an assurance that I would not use it in my report in the *Indian Express* he told me that the statement was changed by the Prime Minister herself at 11.00 p.m. and a new draft was sent to the Speaker. This was the most unfortunate event that changed the course of events and resulted in worsening the situation in Punjab, which ultimately resulted in the *Operation Blue Star* and assassination of Indira Gandhi by her own two Sikh security men.

Indira Gandhi, after the sudden death of her son Sanjay Gandhi, though Rajiv Gandhi had joined politics, had started feeling insecure. Sanjay was a different class and was her right arm. It was because of her this mental state of affairs that people around her like Arun Nehru and a few others had started taking advantage of the situation and misleading her according to their own plans. Arun led a group of those immediate around her, like M.L. Fotedar, P. Shiv Shankar, the then Law Minister, P.K. Kaul, the then Cabinet Secretary and Gopi Arora, the then Joint Secretary in the PMO, all hard-liners on Punjab, and they would use Rajiv Gandhi, who had only lately joined politics, to convince Indira Gandhi on their own plans. On Punjab, it was this group, which had overpowered the thoughts of Indira Gandhi. This group was a great supporter of the then Haryana Chief Minister, Bhajan Lal, who was a great villain in the whole episode. Haryana Assembly elections were due in another few months and this group had impressed upon Indira Gandhi that the statement prepared by the Cabinet Committee with the help of Sardar Swaran Singh would amount to surrender before Akalis and the congress would lose Haryana elections. Another leader who had done great harm to the Punjab cause because of his personal ambitions and his old rivallary with Sardar Swaran Singh and Darbara Singh was Giani Zail Singh, who had become President of the country but he never lost interest in Punjab politics. Three persons—Giani Zail Singh, Jarnail Singh Bhindranwale and Balwant Singh, Akali leader—have done immense damage to Punjab and in particular to the Sikh cause. Giani Zail Singh himself spoke to Indira Gandhi and convinced her that for any settlement with the Akalis, Rajiv Gandhi should be involved in the talks and credit should go to him and not to Sardar Swaran Singh. He was using Captain Amrnder Singh of

Patiala scion and Ravi Inder Singh also to convince Indira Gandhi that any credit for the settlement should go to Rajiv Gandhi and not to Swaran Singh. The two separate lobbies working against any settlement, had forced Indira Gandhi to back out from the understand ding arrived at with Akalis during the day that changed the whole situation and ultimately led the country to the path of destruction. I have gone through the narration of events described by Dr. P.C. Alexander, the then Principal Secretary to Indira Gandhi, who was deeply involved in the talks with Akalis and later decisions of Indira Gandhi, in his book. But I am surprised that Dr. Alexander had not mentioned even a word on the role played by Sardar Swaran Singh, how Indira Gandhi had involved him through the Cabinet Secretary and how the Government backed out at the last minute on the understanding. What Dr. Alexander has written on Punjab is a completely biased version of the events and not honest version. B.G. Deshmukh, a former Cabinet Secretary has also written a chapter on Punjab in his book and this is more accurate, based on facts unlike Dr. Alexander's totally biased narration. Dr. P.C. Alexander may have been a good administrator but he did not understand the Punjab situation at all. He has nowhere even hinted that Jarnail Singh Bhindranwale was the creation of the Congress leadership about which I will be writing in another chapter, whereas B.G. Deshmukh has given enough hints about it.

AMRINDER SINGH'S ROLE IN PUNJAB

After the 4 November statement of the Home Minister in Parliament and the Government backing out on the understanding reached with Akalis, future rounds of talks between the Akalis and the Government, were held not through Sardar Swaran Singh but Amrinder Singh and Ravi Inder Singh emerged as new mediators. For the next rounds of talks, Rajiv Gandhi was involved and not the Cabinet Committee. Amrinder Singh and Ravi Inder Singh were very close to Arun Nehru also. In fact, Amrinder Singh has been very close to Arun Nehru, more than Rajiv Gandhi and Rajiv Gandhi realized this only much later when he fell out with Arun Nehru. Giani Zail Singh was keen that Amrinder Singh should replace Darbara Singh as Punjab Chief Minister and for this purpose; Giani Zail Singh was building up Amrinder Singh. Amrinder Singh's role in the Punjab developments has been questionable and after the Patiala incident in which a sacrilegious act took place in a temple, in which one person supposed to be President of the Hindu Swaraksha Samiti, was involved. The name of Amrinder Singh had figured prominently for cropping up the Hindu Swaraksha Samiti leader, one young man known as Pawan Kumar Sharma. There was a debate in Parliament for about 45 minutes in which this incident figured prominently. The debate was initiated by Dr. Subramanian Swamy. Punjab Congress MPs. had objected to the mention of this. Darbara Singh, the then Chief Minister had got Prem Gupta, the then P.A. to Amrinder Singh arrested. He had sent a taped version of Gupta to Indira Gandhi in which the name of Amrinder Singh had figured. Seema Mustafa, then working for the Telegraph, Calcutta had visited Patiala and interviewed the mother of Pawan Kumar Sharma, who said that she did not understand why the Maharaja Patiala, Amrinder Singh was spoiling her son. She had also stated that Amrinder Singh's car used to pick up Pawan Kumar Sharma. These only show that Giani Zail Singh and Amrinder Singh could go to any extent to get Darbara Singh removed as Chief

Minister. The sabotage of the understanding arrived at with the Akali leaders on 3 November 1982 by the Cabinet Committee with the active help of Sardar Swaran Singh was under these circumstances. The debate in Parliament was held on 9 May 1983 regarding an incident that occurred in Patiala. Indira Gandhi did not have a very high opinion about her own Home Minister and she had told Chanderjit Yadav, a senior leader, a day earlier about her ministers on which I had published a report in the *Indian Express.* Subramanian Swamy while initiating the debate quoting my report wanted the Prime Minister herself to be present in the House during the debate. He said, "I would like to begin with a point of propriety. The Prime Minister, in my opinion, should be present during this discussion because according to the *Indian Express* of the 7 May 1983, carrying a report by Shri G.S. Chawla, who is one of the perceptive journalists, he says that Mrs Gandhi reportedly feels that members of the Cabinet Committee do not have a grip of the situation and their approach is rather narrow. This was amply indicated by her remark to recent suggestion by a leader to Mrs Gandhi that her Home Minister had suggested a division of Chandigarh. She reportedly said, "They do not know anything. Their vision is very narrow."

He said, "If the Cabinet Ministers are a bunch of nincompoops, then it is just necessary that the Prime Minister should be present while this discussion takes place because the Punjab issue is much too serious matter for people who do not know anything, and who have a narrow vision. The Prime Minister should come and say that this is a wrong report."

On the situation in Punjab, he said, "The Government blame the Akalis for what is happening in Punjab," He further said, "The Sikh extremism has been fanned by the Congress (I) leaders. Do you want proof for that? Dal Khalsa, which is charged with Sikh extremism, was founded in the Congress Bhavan in Chandigarh. People like Shri Jagjit Singh Chauhan and Ganga Singh Dhillon who are supposed to be extremists, have met prominent congressmen in 1980. I do not want to name them but if you want I will do it. They cannot deny it. When Shri Jagjit Singh Chauhan visited Delhi in 1980, whom did he meet?"

Dr. Swamy further said, "The issue of Sikh extremism is associated with Bhindranwale. He was given prominence by them on a number of occasions. When he came to Delhi, loaded with armed men, he was received almost like a state guest and they dare not touch him. An impression has been created that there are two states in Punjab, one Bhindranwale state and the other state of Punjab. There are two laws in the country, one for Bhindranwale and one for the rest. I would not blame Bhindranwale under these circumstances. If you build up his ego in this way, he is likely to lose his balance and if he goes to extremism, it is you who encouraged him."

Swamy added, "Similarly, they (Congressmen) have made it almost impossible for Sikh moderates to operate. The moderate elements in Sikhs are under pressure. They do things, which make it easy for the Sikh extremists to gather control of the Sikh community. During the ASIAD, Bhajan Lal announced that he would not allow any Sikh to go to ASIAD and at the checkpoints every Sikh was considered to be an Akali, he was stopped. In many places trucks were confiscated. There was a great deal of harassment of every Sikh."

INDIRA GANDHI'S DIVERSION FROM SECULARISM

About the talks with Akalis, Dr. Swamy said, "After all, it is an attempt at defaming Akalis. They have repeatedly expressed their desire to negotiate. In April 1982, they closed the negotiations. Then the Haryana elections were there. They put it off. Then in November, there was a Cabinet Sub-Committee set up. They were very close to negotiation. In fact, the tripartite talks revealed how narrow the differences were and a common statement was prepared in the room of Dr. Alaxender and after that, suddenly a PAC meeting was called and the whole thing was put off. (This is exactly what I have mentioned that if the Government had not backed out on 3 November 1982, from the understanding reached with Akalis through Sardar Swaran Singh, the situation would have been completely different,) There might not have been the need for the Operation Blue Star and possibly, India would not have lost a leader like Indira Gandhi, which was a greater loss for the country than the Congress party. But unfortunately, the Hindutava forces had started gaining momentum and Indira Gandhi also felt that she should have a better hold on the Hindu votes as they were a majority. For the first time, she tried electoral prospects in the Jammu region in the Jammu and Kashmir elections in 1983 for which preparations had started from 1982 itself and this experiment gave good results to the Congress party. It was the brain work of Arun Nehru and the group he was controlling to divert Indira Gandhi from the path of secularism towards having a better hold on Hindu votes. Not only any settlement with Akalis in Punjab was sabotaged by this group, even the Ayodhya locks were got opened by Arun Nehru in February 1986 during the early years of Rajiv regime.

THE ROLE OF BHAJAN LAL

The role of the then Haryana Chief Minister, Bhajan Lal was in no way less destructive and reprehensible than the roles played by others in sabotaging Punjab talks and also providing provocations in Haryana. Bhajan Lal was known to be very close to M.L. Fotedar, who was then handling political matters at Indira Gandhi's residence, and P. Shiv Shankar, who was Law Minister. Bhajan Lal knew the technique how to keep those around Indira Gandhi in good humour and happy. He was a past master in this game. His role, not only in stopping Sikhs to Delhi during the ASIAD by humiliating them and stopping them from reaching Delhi irrespective of the position they were holding, was one of the major factors that had irritated the entire Sikh community. His role during the communal flare ups in Haryana, especially in Panipat when a Gurdwara was burnt and Sikhs were attacked, and equally in aftermath of Indira Gandhi's assassination, was questionable. His speech at the December 1985 Bombay Congress session in the presence of all Congress leaders including the then Prime Minister, Rajiv Gandhi, threatening not to allow any Sikh to cross Ambala, if Haryana was not given Chandigarh and its share in river waters, was a classic example of the encouragement, he was getting from important congress leaders in flaring up communal sentiments. After this speech, the then Punjab Chief Minister, Surjit Singh Barnala also reacted equally strongly and the sentiments in the Haryana areas adjoining Punjab, had been aroused and there was a serious threat of communal clashes. Then Haryana BJP President, Mangal Sain was more "loyal" to Bhajan Lal than his own leadership and Bhajan Lal was using him and Haryana BJP also to issue provocative statement. By the first week of January 1986, the situation in some parts of Haryana bordering Punjab had become explosive. I, on my usual round of the Home Ministry, met the then Home Secretary, R.D. Pardhan and told him that the

Centre was playing with fire. Both the Chief Ministers, Bhajan Lal of Haryana and Surjit Singh Barnala, were close to the central leadership of the Congress and their provocative statements engulfed the region into a communal flare-up. He dismissed my assessment of the situation and said that he did not agree with my assessment. From the Home Secretary's room, I went to meet S.B. Chavan, the then Home Minister, and repeated my apprehensions. Chavan said, "No, nothing will happen; whatever the two Chief Ministers are saying, it is only for public consumption. The situation will not deteriorate." I was still talking to him when the Home Secretary, Pardhan walked into his room and finding me talking to him, said, "Is he threatening you also?" Chavan just laughed away. I asked Chavan how long had he been in politics? I said, "After arousing the sentiments of the people and taking them to a pitch, how will you be able to control them?" He kept quiet. Only four or five days later, I learnt that the situation in Sirsa and some other areas adjoining Punjab had become volatile and there was a serious threat of communal flare-ups. The administration alerted the army, but the army refused to get involved, unless the army was given full control. Army had experience of 1984 anti-Sikh riots where the civil and police authority had behaved in a most reprehensible manner in the capital. Army authorities were not prepared to listen to any authority. Ultimately, Prime Minister, Rajiv Gandhi himself had to intervene and asked the army authorities to deploy some forces in that area. After whole day's efforts by the civil authorities, it was only around 7.30 p.m. that Rajiv Gandhi had sorted out this matter. Around 8.00 p.m. I rang up Pardhan at his residence to check up the latest position. I must say Pardhan before talking to me on details of the events, first admitted that my assessment of the situation was absolutely correct and they were all wrong. The Home Secretary and the Home Ministry must have been earlier talking to me on the basis of Intelligence Bureau reports. This only shows the kind of assessments the I.B. was giving to the Government.

I am still of the confirmed view that Indira Gandhi and Rajiv Gandhi were surrounded by elements, which have not only destroyed both mother and son but the country also. These elements were responsible for whatever has happened in the country in the last 30 years including the rise of militancy and terrorism of which Pakistan's ISI took full advantage. It was a God-sent opportunity for the ISI of Pakistan, which that country has fully exploited and for which India is paying a very high price.

In a report on the Punjab situation, which was published in the *Pioneer,* Lucknow on 15 October 1988, I had written a paragraph on Rajiv Gandhi's advisors. I had written: "I have been closely following the events in Punjab for the last eight year and I also know the views of some of the advisors of the Prime Minister on Punjab. If an independent commission is appointed on the Punjab problem to find out its causes, some of Gandhi's advisors might have to be put under the NSA instead of Akali leaders and there might have to be a public trial of the RAW bosses who have been ill-advising the central leadership. If Gandhi is honest in solving the Punjab problem, he should first change his advisors on Punjab and think of initiating any step." I must say that Rajiv Gandhi, after he lost the elections in 1989, had learnt a lesson and was a changed leader. He had realized how he used to be misled by those around him. He had been having very frank discussions with me not only on Punjab but on some other important issues also. He was completely a changed leader. He could have come back as Prime Minister in the 1991 elections but unfortunately destiny willed it otherwise and he was assassinated during the election campaign. From their hearts, neither Indira Gandhi nor Rajiv Gandhi were communal. But it was the influence of the forces around them who were responsible and had been misleading them. They both paid a very heavy price.

INDIRA GANDHI'S SENSE OF INSECURITY

As I mentioned earlier, Indira Gandhi had started feeling insecure after the death of Sanjay Gandhi and the biggest culprit in exploiting her for this psychological weakness was Arun Nehru, who was leading a group around her. Both, on Punjab and Jammu and Kashmir, this group was misleading her. She was feeling so insecure that her loyalists like Yash Kapur and Buta Singh were holding *Yagnas* near Yamuna River and somewhere in U.P. through some *Tantriks* to counter any evil design against her by her political rivals. Whatever Congress leaders may claim about their secular credentials, many of them at the senior level, believed in *Tantriks* and used them very frequently not only for their own well-being but against their political rivals also. *Tantriks* had been having a good time.

In the statement prepared by the Cabinet Committee and approved by the Akali leadership, the Government was not giving any concession to Akalis. It was only gaining time and averting further confrontation with the Akalis. But the statement was providing a face-saving device to Akalis to wriggle out of the announcement they had made to declare their programme for the agitation. The hard-liners around her considered even this as surrender to Akalis, which they felt would annoy the Hindus. This was absolutely misreading of the situation and exploitation of Indira Gandhi's weakness.

Akalis who were waiting for the Home Minister's statement, were greatly disappointed and announced boycott of the Asian Games that were to be inaugurated on 19 November 1982, a few days later, and also demonstration and disruption of games. Bhajan Lal, the then Haryana Chief Minister and a loyalist of Arun Nehru-Fotedar group, instructed Haryana Police not to allow any Sikh to cross Haryana territory to reach Delhi.

BHAJAN LAL'S WORKINGS

R.C. Sharma, who retired as Director of the CBI and belonged to Haryana IPS cadre and was a trusted man of Bhajan Lal, confided in me some years later that he was heading the Ambala Police and was told by Bhajan Lal that Indira Gandhi had asked him not to allow any Sikh to reach Delhi. I was not prepared to believe this statement. It was possible that Indira Gandhi might have asked Bhajan Lal not to allow possible agitators to reach Delhi but I was not prepared to believe that Indira Gandhi would have given instructions to stop every Sikh to Delhi. It was Bhajan Lal, under instructions from Arun Nehru, who could have given any such instructions but not Indira Gandhi. How every Sikh, irrespective of the position he was occupying, whether he was a High Court Judge, a senior Army General or a Police Officer in civil dress, was taken out of moving buses and cars, questioned, humiliated and stopped from reaching Delhi. This had angered the entire Sikh community and the situation became worse. But the Government showed no remorse though this was condemned even in Parliament by many opposition leaders. Even outside India, in countries like USA, Canada and

U.K., Sikhs living in a very large number felt anguished and Indira Gandhi became a target of hatred among Sikhs living abroad, who started supporting the Akali agitation in Punjab and sending financial help to a man like Bhindranwale to fight against the Government.

Following is the text of the statement made by Home Minister, P.C. Sethi in Lok Sabha on 4 November 1982.

Government has been deeply distressed over the situation in Punjab. The Prime Minister and senior members of the cabinet have met delegations of the Akalis several times. The Prime Minister has indicated to them that practically all religious demands could be accepted subject to details being worked out but this could not be finalized because of their other demands.

During the recent agitation, Government made further efforts to resolve the crisis and has been considering the demands conveyed recently by the 5-members committees of Akali leaders through Sardar Swaran Singh. Certain areas of agreement have been identified in respect of some demands. The others concern various States also. Therefore, consultations have to be held with the Punjab and other concerned Governments and also with representatives of other communities before a decision can be taken. This process of consultation has been initiated and I have been in touch with the respective Chief Ministers and others including leaders of opposition parties and Members of Parliament. It is likely that this process will take some more time.

In taking any decision, the Government cannot ignore the overall interest of national unity, integrity and the welfare of all sections of the people.

Government hopes and trusts that representatives of the Akali Dal will look at their problems in the larger context. We repeat our invitation to them to come for further discussions and to create the right atmosphere for this by calling off or suspending their agitation. I hope that in the present circumstances nothing will be done which may escalate tension or give rise to violence and suffering. I appeal to all parties to extend their cooperation."

It was a complete redraft of the earlier statement prepared by the Cabinet Committee and approved by the Akalis. The earlier draft was brief and vague but very polite and that could not have created any impression of government surrender before Akalis. It was the group around Indira Gandhi, which had given her this impression. Giani Zail Singh was keen to ensure that no other Sikh leader, especially Sardar Swaran Singh, got any credit and in the eyes of the Sikh community, became more important than Giani Zail Singh. Giani Zail Singh had already succeeded during the emergency in conspiring and manipulating the exit of Sardar Swaran Singh from the cabinet by poisoning the mind of Indira Gandhi against Sardar Swaran Singh about which I will be writing in another chapter.

The group surrounding Indira Gandhi had not only sabotaged any settlement with Akalis on Punjab, how at every stage they had created hurdles, they had also sabotaged implementation of the Rajiv-Longowal accord and what happened in the aftermath of Indira Gandhi's assassination. Indira Gandhi had been assassinated but Rajiv Gandhi had realized only after his defeat in the 1989 elections that how some of those around him had destroyed first Indira Gandhi and later him. He had distanced away from Arun Nehru in 1986 itself, which gave a big shock to Arun Nehru and he suffered a heart attack in Srinagar, but discovered about others including Gopi Arora who was the biggest beneficiary of Gandhi family rule. He always got good postings and rapid promotions. But later on, Rajiv Gandhi discovered how Gopi Arora was keeping a line open with Arun Nehru and V.P. Singh. Rajiv Gandhi was so much annoyed with Gopi that a few months before Rajiv's assassination, Gopi had come to Delhi on leave and wanted an appointment with Rajiv but Rajiv refused to meet him though Gopi was waiting for the appointment for one month.

TALKS BETWEEN THE AKALIS AND GOVERNMENT

3 November 1982 was a very important day for the talks between Akalis and the government in Delhi. Four Akali leaders—Prakash Singh Badal, G.S. Tohra, President of the S.G.P.C., Jagdev Singh Talwandi and Balwant Singh—had come to the capital and on 2 November 1982, there had been talks between the Government representatives and Akali leaders and many issues had been sorted out. There was every hope of the talks succeeding in some settlement. The Government had agreed to accept all religious demands of Akalis including relaying of Gurbani from the Golden Temple, enactment of an All India Gurdwara Act and carrying of a small *Kirpan* in the internal flights of airlines and closure of tobacco, meat and liquor shops up to a particular area in the walled city of Amritsar. There was an agreement on some political demands also. But still certain modalities had to be discussed with the Akalis. Other states had also to be consulted. There was some understanding on the Chandigarh issue also. After these talks, Tohra and Talwandi left for Amritsar in the early morning of 3 November, and Badal and Balwant Singh left by 11.30 flight for Amritsar. On 3 November, there were two

meetings of the Special Committee on Punjab with Sardar Swaran Singh. Sant Harchand Singh Longowal had called a meeting of district Jathedars and working committee members on 4 November at Amritsar to decide the next course of action. Sardar Swaran Singh was pleading with the Cabinet Committee to make some official announcement on the morning of 4 November in Parliament on the understanding arrived at with the Akalis. His plea was that Akalis should be given some way to put a stop to their agitation and not to announce any further escalation of the agitation. For the second time, the Cabinet Committee met in the afternoon of 3 November in the room of P.V. Narsimha Rao in Parliament House and the meeting was also attended by Sardar Swaran Singh besides senior officers dealing with the Punjab situation, Cabinet Secretary, Krishnaswamy Rao Saheb, Home Secretary T.N. Chaturvedi and Special Secretary in Home Ministry, P.P. Nayyar who was handling the Punjab situation. In the meeting, it was decided that the Home Minister, P.C. Sethi will make a statement in Parliament next morning on the Government stand on Akali demands and a draft of statement was prepared. It was a brief statement. It was read out to the Akalis on phone in Amritsar and they approved the statement.

II

Akali-Congress Rivalry

The fight between the Akalis and the Sikh congress leaders of Punjab over the control of Sikh Gurdwaras through the Shiromani Gurdwara Parbandhak Committee (SGPC) has been going on for a very long time much before the partition of the country in 1947. Initially, much before1947, when the Akalis were fighting for the control of gurdwaras, Mahatma Gandhi had supported the Akalis as it suited the Congress party. Akalis had two very important and highly respected leaders—Baba Kharak Singh and Master Tara Singh—who were fighting for the identity of the Sikhs. Master Tara Singh ruled over the Sikh politics as an undisputed leader for almost 50 years and throughout his political career, not even once, there was any allegation against him, which for a politician is a remarkable and unbeaten record. It is well-known that Sikh politics is controlled more through the Gurdwaras control and it is for this reason that Sikh congress leaders have been always keen to have control of the Sikh Gurdwaras through the SGPC elections. For many years, this tussle has been going on and there have been occasions when Congress was in control of the SGPC but for almost five decades, now the Akalis are in full control of the SGPC. They have complete hold on the Sikh Gurdwaras. In 1957, Partap Singh Kairon, the then Chief Minister of Punjab, and Giani Kartar Singh, who was once known as brain of the Akali party and a minister in the Punjab

Government as a result of an alliance between the Congress and the Akali party, but later on he resigned from the Akali Dal and joined the Congress party. Partap Singh Kairon and Giani Kartar Singh joined hands to fight the SGPC elections under the banner of Sikh Sangat Board against the Akalis in 1957. But the Congress suffered a humiliating rout as the Congress could get only less than half a dozen seats out of 132 seats in the SGPC and the Akalis got almost all the remaining except a few. This had a very demoralizing effect on Partap Singh Kairon and Giani Kartar Singh. I remember soon after these elections, I was in Ludhiana and I learnt that Kairon had come to Ludhiana and was staying at the PWD Rest House. I, alongwith Joginder Pal Pandey and Sat Paul Mittal went to the PWD Rest House to meet Kairon late in the evening. Kairon was alone in his room and except the chowkidar of the Rest house and a policeman as a guard, nobody else was there. When we entered Kairon's room, we found Kairon was taking turns and feeling extremely shaken. All the time, more than 45 minutes that we spent with him, he was lying in his bed and talking to us. He said, "Mundio, Mainu Koi Aisa Tareeqa Dasso Keh Main Master Tara Singh Noo Chor, Uchaka Ate Daku Sabat Kar Sakan." (O young boys, tell me a way that I could prove Master Tara Singh as a thief, vagabond and a dacoit). This amply showed the mental state of Kairon after his humiliating rout in the SGPC elections. Kairon was a great fighter and he never lost his nerves.

KAIRON'S STRATEGY TO OUST TARA SINGH

After this defeat, he started planning new strategies to finish Master Tara Singh politically within the Akali Dal. It was Partap

Singh Kairon who introduced in Akali politics the theory that Akalis were being ruled by a non-Jat Sikh and he also gave a slogan of rural and urban Sikhs and started giving feelings that Akalis should be led by a Jat from rural areas. At the same time, he involved two Sikh businessmen, Uttam Singh Duggal, a leading builder from Delhi and Lachhman Singh Gill who was from Punjab but was staying in Delhi, another contractor, to find a Sikh, prop him up and build him to replace Master Tara Singh. Sant Fateh Singh was the creation of Partap Singh Kairon, through Lachhman Singh Gill and Uttam Singh Duggal. He was brought from Ganga Nagar in Rajasthan and planted on the Akalis. A large Sikh population had settled in Ganga Nagar and Fateh Singh was preaching in that area. During the Punjabi Suba agitation in 1955-56, he was brought to Punjab and he joined the agitation, launched by the Akali Dal under the leadership of Master Tara Singh. During the agitation, he rose to become the Vice-President of the Akali Dal. Sant Fateh Singh led the Punjabi Suba agitation in Delhi in March 1959. There were a number of meetings held between the then Prime Minister, Jawahar Lal Nehru and the Akali leaders on their demands but no solution could be found. Master Tara Singh's health started deteriorating as his age was catching up with him. But still he was fighting a relentless battle. His decline started in 1961 when he went on fast unto death after a prayer at the Akal Takhat. It was here that Partap Singh Kairon's strategy worked to hit at Master Tara Singh. Kairon was Chief Minister Punjab. He knew the Sikh tradition that if Master Tara Singh broke his fast without achieving anything, this would be the end of his political career. Kairon was making all efforts to somehow manipulate the breaking of Master Tara Singh's fast. When the fast had crossed 40 days and was still continuing, Kairon got worried about the developing situation and his purpose of finishing Master Tara Singh politically was not going to be served. As a very shrewd politician, Kairon rang up the then Defence Minister, Krishna Menon and asked him to call Master Tara Singh's son-in-law, Wing Commander Kanwaljit Singh, who was posted in Delhi and was in the Air Force and pressurized him to get his father-in law's fast broken and this worked. Master Tara Singh's daughter was in Amritsar looking after him. Kanwaljit Singh rang up his wife in the Golden Temple complex and told her that all those around her father wanted her father to die. But she should ensure that he must break his fast; she should not allow others' plans to succeed. Kanwaljit's talk with his wife was firm and it was evident from the talk that she would now persuade her father to break the fast. On the other hand, leading Sikhs like Malik Hardit Singh and late Maharaja Yadvindra Singh of Patiala, father of Amrinder Singh, were also trying to persuade Master Tara Singh to break his fast. They were in touch with Jawahar Lal Nehru and the then Home Minister, Lal Bahadur Shastri, Both of them were well-meaning persons with good intentions. But the source Kairon had used through the Defence Minister was Kairon's master stroke. When Master Tara Singh had undertaken this fast, I was staying in the Raisina Hostel, opposite the Chelmaford Club, New Delhi. Krishan Kumar, another journalist working for a foreign news agency, was also staying in the same Hostel near my room. His elder brother, Raghunath Sharma was working in Delhi Police CID Branch handling Punjab and Sikh affairs. He used to visit his brother very frequently. One day he had come to see his brother and then he met me also and told me that Master Tara Singh would break his fast in a day or so. I was surprised at this information. He told me that they were intercepting all telephone calls in the Golden Temple and were also aware of some talks and the strategies Kairon was using to get this fast broken. He narrated me the entire story about Kairon talking to Krishna Menon and then Menon calling Kanwaljit Singh and asking him to get this fast broken. The police was also aware of the conversation Kanwaljit Singh had with his wife on phone in Amritsar. Two days later, on the 48 day of Master Tara Singh's fast, Maharaja Yadvindra Singh and Fateh Singh gave a glass of juice to Master Tara Singh and the fast was broken. Since Master Tara Singh had broken his fast without achieving the objective for which the fast was undertaken, this gave the biggest opportunity to Partap Singh Kairon to use his sources within Akalis to bring down the image of Master Tara Singh. This was the biggest success Kairon had achieved against Master Tara Singh in his life. With this, Master Tara Singh's political career started declining and Sant Fateh Singh started asserting. But the fact remained that the fight between the Akalis and the Sikh Congress leaders of Punjab was on the control of the Gurdwara politics, which dominated Punjab politics.

Master Tara Singh also hit back at Partap Singh Kairon. People might not be aware that the motivating spirit behind the charge-sheet against Partap Singh Kairon on corruption charges given by Maulvi Abdul Ghani and others, was Master Tara Singh. Kairon was indicted by the Dass Commission and he had to quit as Chief Minister of Punjab. Three opposition leaders from Punjab—Harkishan Singh Surjeet, CPM leader, Maulvi Abdul Ghani and Jagat Narain—had entered the Rajya Sabha with the support of the Akalis. While Jagat Narain betrayed the Akalis who had supported him, Abdul Ghani Dar and Harkishan Singh Surjeet remained indebted to the Akalis for their support. Master Tara Singh was staying at Gurdwara Rakab Ganj in New Delhi and I was sitting with him when Maulvi Abdul Ghani came to see him. Master Tara Singh was a very simple man who on his visits to Delhi used to stay in a room just near the gate of the Gurdwara, which neither had a telephone connection nor an attached bathroom. He used to sleep on a rough cot and his two meals used to come from the Gurdwara *Langar.* Though many important Delhi Sikh leaders including leading businessmen used to visit him and were keen that Master Tara Singh should stay with them but the Master always refused to oblige them and always preferred to stay in the Gurdwara Rankab Ganj. Master Tara Singh asked Maulvi Abdul Ghani Dar to find out some serious charges of corruption against Partap Singh Kairon and submit a memorandum to the Prime Minister demanding an enquiry commissioner against Kairon. Maulvi took the help of R.P. Kapur, an ICS Officer of the Punjab Government who had just retired and was against Kairon. Ch. Devi Lal also joined them. Main work on the charge sheet was done by R.P. Kapur with some inputs from Maulvi Abdul Ghani. It was on this charge-sheet that Jawahar Lal Nehru who was a great supporter of Partap Singh Kairon, was forced to appoint a Commission which indicted Partap Singh Kairon on some of the charges, though not directly involving him, and Kairon had to quit on the Commission's report. By that time, Jawahar Lal Nehru had died a few months earlier and Lal Bahadur Shastri, then Prime Minister, and Gulzari Lal Nanda had no sympathy for Partap Singh Kairon. So, Master Tara Singh had succeeded in avenging the attack Kairon had launched on him. But by that time, Master Tara Singh was very old and his health had further started deteriorating. He was no more in a position to exert and this left an open field for Sant Fateh Singh. But there was no comparison between Master Tara Singh and Sant Fateh Singh, Master Tara Singh being a far superior human being in every aspect.

CONSPIRACY TO KILL PRATAP SINGH KAIRON

Master Tara Singh died on 22 November 1967 when he had crossed the age of 80 and Partap Singh Kairon was killed near Sonepat by two assailants three years earlier. Kairon had come to Delhi to meet Lal Bahadur Shastri and after staying in the capital for about a week, he was returning to Punjab when he was killed near Sonepat. Kairon's killers had been planning and selecting the place for their target. His programme for his Delhi visit had been published in newspapers. He was staying at the residence of Sardar Bahadur Ranjit Singh on Kasturba Gandhi Marg. While his killers were selecting a place near Sonepat, their car developed some trouble and they came to Delhi to pick up a mechanic. They took one Hanif, a mechanic from Sabzi Mandi area, for the repair of the car. While the mechanic was working on the car lying under it, he heard those who had brought him talking; "This is the right place to kill him on the G. T. Road." They were carrying some fire arms in a *jhola* (bag). The mechanic repaired their car and he was dropped at his workshop in Sabzi Mandi. He felt that they were planning to kill some big leader as he had assessed from their conversation and went to the residence of Gulzari Lal Nanda, then Home Minister of India, and narrated the sequence. Nanda called the IG, Delhi police and asked him to investigate the matter. Nanda got a feeling that perhaps they could be Kairon's men wanting to kill him (Nanda) or the Congress President, K.

Kamraj. I was sitting in the Daily Partap office and writing a report when Raghunath Sharma, Delhi Police DSP, CID whom I knew through his younger brother, a journalist colleague of mine, came and asked me if I knew where Kairon's two sons, Surinder Singh and Gurinder Singh used to stay in the capital. I did not know about that and I asked him why he was trying to find out their whereabouts. He narrated the story of Hanif, the mechanic, meeting the Home Minister, Gulzari Lal Nanda and Nanda apprehending that Kairon was perhaps trying to get him or the Congress President killed. Two or three days later, Delhi Police sent a report to the Intelligence Bureau suggesting that the IB should make enquiries from the Rohtak Police as at that time Sonepat area came under the Rohtak District Police. I published a report in Daily *Partap* with Rohtak dateline that the police and IB were making enquiries about a report by a mechanic to Gulzari Lal Nanda about the possibility of a big man to be killed on the G. T. Road. Just a few days later, Kairon was killed on that spot. It was a very sensational murder of a very important political personality and the police officers from Punjab, UP, Delhi and Rajasthan, used to meet daily at Canal Rest House in Delhi to review the progress in the investigation. A few days later, someone in the meeting pointed out the report I had published in Daily *Partap* and one Delhi police DSP, Pritam Piara was deputed to find out the source of the report. Raghu Nath Sharma was also sitting in the meeting and he got worried that I may not disclose the source of the report, which he himself was. He rang me up from somewhere outside and told me how this matter came up and Pritam Piara was deputed to find the source. Since the report was datelined Rohtak, I met K. Narendra, Editor-Proprietor of Daily *Pratap* and told him that this was my report and if any police officer came to him to know about it that he should just say that he had received a letter in which some details were mentioned and he gave that letter to me. I told him that he should send that police officer to me and I would handle that. Pritam Piara met Narendra twice to question him on the report and ultimately Narendra suggested him to talk to me. I was at a diplomatic cocktail party when K. Narendra also reached there and after seeing me he called the waiter and asked him to pour a stiff drink and he handed over that drink to me. After some time, he got another strong drink for me and then asked me to go to the office as the Police DSP was waiting for me. I reached the office around 9 p.m. and the news editor told me pointing towards a plain-clothes man that he was waiting for me. I took him to the manager's cabin and asked him the purpose of his visit. He did not disclose his identity and straight away asked me about the source of that report. I asked him if he was the same police officer who had been questioning K. Narendra and he said yes. I flared up and asked him to leave the office immediately. I sent him out of the cabin and then asked him to seek my permission before entering the cabin. I shouted at him and told him that he did not deserve to be in the department he was serving. I told him that if he was a competent man, he should have first introduced himself and then explained the importance of the investigation and should have sought my help. That approach would certainly have forced me to help him. After snubbing him, I became polite and told him that no records of such letters were kept in Urdu newspapers and I sent him away. Next morning, at the police officers' meeting, he narrated exactly how I had treated him and he withdrew from the investigation. Then, an SP from the IB, Harbans Singh, who was dealing with the press, was deputed to contact me and try to extract the source. Harbans Singh came to my house twice for this purpose and pleaded with me that if I could give him the source of my report, he would immediately get next promotion. He was still in the process of making these efforts when Gulzari Lal Nanda narrated the entire story of Hanif mechanic at the *Press Club* function.

ARREST OF KAIRON'S KILLER

Partap Singh Kairon's killer, Sucha Singh was arrested from Nepal. Ashwini Kumarwho later retired as DG, BSF, was leader of the team to arrest Sucha Singh. Kairon's sons had petitioned to the Home Minister that Kairon's murder was politically motivated and they had pointed finger at Darbara Singh who was then the Home Minister of Punjab in the Ram Kishan Ministry. Wagh, a Joint Director of the IB, was deputed to go into this complaint and Wagh in his six-page report said that on the basis of material before him, he could say that there was no political motivation behind Kairon's murder. However, I saw the report with Gulzari Lal Nanda, published it. Nanda had handed over this report to Ram Kishan who did not show it to Darbara Singh. Darbara Singh came to k now about it from my report only.

The fight between the Akalis and the Congress has been a long driven battle for power in Punjab. The Congress was not prepared to tolerate any other political party coming to power. Soon after the merger of princely states with India, in Punjab, eight such states were clubbed together and a new province 'PEPSU' (Patiala and East Punjab States Union) was created. This was a Sikh-dominant area. But the Congress did not allow the Akalis to come to power in this state also though in the first elections in 1952, the Akalis had got a majority in this small state but the Congress arranged defections and did not allow the Akalis to form their Government.

AKALI'S LAUNCH OF AGITATION

The Akalis had launched an agitation for reorganization of the states on the basis of linguistic population. The Central Government appointed a States Reorganization Commission in 1953. Though this Commission made recommendations for recoganization of some other states in the South and West, yet in the case of Punjab, it rejected the demand of the Akalis and instead recommended adding of more areas to Punjab from Himachal Pradesh and merger of PEPSU into Punjab. The Central Government accepted the recommendations of the States Reorganization Commission, though on face of it, its recommendations were biased and unjustified. The Central Government also appointed a First Census Commission of India in 1951 under a very straight forward ICS Officer, G. Gopalaswamy. The Congress-Arya Samaj leaders of Jalandhar Division launched a full-blast campaign against Punjabi language and appealed to Hindus in the state to record their mother-tongue as Hindi though they were all speaking Punjabi. The role of Jalandhar Division Congress—Arya Samaj leaders like Jagat Narain, Yash, Mahasha Khushal Chand and Varindera, all running urdu newspapers, was most reprehensible and they were responsible for polluting the communal atmosphere in Punjab. Their campaign against Punjabi was so virulent that even Jawahar Lal Nehru had to say in a public meeting that some people in Punjab were fighting for Hindi but their fight was through urdu newspapers. The attitude of some of the top Hindu leaders in the Central

Government was sympathetic towards the Hindi protagonists. The Census Commissioner, Gopalaswamy was so upset with the campaign launched by the Hindi protagonists that he met the then President, Dr. Rajendra Prasad and reported to him that though the Hindus in Punjab were speaking Punjabi but they were giving their mother-tongue as Hindi, which was a lie. Dr. Rajendra Prasad put him off by saying, “it is their choice, what can we do?” This is confirmed by Gopalaswamy’s son, G. Parthasarthy, who retired as India’s Ambassador to Pakistan and is now a days a leading commentator on Pakistan and its sponsored terrorism. Even Sikh Congress leaders like Partap Singh Kairon were most unhappy with the anti-Punjabi campaign of the Congress leaders belonging to Arya Samaj. Later, when Kairon became Chief Minister, 1957, Jagat Narain, Prof. Sher Singh and some others launched an agitation against Regional Formula and for propagation of Hindi. Kairon crushed this agitation with full force and after that, during the entire regime of Kairon, these leaders did not have the courage to start another agitation.

In Punjab, there had never been any feeling whether someone was Sikh or Hindu. There was no word Hindu or Sikh, instead what used to be described was Sikh and a clean-shaven. And in almost every family, some members were supporting long hair and beard and some were clean-shaven. For bringing this cleavage between Hindus and Sikhs, a section of Akalis and the Congress leaders with Arya Samaj background of Jalandhar Division were responsible. The role of both these section was most reprehensible. In a majority of families in Punjab, even now there is no thinking on the lines whether somebody is Hindu or a Sikh. Even today mixed marriages are taking place. It is for this reason that terrorism could not succeed in Punjab despite all the efforts by Pakistan and at that time by the CIA also. The ISI and the CIA were working in tandem and both were responsible for bringing terrorism to Punjab.

OPPOSITION OF PUNJABI LANGUAGE

The report of the States Reorganization Commission and later the attitude of the Arya Samaj Congress leaders from Jalandhar Division in opposing Punjabi language gave a further feeling of grievances to the Akalis in Punjab. Jagat Narain was projecting himself as the champion of Hindu cause. There was no danger to the Hindus or anybody else and Jagat Narain's tirade against Akalis and Sikhs was so virulent and poisonous that it was equally responsible for spoiling the communal harmony in Punjab as propaganda of Bhindranwala. He was doing it more for his commercial interests to run his two newspapers whose circulation with such campaigns, was increasing. As a result, his Hindi newspaper, *Punjab Kesri*, became number one in Punjab. Thus, he earned more money and became rich by inciting the sentiments of people in Punjab against the Akalis. When he had started his newspaper, he did not have money even to pay salaries to his staff who frequently used to go on strike, for non-payment of wages. With the increase in circulation of his newspapers, he became more and more virulent against Akalis and the Sikh cause. Ultimately, he was killed near Ludhiana on 9 September 1981 and three years later, his son Romesh Chander, who was known as a better person than his father, was also killed by militants in Jalandhar on 12 May 1984, Romesh Chander was known as a decent human being and had good relations with all the communities. But he had to pay the price for being the son of Jagat Narain, who was mainly responsible for polluting the atmosphere in Punjab.

There were long drawn battles between the Akalis and the Congress leaders for almost two decades during which period the Akalis led many agitations for the creation of a separate state based on language. They had courted arrests of thousands of workers during these agitations. For the first time after independence during the regime of Bhim Sen Sachar, police entered Golden Temple to arrest Akali leaders on 4 July 1955. Three weeks later, Sachar apologized from the Sikh community and had to resign as Chief Minister and Kairon took over from him. There were many agitations by Akalis during the regime of Partap Singh Kairon also. On the intervention of the Central Government, personally by Jawahar Lal Nehru, a regional formula was devised under which Punjab-speaking areas were to have teachings in Punjab and the Hindi speaking region was to have teaching in Hindi. But the Arya Samaj section of the Congress leadership in both the regions opposed this formula and started an agitation under the banner of Hindi Raksha Samiti. Jagat Narain and Prof. Sher Singh were the leading lights of this agitation, which was crushed by Partap Singh Kairon. Even at personal level, Jagat Narain and Kairon had strained relations. This had given further rise to the feelings among Akalis that the Congress leaders were not prepared even to have Punjabi in the Punjabi dominant areas and this resulted in bringing out communal feelings from both sides. The Akalis felt that the regional formula was no solution and they came back to their demand for a separate Punjabi-speaking state. As a result of a compromise between the Congress leadership and the Akalis on the regional formula, the latter had joined the Partap Singh Kairon Government, Akali representative being Giani Kartar Singh and Gian Singh Rarewala. Though, later the Akalis revived the political status of the Akali Dal, after the

Hindu Congress leaders were opposing the Regional Formula and launching an agitation for Hindi, Giani Kartar Singh and Gian Singh Rarewala remained in the Government as congressmen. Ultimately, it was in 1965, just before the start of Indo-Pak war, that Sant Fateh Siingh had announced to sit on a fast to achieve Punjabi Suba and he declared that if the Government did not concede his demand, he would go in for self-immolation on 25 September. Soon after, Indo-Pak war was declared. But on 9 September, on a message from the then Prime Minister, Lal Bahadur Shastri and the intervention of Maharaja Yadvindera Singh of Patiala, Sant Fateh Singh broke his fast and appealed to the Sikhs to make all efforts to resist the Pakistani attack as the country was in danger. This helped the fighting forces so much that the country would never have seen such mobilization of masses in Punjab that every family in the state stood up to support the fighting forces. I remember that when we went to the border areas, across the border within the shelling range when the fighting was on its pitch on 11 September along with the then Home Minister, Gulzari Lal Nanda and Congress President, Kamraj, there was so much enthusiasm among the masses that all women folk were doing the cooking in villages and the truck-drivers, fearlessly, were taking hot food, tea and *pakoras* right up to the fighting forces, which for the forces was a great morale booster. It was on that day a Pakistani Major General was killed in the Khem-Karan Sector. Giani Gurmukh Singh Musafir, a highly respected Punjab Congress leader, Dr. Anup Singh and Surjit Singh Atwal, Members of Parliament were also with us. It was on that morning that Subedar Raju had shot down two Sabre Jets of Pakistan and the people of Amritsar were highly appreciative of Subedar Raju.

MOBILIZATION OF MASSES

India would never see such mobilization of masses against an enemy country again. Pakistani Para shooters were killed by villagers with their *lathis* only. The entire Punjab had stood like one man to fight against the enemy. There were graveyards of Patton tanks in the Khem Karan and Sialkot sectors. Patton tanks supplied to Pakistan by Americans were the pride of Pakistan forces. But Indian forces had smashed these tanks.

Lt. Gen. Harbax Singh was the Western Command Chief, leading the forces against Pakistan. The Air Force was commanded by Air Chief Marshal Arjun Singh, who himself was one of the great air force fighters and had led the first attack against Pakistan in Chumb-Jaurian sector where Pakistani forces were advancing. While the entire country was praising the Sikh armed forces, Jagat Narain was not prepared to stomach even this praise and was still writing that Sikhs were not the only brave soldiers; soldiers from other communities were equally brave. His tone and tenor of writing was only to slight Sikh forces.

The war with Pakistan was over in three weeks and just two days after the ceasefire, Lal Bahadur Shastri fulfilled his assurances to re-examine all the grievances of the Akalis and announcing this in Parliament, a cabinet committee was appointed to go into this matter. Indira Gandhi, then a Minister, was a member of this committee and the Government also requested the Speaker of the Lok Sabha and Chairman of the Rajya Sabha to set up a Parliamentary Committee, to look in to this matter and find a satisfactory solution to the issues raised. Gulzari Lal Nanda was the Home Minister. Though he was known as Gandhian but he was not honest and above board in this matter. He was certainly biased. On the basis of the report of the Parliamentary Committee, submitted in March 1966, Indira Gandhi, who had become Prime Minister of the country in January 1966 after the sudden death of Lal Bahadur Shastri in Tashkent, agreed to the demand for creation of a Punjab-speaking state, and a Commission was appointed to demarcate the new states of Punjab and Haryana. The Parliament passed the Punjab Reorganization Bill in September 1966 to carve the two states from 1 November 1966. But there was still a dispute on the status of Chandigarh as the Shah Commission had awarded Chandigarh to Haryana, which was not an honest decision. The role of Gulzari Lal Nanda in favouring Haryana was evident. Nanda had been rejected by Gujarat, from where he used to contest Lok Sabha elections, and was keen to fight from Haryana. He had started taking very keen interest in Haryana affairs. Those days, I was working for *The Tribune*, Chandigarh and Nanda was cultivating with me and had given free access to me. I used to visit him almost every evening. One evening when I went to see him, Krishan Bhatia, the then editor of the *Hindustan Times*, was waiting to see him. Nanda came from inside his room, took me aside, and asked what do leaders of Haryana think of him. I told him that he should not have asked me that because I was not his informer but since he had asked I must tell him the truth, and I said that truth was that Haryana leaders considered him as a representative of the Jan Sangh. He flared up and said "was he a Jan Sanghi"? Thereafter, he got into his car and left the place even without meeting Krishan Bhatia. Krishan Bhatia asked what did I say that made him angry, and I narrated what I had told him. From next day, I stopped going to Nanda's house. A few days later, I had gone to see U.N. Dhebar, senior Congress leader, whom I used to meet almost daily, when Gulzari Lal Nanda also arrived. Dhebar asked Nanda, "Nanda Ji do you know Chawla Ji, he is a good journalist and an expert on Punjab." Nanda said, "Yes, he is a friend of mine" but pointing at me he asked, "why I have stopped going to his house? I said, "Nanda Ji I made a mistake of speaking the truth which made you angry." He said, "No, these things keep on happening but you should not stop coming to my house." U.N. Dhebar was one of the most honest and straight forward Congress leaders and a real Gandhian who was respected by all. Giani Gurmukh Singh Musafir, a highly respected Congress leader from Punjab, was the first Chief Minister of newly created Punjab but a few months later when elections were held in Punjab, the Akalis came to power for the first time and in March 1967, Justice Gurnam Singh became the first Akali Chief Minister. Justice Gurnam Singh was not only respected by Akalis, especially Sant Fateh Singh but by Indira Gandhi also.

GURNAM SINGH VS. PRAKASH SINGH BADAL

Justice Gurnam Singh was not a mass leader whereas Parkash Singh Badal was a mass leader having a complete hold on Akali politics. While Gurnam Singh was a more straight-forward bold and courageous Akali Chief Minister whereas Badal was a mass leader but not bold and courageous. Justice Gurnam Singh as an administrator, had a much broader view than that of Badal. Justice Gurnam Singh was the only Chief Minister of a state who had the courage to write to Indira Gandhi about her Home Minister, Gulzari Lal Nanda that, "Your Home Minister is communal. Do you want Punjab to secede from the country?" this was what he wrote to Indira Gandhi in early 1969 complaining against the Home Minister on taking sides on Chandigarh. I was those days writing for The Tribune and I had an understanding with Justice Gurnam Singh that he used to send me copies of the letters he used to write to the Central Government. B.S. Dhillon who later on became a judge of the Punjab and Haryana High Court, was Advocate General of Gurnam Singh Government. B.S. Dhillon was a trusted man of Justice Gurnam Singh. They used to send a special messenger with a copy of the letter. It was left to me to use those letters from Delhi according to the situation I thought will be proper for publication. When I got a copy of this letter, it was published on front page of *The Tribune.* When journalists in Chandigarh confronted Justice Gurnam Singh with *The Tribune* report on the letter, he said, "The contents of the report are correct but heading is not." So, he did not deny having written the letter. He was the only Chief Minister in the country who had the courage to write such letters to the Central Government. On the other hand, Badal was the Chief Minister even in 1978 when the Akalis were an alliance partner in the Central Government and he had not written even a single letter to the Central Government on Punjab's demands. In 1978, he under the influence of Harkishan Singh Surjeet invited Chief Ministers of opposition parties for a conclave at Chandigarh on the issue of more autonomy to the states but when Morarji Desai, who was the Prime Minister, learnt about it, he asked Badal to cancel this conclave immediately and Badal did not have the courage to defy Morarji Desai. Even on the Nirankaris issue, after the clash in Amritsar between Akalis and Bhindranwala and *Akhand Kirtni Jatha* in which 13 persons were killed, Badal banned the Nirankari book but on a telephone call from Morarji Desai, he withdrew the ban immediately. This was the difference between Justice Gurnam Singh and Parkash Singh Badal. Congress in Punjab led by Giani Zail Singh brought defections among the Akalis and supported Lachhman Singh Gill to form the next Government in Punjab. Dr. Jagjit Singh Chauhan, who was the protagonist of "Khalistan" under the influence of the CIA-ISI nexus, was the Finance Minister in the Lachhman Singh Gill ministry. Congress support was not based on any principle but Lachhman Singh Gill was looking after the interests of Giani Zail Singh, which suited both. But later on, many Congress leaders from Punjab had complained to the then Congress President, S. Nijilingappa, who later on announced withdrawal of support to the Gill Ministry despite best efforts by Giani Zail Singh to save the Ministry. Giani Zail Singh and Lachhman Singh Gill had both come to see the Congress President. They had just come out after meeting the Congress President separately and were still in the compound of the Congress President that I met him and he said, "You can write now that I have decided to withdraw support from the Gill Ministry." I rushed to *The Tribune* office in Connaught Place and dictated the story on the teleprinter itself to the operator so that it could come in the *The Tribune* edition, which comes to Delhi. Delhi edition of The Tribune used to be published a few hours before the main edition as it used to be sent to Delhi by a taxi service.

THE ROLE OF DARSHAN SINGH PHERUMAN

The only leader who really made great sacrifice for Punjab was Darshan Singh Pheruman, who was not an Akali but a Congress supporter but he felt that the Central Government had done great injustice to Punjab in not giving Chandigarh to Punjab. He undertook a fast unto death on 15 August 1969 to demand transfer of Chandigarh to Punjab. He stuck to his resolve and showed no sign of weakness and preferred to die than breaking his fast. His fast continued for almost over 70 days. Indira Gandhi was worried about Pheruman's fast. She sent Giani Gurmukh Singh Musafir to Amritsar to persuade Jathedar Pheruman to break his fast. Giani Gurmukh Singh Musafir and Jathedar Pheruman were very close to each other. When Musafir went to Amritsar to meet Pheruman, the latter refused to meet him. He said he knew that he had been sent by Indira Gandhi and he would try to persuade him to break his fast. Since he was not going to waver from his resolve, he would not like to disappoint his dear friend. Therefore, he would not meet him. Tears rolled down Musafir's eyes to see the resolve of Pheruman. He knew that Indira Gandhi was not going to accept Pheruman's demand and Pheruman being a man of strong will, would ultimately die. This was exactly what happened. No other Akali leader had made such a supreme sacrifice as Pheruman had done. Still Akalis have completely forgotten him, it is difficult to imagine how torturous it is to remain on fast for such a long time. It is a very painful process through which one had to go during the fast unto death. But Pheruman proved himself as a man of word and principle, which no other Akali leader could do. But now, it is the Akali leadership that is enjoying the fruits of the sacrifice made by leaders like Jathedar Darshan Singh Pheruman.

Congress once again came to power in Punjab after the 1970 war with Pakistan with Giani Zail Singh as Chief Minister. Giani Zail Singh was allergic to the Jat dominated Akali leadership. He was a shrewd politician who could resort to any method to achieve his goal. He also tried to fight the Akalis through religious means but not through the SGPC elections and organized Guru Gobind Singh Marg from Anandpur Sahib to Talwandi Sabo (Damdama Sahib) on the route Guru Gobind Singh, the tenth Guru of Sikhs had traveled when he left Anandpur Sahib. He organized a huge procession for the entire route and the celebrations went on for a few days. He knew the Sikh sentiments as he himself had started his career as a preacher in a Gurdwara in Faridkot, where he was imprisoned by the Maharaja of Faridkot on charge of embezzlement of Gurdwara funds for which Giani Zail Singh never pardoned the Faridkot Maharaja. Giani Zail Singh was so vindictive that during an Akali agitation in early 1960s, Zail Singh met the Home Minister twice and pleaded with him that the Akali agitation was being financed by the Faridkot Maharaja and the Government should stop the pension the Maharaja was getting from the Government following an agreement with princely states. Maharaja Faridkot was not interested in politics and he was not helping the Akalis at all. This was only to avenge his arrest by the Maharaja, which was a blot on Giani Zail Singh. I happened to accompany Surjit Singh Atwal, then a Rajya Sabha member from Punjab and a friend of mine, to the Deputy Home Minister who was from West Bengal and close to Atwal. He asked me why Maharaja Faridkot was giving financial support to the Akalis. It just struck me that Giani Zail might have complained against the Maharaja. I asked the Deputy Home Minister if Giani Zaiil Singh had made any complaint. He revealed that Giani Zail Singh had met the Home Minister twice in this connection and was pressing to stop Maharaja Faridkot's pension. I told him that I did not know Maharaja Faridkot but knew this much that he was not at all interested in politics and Giani Zail Singh was campaigning against him because the Maharaja had arrested Giani Zail Singh when he was a preacher in a Gurdeara in Faridkot on charge of embezzlement of Gurdwara funds. The Deputy Home Minister said that the file was with him and he had to send that file to the Home Minister on that day itself. He said, "You have saved an innocent man being unnecessarily dragged in the Akali agitation. Giani Zail Singh did not believe in any scruples. He was a successful Chief Minister who knew the leadership of the Congress party, especially those around Indira Gandhi and Sanjay Gandhi.

After the emergency when Lok Sabha elections were held in 1978 and also Punjab Assembly elections were held, Morarji Desai became the Prime Minister at the Centre and the Akalis were an alliance partner at the Centre as well as in Punjab; Parkash Singh Badal became the Chief Minister of Punjab.

When Giani Zail Singh became the Chief Minister in 1971, Darbara Singh, another Congress leader, but not Darbara Singh who later succeeded Zail Singh as Punjab Chief Minister in 1980, had become Speaker of the Punjab Assembly. That Darbara Singh who during the NDA Government was appointed as Governor of Rajasthan, was close to S. Sawarn Singh and Giani Zail Singh wanted Darbara Singh removed as Speaker of the Punjab Assembly. Zail Singh appointed Harchand Singh Committee to go into the charges of some extra land with Darbara Singh and that Committee gave a report against Darbara Singh. Uma Shankar Dixt, then Home Minister, called Darbara Singh to Delhi to ask him to resign as Speaker of the Punjab Assembly. But Darbara Singh was saved by the combined efforts of Sawarn Singh and Giani Gurmukh Singh Musafir, who started feeling that if Zail Singh succeeded in his mission, then they would be his next targets. They knew the working of Zail Singh and his thinking. After this, Zail Singh was waiting for an opportunity to attack S. Sawarn Singh directly. It was known that in the first cabinet meeting on the early morning of 26 June 1975, when emergency was formally imposed, S. Sawarn Singh had opposed this move and said in the meeting. "This will be too harsh a step and people will not accept it." Zail Singh was then the Chief Minister of Punjab and Naranjan Singh Talib was the President of the Punjab Congress and Talib was playing into Zail Singh's hands. Zail Singh's strategy was to exploit the remarks made by S. Sawarn Singh in the cabinet meeting and to poison the mind of Indira Gandhi against him. Zail Singh would first send Talib to meet Indira Gandhi and tell her, "*Bahenji,* S. Sawarn Singh is our senior leader but what he is telling people these days is not good. He is telling people that how long this *Thanedari (Emergency Danda)* will last?" After Talib's meeting with Indira Gandhi, a few days later, Zail Singh himself used to call on Indira Gandhi and when she enquired if what Talib had told her was true, he used to say, "Yes, unfortunately this is true." Zail Singh was also using a Communist leader from Punjab who was a frequent visitor to Indira Gandhi to convey the same thing. Yash Paul Kapur, a trusted aide of Indira Gandhi learnt about the game being played by Giani Zail Singh against Sawarn Singh. Kapur disclosed this to B.R. Bowry, then attached to the Prime Minister as DPIO from the Information and Broadcasting Ministry. Yash Paul Kapur and Bowry were very close to each other. Bowry was a very well informed officer and had a good reputation among the journalists. He had been equally close to me. During the emergency, one day when I went to see Bowry in the PIB office, he disclosed to me how Zail

Singh was poisoning Indira Gandhi, against Sawarn Singh and what was happening. His assessment was that Sawarn Singh was having only numbered days in the cabinet, though Bowry himself had very high regard for Sawarn Singh. Sawarn Singh was one of the ministers, who used to pick up his unlisted telephone number at his residence himself and in his absence, his wife only and no other family member was allowed to use that telephone. He had given me that number to talk to him. I rang him early in the morning and told him that I wanted to see him urgently, and he immediately called me to his residence. When I went to meet him, K.L. Rao, the then Minister for Water Resources was sitting in his drawing room waiting to see him. I had never gone to his house earlier and he realized that there must be some thing really urgent for which I wanted to meet him. He came out of his drawing room, took me aside, and asked me the purpose of the visit. I told him what I had learnt. He did not believe it. He said he could not believe that Zail Singh would succeed in poisoning her mind as for every cabinet sub-committee, she was appointing him as a convener of the Cabinet Committee, even though he said he had nothing to do with that subject. I told him that it would be good if it does not happen but he has to be on the watch. Only about a week later, he had gone to Kurukshetra for some function when he got a message from the Prime Minister to see her urgently. He came back and went straight to see Indira Gandhi. She asked him, "Sardar Sahib, how about your going to Moscow as our Ambassador?" Sawarn Singh understood that time had come for him to quit and he told her, "I would not like to go to Moscow and I understand that you want me to quit, here is my resignation, and I will not advise you to send a Minister rank politician to Moscow as Ambassador. Because if you do that, then you will have to raise the status of our Ambassadors in USA, UK and France also." He took a paper, wrote his resignation on the spot, and handed over to her. From there, he straight came to my house on Shah Jahan Road and narrated the entire development. He said, "Your information and assessment was correct and I was wrong in assessing her," Zail Singh, though semi-literate, was a past-master in such conspiracies. He could go to any extent to manipulate things and conspire to achieve his political objective.

III

Bhindranwale and Dal Khalsa

The coming years beginning from 1978, when Morarji Desai became Prime Minister at the Centre and Akalis came to power in Punjab with Parkash Singh Badal as Chief Minister, saw the fight between Akalis and the Congress escalating. As Morarji Desai did at the Centre to start investigations through the Shah Commission into excesses committed during the emergency in Punjab, the Badal Government arrested a large number of Congress leaders and started investigations into the emergency excesses including against Giani Zail Singh. A number of Congress leaders were arrested including some former ministers in the Zail Singh Government and Congress party office-bearers; they were put in jails and tortured. It was at that time that Giani Zail Singh with the consent of Sanjay Gandhi thought of fighting the Akalis on religious grounds and started cultivating with Jarnail Singh Bhindranwale, who had only a year ago become Head of the Damdami Taksal, based at Gurdwara Gurdarshan Prakash at Chowk Mehta, about 25 km from Amritsar. Earlier in April 1978, Bhindranwale had announced to lead a Sikh protest against the Nirankaris at their congregation at Amritsar but at the last minute, he did not participate and Akhand Kirtani Jatha led the protest in which 16 persons were killed in the clash with Nirankaris, mostly of the Akhand Kirtni Jatha because Nirankaris were sitting fully armed expecting an attack from Bhindranwale and Akhand

Kirtani Jatha. This happened during the Akali Government led by Parkash Singh Badal. Congress leadership in Punjab thought of using Jarnail Singh Bhindranwale against the Akalis to build him up to give a fight to Akalis. At the same time, Punjab Congress leaders led by Zail Singh propped up a Sikh working with the Congress M.P., V.N. Tiwari in the Punjab University to set up a new radical organization *Dal Khalsa*. *Dal Khalsa* was set up in August 1978 at Gurdwara Akal Garh in Chandigarh and in a press conference, it announced its objective of establishing an independent Sikh state. After the press conference, next day many Punjab newspapers had published reports that the bill for the expenses at the press conference was paid by the Punjab Congress leaders. This had attracted controversy for some time. The same *Dal Khalsa*, established with the help of Punjab Congress, later became a dangerous radical organization and it was banned by the Government of India.

BHINDRANWALE'S ATTACK ON AKALI LEADERSHIP

Jarnail Singh Bhindranwale was initially a religious preacher only. He was confining his activities to rural areas only, preaching the Sikh religion. Though he was not well-educated but he had picked up *gurbani* well and became a good speaker on Sikh religion. He was not indulging in any violence. For a long time, for almost two years, he was giving the impression of a sober person. It was only after the clash with the Nirankaris and his close contacts with the Congress leadership in Punjab that he started becoming aggressive. In the clash with Nirankaris, 13 from the Akhand Kirtani Jatha and 3 from the Nirankari were killed. The Akali Government had prosecuted 64 Nirankaris including the Nirankari head Baba Gurbachan

Singh and they were tried in the sessions court, Karnal. All the 64 were acquitted and released in January 1980. After his close association with the Congress leadership and the clash with Nirankaris, Bhindranwale became highly critical of the Akali leadership. In the 1978 Akali conference at Ludhiana, Bhindranwale spoke briefly and attacked the Akali leadership, especially the then Akali Dal President, Jagdev Singh Talwandi without naming him. Bhindranwale after finishing his speech, left the dias and started moving out of the conference when Talwandi shouted at him and asked him not to run away but wait for the reply. However, Bhindranwale did not stop as he was scared of Talwandi and left the Conference.

In January 1980, Congress came to power at the centre and Giani Zail Singh became the Home Minister. Soon afterwards, some of the non-Congress State Governments including the Akali Government in Punjab, were dismissed and states brought under the central rule and some State Governors appointed by the Morarji Desai Government, which immediately after taking over had dismissed some Congress ruled State Governments and had also removed Congress appointee State Governors. Fresh assembly elections were held in Punjab and Congress came to power with Daraba Singh as Chief Minister. During the Lok Sabha polls in January 1980. Bhindranwale had campaigned actively for at least three Congress candidates including Gurdial Singh Dhillon and R.L. Bhatia. The coming to power of the Congress party at the centre and in Punjab, Bhindranwale who till then was a submissive and a humble preacher, became more bold and started taking aggressive postures. He and his other friends having radical views were not happy over the acquittal of the

Nirankari Guru and other nirankaris and they were keen to strike at Nirankaris. Nirankari Guru, Baba Gurbachan Singh was killed in Delhi on 24 April 1980, only four months after the Congress came to power at the Centre. This had embarrassed Indira Gandhi. In the FIR on the killing of the Nirankari Guru, Jarnail Singh Bhindranwale was named as an accused. The case was given to the CBI and a committee under the Lt. Governor of Delhi was set up to monitor the investigation. Though Bhindranwale was moving in Punjab freely with his armed supporters, nobody had the courage to arrest him. It was not because Bhindranwale had a large following, but because he was close to the Congress leadership and the Congress leadership was using him against the Akalis. Till then, Akalis were not openly supporting him. The letter written by the Lt. Governor of Delhi to Punjab Chief Minister, Darbara Singh on 5 September 1980, on this murder is revealing. The letter stated, "Evidence has been collected to the effect that all the 20 persons against whom notices have been issued and the three persons against whom warrants have been issued, either belong to Sant Bhindranwale Jatha or are his close associates/relatives who are hiding under his protection." The letter further said that "the experience of the investigating team has been that the local police have failed to serve notice or execute even one warrant despite the lapse of such a long period. The request from the CBI to return the unserved notices along with a report has also met with no success. This has resulted in the stalemate as the required witnesses, suspect and accused have remained non-available and the arms required for examination and expert opinion also not been presented before the investigating team." This shows the clout Bhindranwale had with the Congress leadership. Bhindranwale was moving about in the state at will, addressing congregations. Jagmohan was the Lt. Governor of Delhi, who was known to be close to Sanjay Gandhi. The letter was written to discredit Darbara Singh who was the Chief Minister and whose relations with Giani Zail Singh were not good. In fact, they were political rivals within the Congress. Zail Singh wanted to show that Darbara Singh Government was not taking action against Bhindranwale whereas the fact remained that Zail was close to Bhindranwale and was patronizing him.

BHINDRANWALE'S ACTIVITIES IN PUNJAB

The fact that Bhindranwale was being propped up by the Congress leadership against the Akalis in Punjab was known to everybody. Dr. P.C. Alexander, former Principal Secretary to Indira Gandhi, who was one of the main negotiators in the Government-Akali talks during Indira Gandhi's regime, had written pages after pages on the Punjab situation in his book, "Through the Corridors of Power" projecting Bhindranwale as the main culprit to have spread violence in Punjab but at nowhere he has even hinted that Bhindranwale was put up by the Congress leadership though Alexander knew everything. It has been a biased writing like his views on Punjab. But another senior Bureaucrat, B.G. Deshmukh, who was Cabinet Secretary during Rajiv Gandhi's regime and later Principal Secretary to the Prime Minister also, had been more truthful in his writings. In his book "A Cabinet Secretary Looks Back," Deshmukh writes in Chapter 32 on Punjab (Page 359). In the first Para on Punjab itself, he says: "As Additional Secretary in the Home Ministry from May 1981, I had to deal with police and law and order. Jyothish Pandey, Joint Secretary, reported to me and was highly apprehensive about Bhindranwale's activities in Punjab and the "dangerous game the Congress was playing by openly patronizing the Sikh leader." I wonder if Dr. Alexander had read what B.G. Deshmukh had written in his book. When Bhindranwale was arrested on 20 September 1981 in the Jagat Narain murder, at the Chowk Mehta congregation before his arrest, Jathedar Santokh Singh, President of the Delhi Sikh Gurdwara Committee, who was also patronized by Indira Gandhi, made a very provocative speech, which aroused the sentiments of crowd resulting in violence and deaths of six persons. Indira Gandhi was worried over the growing violence in Punjab but was not aware that her own party leaders were behind this violence. There was a proverbial dog-fight between Zail Singh and Darbara Singh and both of them were not missing any chance of attacking each other. When Indira Gandhi paid a hurried visit to Chandigarh to address an all party meeting on 22 September 1981 just before leaving for abroad, at the meeting Parkash Singh Badal had pointed out how her own supporter, Jathedar Santokh Singh had made a provocative speech in support of Bhindranwale, which resulted in violence. Mrs Gandhi felt a little embarrassed.

Bhindranwale was initially a very humble person but he became aggressive only when he got full support from the Congress leaders. Jagat Narain was killed near Ludhiana on 9 September 1981. Bhindranwale was in village Chando Kalan in Hissar district. Three persons close to him were named in the FIR. After Jagat Narain's murder, Darbara Singh as Chief Minister made an announcement that all the three giving their names also have been arrested. But later on, the Punjab Government changed its stand. The police got Bhindranwale's arrest warrant and the police party headed by DIG, D.S.

Mangat was sent to arrest him from Chando Kalan. Even before his arrest, news came on *AIR* news bulletin about the police obtaining his arrest warrant. Bhindranwale left the village in a bus along with some of his supporters for Chowk Mehta. Bhajan Lal was Chief Minister of Haryana and he was told by Zail Singh, then Home Minister of the country not to involve himself by arresting Bhindranwale in the state. He travelled almost over 300 km to reach Chowk Mehta at his headquarters on the night between 13-14 September 1981 and there were many police check posts on the way but nobody even questioned him. This was the patronage he was enjoying of the Congress leadership ruling at the Centre, Punjab and Haryana. When he was arrested on 20 September 1981 in this case, he was brought to Ludhiana and kept in a Canal rest House at Sidhwan Bet and later moved to Canal Rest House, Garhi village. He was interrogated by the police in these two rest houses. I got a copy of the interrogation report and gave it to Khushwant Singh, which he later used in his column in the *Hindustan Times* and described how with every sentence during the interrogation, he was addressing investigating officer as *Janab* (Sir). But after a year or so, the same Bhindranwale became a terror in Punjab and his name was enough to threaten any police officer or a judicial officer. On 15 October 1981, Zail Singh made a statement that nothing was found against Bhindranwale and he was released. How could he move about openly with his supporters carrying lethal fire-arms for which licences had been issued by the Government unless he had full support from the ruling party? The same Bhindranwale, who was addressing the interrogating police officer of the rank of an Inspector only as *Janab*, could threaten the top officers of the state police, bureaucrats and even judicial officers and lawyers;

and there was so much of this fear that his simple threat used to be enough to threaten anybody in the Government. Why was the Government giving him such a long rope and was not taking any action? He could have been arrested anywhere in Punjab or Chandigarh. Although the Punjab Government had asked people to surrender their licensed arms after the anti-tobacco procession 31 May 1981, Bhindranwale directed his men not to surrender their arms. Bhindranwale, addressing a congregation at the Sector 11 Gurdwara in Chandigarh, reiterated that his men would not surrender arms. But the Government was a silent spectator. Why? Not only he has been openly moving about with armed men in Punjab, in the first week of April, 1982, Bhindranwale came to Delhi on the invitation of the Congress controlled Delhi Sikh Gurdwara Committee along with bus loads of armed men and they were moving about in the capital, his armed men sitting on the roof of the bus. There were reports that Giani Zail Singh had met Bhindranwale at the residence of Jathedar Santokh Singh, President of Delhi Sikh Gurdwara Committee. I had given all these facts in my article in *Illustrated Weekly* of Bombay, in the issue of 26 September 1982.

GOVERNMENT'S HESITANCY IN ARRESTING BHINDRANWALE

Three months later, when some of Bhindranwale's men were arrested, he started apprehending his own arrest also so, he moved into the Golden Temple premises on 19 July 1982 and took shelter there. But what had stopped the Government from arresting him when he was moving about openly in Punjab and Delhi? The Government had all the information as to what Bhindranwale was doing and how he was arming his men. If the

Government could order operation *Blue Star*, why the Government could not take out Bhindranwale from the Gurdwara at the initial stage itself? Then Punjab Chief Minsiter, Darbara Singh had told a group of Punjab M.Ps. (*Illustrated Weekly* of 26 September 1982) in Delhi that "according to the State Government's information, not only extremists were hiding in the Gurdwara but even arms were being manufactured on the fourth floor of Nanak Niwas, adjoining the Golden Temple." Still no action was taken. Akalis were scared of Bhindranwale. However, Bhindranwale had the support of G.S. Tohra, President of the SGPC. Bhindranwale could not have stayed in the Golden Temple complex without the support of Tohra. But other Akali leaders, Sant Harchand Singh Longowal, President of the Akali Dal, Parkash Singh Badal and Jagdev Singh Talwandi were opposed to Bhindranwale and his style. But they did not have the courage to oppose him publically as Bhindranwale was becoming popular among Sikh youth, as he was speaking the language of rural Sikh youth. Once inside the Golden Temple, he had started feeling protected and secure and when he found that his writ was running and the State machinary was scared of him, he was becoming more and more aggressive and had started indulging in giving "orders" to the administration from his hide-out within the Golden Temple complex. He had further moved to the Akal Takhat, considered as the holiest place of the Sikhs, thinking that he would be more secure there. He had started considering himself as the monarch who could not be challenged and from his hide-out, he was announcing the names of persons who should be killed. He was giving judgements from his hide-out. It was a complete *jungle raj* in Punjab. But the Government was still a silent spectator. Now, within the temple complex, RAW and IB officials were in close touch with him, acting as emissaries of the Government. Dr. P.C. Alexander himself admits in his book: "The Government began to receive information about the growing rift between Longowal and Bhindranwale. Bhindranwale had by then turned openly hostile against the ostensibly moderate "style" of the Akali leaders. He branded them as agents of the Government in his diatribes. What he wanted was an all out war against the Government as well as communal clashes, which could lead to a massive exodus of Hindus in Punjab. Longowal was basically against instigating communal conflicts; he wanted the agitation directed only against the Central Government and the State Governments. At the same time, he was becoming increasingly anxious about the propaganda unleashed against him by Bhindranwale. Consequently, he felt obliged to intensify the agitation in order not to be overshadowed." Bhindranwale was surrounded by many extremist elements and also by unemployed youth and some undesirable elements whose main plank was crime. He had started feeling apprehensive that he might be arrested, especially after his quarrel with Longowal and on 15 December 1983, he along with his men shifted to the Akal Takhat where he felt more secure and with the help of retired Major General Shehbag Singh who had trained Mukti Bahni in Bangla Desh against the Pakistani army and was known as a competent army officer, started building a defence network. His shifting to the Akal Thakat and preparing a defensive network were both sacrilegious act. But nobody had the courage among the Akalis to oust him from the Akal Takhat.

As I have written earlier, within the Golden Temple Complex, RAW and IB both were directly in touch with

Bhindranwale. There was every attempt by the Government to keep Bhindranwale in good humour. Why was the Government not moving against him and why was the Government giving him a long rope to create more havoc in Punjab, waiting for an opportunity to show a bigger strength of the Government to cow down the Akalis? What was the real purpose behind all these moves?

THE KILLING OF DIG OF POLICE

A.S. Atwal, DIG of Police, Jalandhar Range in Punjab was killed on 25 April 1983 by supporters of Bhindranwale, just at the entrance of the Golden Temple, when Atwal was coming out of the Golden Temple after paying obeisance there. He was carrying holy *prasad* he had received from the Golden Temple priest in both his hands and was coming out of the temple when he was shot dead just at the steps of the Golden Temple and killed on the spot. Atwal was a highly respected police officer and Amritsar district fell under his range. A month or so earlier, Amritsar Police under Atwal's range under A.P. Pandey, the then SP Headquarters at Amritsar, had put up a *Naka* at 4 a.m. at Mannewala on way to Chowk Mehta, to arrest some supporters of Bhindranwale. Bhindranwale's men travelling in a vehicle threw a grenade on the Police party and encounter ensued in which one Hardev Singh Chinna was killed and three persons injured. This had made Bhindranwale furious and he was threatening more deadly attacks on the Police. A senior Sikh RAW officer, who was in touch with Bhindranwale, went to Amritsar and after meeting Bhindranwale, whom he found highly agitated, rang up A.S. Atwal in Jalandhar and asked him to reach Amritsar urgently. This RAW officer was staying at Canal Rest House. Atwal reached there and the RAW officer told him that he was sent by the Central Government to convey him that Bhindranwale was very agitated over the encounter with his men and the Centre wants Atwal to go with the RAW officer to meet Bhindranwale and apologize from him. But Atwal refused point blank and told him that he would not apologize for the action taken by his men. However, early in the morning, he got ready and since he was in Amritsar and was a devoted Sikh, went to the Golden Temple to pay his obeisance at the Darbar Saheb, which he always did. It was at that time that when he was coming out of the temple, he was shot-dead at the foot-steps of the Golden Temple. This came as a big shock for the then Prime Minister, Indira Gandhi. She was extremely worried over the developments. She sent the then CBI Director, J.S. Bawa to Amritsar to study the situation and report to her. Bawa was a very straight-forward and honest officer. He personally went to Amritsar and visited the Golden Temple also. He discussed the situation with local officials also. He came back and reported to Indira Gandhi that the killers were still within the Golden Temple Complex and were men of Bhindranwale. After his meeting with Indira Gandhi, I met Bawa with whom I was in touch almost on daily basis and he told me that he had briefed the Prime Minister and told her that the killers were still in the Golden Temple complex. I asked him if he had given this report in writing, he said, "Such reports are not given in writing." These are personal level briefings and I have done that." I asked him what was Prime Minister's reaction when he told her that the killers were still in the Golden Temple complex, he said, "she kept quiet."

When Atwal was killed at the foot-steps of the Golden Temple, there was a great anger among the people of Punjab including Sikhs against Bhindranwale and that was the best opportunity for the Government to enter the Golden Temple and arrest Bhindranwale and his men. Even the Akalis would have been forced to cooperate with the Government. In fact, they would have been happy over riddance from Bhindranwale, who had made their lives also miserable. But the Government did not move in the matter at all. If the Government had acted even at that stage, there would have been no need for Operation Blue Star and possibly, Indira Gandhi would still have been alive. But it was her misfortune that she was surrounded by such persons who were advising her and playing some other game. This is the biggest weakness of every politician. When they are in power, they trust certain people without realizing that those whom they are trusting might be, wittingly or unwittingly, leading them to the wrong path. This is what was happening with Indira Gandhi and later with Rajiv Gandhi also. Whenever, anybody complained to Indira Gandhi against such persons, she used to get annoyed. She was a good leader, India had but this was her biggest weakness. Now, same mistake is being committed by Mrs Sonia Gandhi. These leaders never try to learn any lesson from the past experience, though Rajiv Gandhi had started realizing that some of those around him, when he was the Prime Minister, were responsible for his defeat in the 1989 Lok Sabha polls, and he had become very cautious. There should be a commission of enquiry to find out the causes of rise of terrorism in Punjab but not by judges like Ranganath Mishra, who looked into anti-Sikh riots of 1984 or the Thakkar Commission. It could be even a secret study through some independent agency from which the Government could at least learn some lessons.

Even Dr. P.C. Alexander has mentioned in his book on page 241 that for the first round of talks with the Akalis on

16 October 1981, Indira Gandhi did not want to involve Home Minister, Zail Singh; consequently, no other minister was invited. A pertinent question has often been asked as to why Indira Gandhi did not bring in Zail Singh the first time around or on all subsequent occasions, except one, even though some other senior Cabinet Ministers were actively involved. One of the reasons could be that she harboured serious apprehensions that the presence of Zail Singh might lead to a stiffening of the attitude of the Akali leaders participating in the talks. The seniormost among them heartily disliked Zail Singh; this dislike had been aggravated during his tenure as the Chief Minister of Punjab. The Akalis seemed to believe that Zail Singh would be more interested in breaking the unity among the Akalis than in finding a solution to the problems. In fact, they believed, rightly or wrongly, that Zail Singh had been secretly grooming Bhindranwale to become a rival power centre in Punjab in order to weaken the Akalis' "hold over the Sikh community."

The dislikes by the top Akali leadership of Giani Zail Singh had been from the time even before he was Chief Minister of Punjab. This had more to do with the psychological feeling of Jat Sikhs of Punjab. Akali politics after the death of Master Tara Singh became Jat dominated and this shift had taken place soon after death of Master Tara Singh. Jat Sikhs in Punjab had always a certain dislike for the scheduled caste and backward class Sikhs as the Jats considered themselves much superior to other Sikh communities. Zail Singh belonged to the Ramgarhia community and the Akalis in their private talks used to describe Zail Singh as *Gulli Ghad.* Zail Singh knew about it and when he became Chief Minister, he used to ensure that the Jat Sikh leaders, especially when they used to come to meet him, wait for long and if any Akali leader enquired why the Chief Minister was so busy, Zall Singh used to convey to them that he was busy in *Gulli Ghad.* Though the scheduled caste and backward classes population in Punjab is much more than the Jat Sikhs of the State, yet Akali leadership never liked them from their hearts. They accommodated these classes only for political reasons but from their hearts, they disliked them. About two decades ago in the late seventies, the Jat Sikhs in Punjab were feeling aggrieved and agitated and it was well known in Chandigarh that some Jat Sikh officers, at their closed door "evening get together," used to criticize even the Ten Sikh Gurus for not promoting any Jat among the Gurus. They considered the Ten Gurus as biased against Jats. They used to name many Jat devotees of the Gurus who could have been promoted as Guru. This was the mental state of affairs of the Jat Sikhs. Even Partap Singh Kairon was known for promoting Jat lobby and in fact, he had, through some Akali sources, given the idea to the Akalis to replace Master Tara Singh with a Jat leader and the Akali Dal should be led by the Jat Sikh. It was this inside hatred between Zail Singh and the Akali leadership more than even political circumstances. The Akalis in their private talks, describing him as "Gulli Ghad," had created a hate in him against the Jat Sikh leadership. As Chief Minister, within the Congress party, he humiliated the then Speaker of the Assembly, Darbara Singh, who later died when he was Governor of Rajasthan during the NDA Government, and also conspired the exit of a tall leader like Sardar Sawaran Singh from the cabinet by poisoning the mind of Indira Gandhi against him. Zail Singh was much shrewder than the Akalis. Despite his dislike for the Akalis, he was keeping close links with some senior Akali leaders like G.S. Tohra.

Alexander also wrote, "While violence and terrorist activities were spreading like wildfire across the state, the Chief Minister of Punjab and Giani Zail Singh, the Union Home Minister, continued fighting unabated, thereby seriously impairing the effective handling of the situation. Darbara Singh levelled a serious charge, confidentially, to the Prime Minister against Zail Singh that he had helped Bhindranwale to escape from Chando Kalan. For his part, Zail Singh accused Darbara Singh of ineptitude in handling the whole affair."

When Indira Gandhi knew that her Home Minister, Zail Singh was propping up Jarnail Singh Bhindranwale and this was known to everybody, Akalis and Chief Minister Darbara Singh and the entire Punjab, why was she not asking Zail Singh not to have any link with Bhindranwale? When Bhindranwale was disturbing peace in Punjab and giving birth for the first time to rise of terrorism in the State, why was she ignoring Zail Singh's connections with Bhindranwale? If they had not sponsored Bhindranwale against the Akalis, the situation in Punjab would not have taken the kind of turn it took from 1980 onwards. Why does the Government accuse the Akalis for the acts of Bhindranwale when it was well known that Bhindranwale was the creation of the Congress leadership?

When Bhindranwale was arrested in the Jagat Narain murder case, the decision to release him a few days later was not of any court but of the Central Government. It was the Central Government, which announced that there was no charge against Bhindranwale. An *Indian Airlines* plane was hijacked on 20 September 1981 in which *Dal Khalsa* members were involved and they demanded the release of Bhindranwale. This was the same *Dal Khalsa* that was set up in Chandigarh in 1978 and there were allegations that the bill for the press conference of the Dal Khalsa was paid by the Punjab Congress. The same *Dal Khalsa* had become a deadly radical organization, which was banned by the Central Government.

The Government of India had reports for months together that Bhindranwale was collecting arms inside the Golden Temple complex and he was creating defences with the help of retired Major General Shehbagh Singh. Shehbagh Singh had serious grievances against the Central Government that he had trained the Mukti Bahni in the former territory of Pakistan known as East Pakistan, now Bangladesh, to fight against the atrocities being committed by the Pakistani army against the people of Bangladesh and Mukti Bahni had given great help to the Indian army during the 1971 war with Pakistan. But Shehbagh Singh was cashiered from service on corruption charges. He was a highly trained army officer who was out to strike back at the Central Government. It was all his planning of defences within the Golden Temple complex, which gave a lot of resistance to the entry of armed forces during Operation Blue Star. Shahbegh Singh was a good fighter.

A few days after *Operation Blue Star,* in the middle of June, the Central Government took a press party to Amritsar for on-the-spot view of the Operation Blue Star, where the army authorities were to brief the press. There were about 45 journalists taken to Amritsar in a special plane, and I was one of them. Those days, I was working for the *Indian Express.* Army was present all around the Golden Temple.

I spoke to some of the senior army officers about their view of the situation and I found they were not happy how the situation had ultimately developed. There were also question marks on the death of Bhindranwale, whether he had died fighting or was caught by the army and later liquidated. There were hushed voices and this was a mystry.

Two days after the Operation Blue Star, exactly on 8 June, the Central Government had planned that some journalists should be taken to Amritsar. Three journalists were selected. M.K. Dhar of *Hindustan Times,* R. Rangarajan of the *UNI* and myself from the *Indian Express*. I was rung up by Sharda Prasad, the then Press Secretary to the Prime Minister, at 6 a.m. on 8 June and told to be ready to go to Amritsar by 8 a.m. by special plane. I was told that only three of us will be going. I immediately rang up B.G. Verghese, who was editor of the *Indian Express,* at his residence and informed him about the telephone call I had received from Sharda Prasad. Verghese asked me to take a camera and a few films from the office with me and take as many pictures as I could from the spot, at the Golden Temple. But the government did not want any of us to take any camera with us. After about an hour, I got another telephone call from Sharda Prasad saying that the trip to Amritsar has been cancelled as the plane that was supposed to take us to Amritsar, has been taken by Giani Zail Singh, who wanted to go to Amritsar. Giani Zail Singh also wanted me to accompany him but I declined to accompany him as I held him fully responsible for whatever had happened. I knew Zail Singh very intimately for over 40 years, and even as President of India, he used to ring me personally and never through his P.A.

ZAIL SINGH'S VISIT TO AMRITSAR

During his visit to Amritsar, Zail Singh met the Sikh head priests of the Golden Temple and heard their complaints. The *Jathedars* were highly critical of the role of the army during Operation Blue Star. When the head priests were criticizing the army role, some Army Generals were also present. After his meeting, there was resentment in the army hierarchy against Zail Singh that as President of India, he was the supreme commander of the armed forces and when the head priests were criticizing the army role, he did not defend them. This resentment reached Indira Gandhi also who was not happy over Zail Singh's visit to Amritsar so soon, after *Operation Blue Star.* The relations between Zail Singh and Indira Gandhi had already become sore. The relations between Indira Gandhi and Zail Singh had not been very cordial right from the beginning of Zail Singh taking over as President of India on 25 July 1982. Zail Singh, who during his election campaign for the Presidentship of India, had said that he was prepared to broom the floor if Indira Gandhi wanted, had started showing colours soon after becoming the President of India. There was a general impression that Zail Singh will be a rubber stamp President but in my article in the *Illustrated Weekly* of India of 25 July 1982, I had said, "To say that Zail Singh will be a rubber stamp President, will be to underestimate him. He is quite capable of showing his true colours once he is on his own. He does believe in giving unstinted loyalty to the leader. But, in Rashtrapati Bhavan, he will be his own leader and have full freedom to act within the constraints imposed by the constitution and convention. Zail Singh had become President with the help of R.K. Dhawan but Dhawan's loyalty was more with Indira Gandhi than Zail Singh. There were allegations that the Government was tapping the telephones of Rashtrapati Bhavan but the Government had denied this. Even A.B. Vajpayee as leader of the BJP and L.K. Advani had held a press conference on 23 June, 1985 where they had alleged that Rashtrapati Bhavan telephones were being tapped and they had given a few names of some journalists also whose telephones were being tapped and that list included my name and the name of Kuldip Nayyar also. The BJP has been having its sources deep into the Intelligence Bureau for a long time and those sources have been very helpful to Vajpayee and Advani. There were reports that following the Operation Blue Star, on June 7, 1984, only a day after the operation, about 500 Sikh soldiers belonging to the Sikh Regiment based at Ganganagar in Rajasthan, had mutinied, and had seized the army vehicles and were out shouting slogans against the Government. This was followed by incidents of mutiny by Sikh soldiers at some other places also. In Ramgarh in Bihar at the Sikh Regimental Centre, large groups of Sikhs recruits also revolted, took out arms from the government armoury and vehicles and drove towards Amritsar raising slogans. They first killed Brigadier S.C. Puri, who was heading the Sikh Regimental Centre. There were revolts by Sikh soldiers from some other places also. This had panicked the Prime Minister, Indira Gandhi. Indian army was known for discipline and loyalty and no one could ever have thought of mutiny by Sikh soldiers. The armed forces moved swiftly and soon normalcy was restored. The fact remained that the Rashtrapati Bhavan telephones were being tapped and the Government was keeping a close watch. During the telephone tapping of Rashtrapati Bhavan, the Government found a telephone call made from Rashtrapati Bhavan to Patiala to someone conveying Zail Singh's message to Amrinder Singh asking him to resign from Parliament immediately. Zail Singh was taking precaution that no call was made direct to Amrinder Singh for this purpose as he knew that Rashtrapati Bhavan telephones were being tapped. This call was made to Patiala in the early hours of the morning.

Amrinder Singh soon after this call, left for Delhi to submit his resignation to the Speaker of the Lok Sabha. The IB had intercepted this call and informed the Prime Minister. Some security men were posted at the Tilak Marg residence of Amrinder Singh to bring him to the Prime Minister's residence as soon as he reached Delhi. But Amrinder Singh after reaching Delhi, did not go to his residence but to some other friend's house and then drove straight to the Speaker and handed over his resignation from the Lok Sabha as protest against the Operation Blue Star. Soon afterwards, the news of his resignation spread as copies of his resignation letter were distributed to some journalists. This disturbed Indira Gandhi a lot. In the evening, she called on Zail Singh and requested him to make an appeal to the Sikh soldiers, as supreme commander of the armed forces, to remain in discipline. During the talk with Zail Singh, she took out a cassette and asked Giani Zail Singh to listen to the conversation in which it was stated that Giani Ji wanted Amrinder to resign from Lok Sabha immediately. She told Zail Singh that a telephone at Patiala was being tapped in which this conversation was tapped. Zail Singh realized that he had been caught and had no escape route. From next day, his Deputy Press Secretary, Tarlochan Singh, who had conveyed his message at Patiala and who was known as a confidante of Zail Singh, was sent on one month's leave and Zail Singh recorded his telecast appealing to the Sikh soldiers to remain loyal to the forces. According to reports then emanating from circles close to Zail Singh, he was given some brandy in milk before recording his speech because he was feeling very low. Zail Singh's message to the forces was telecasted on 17 June. After about two weeks, he started conveying to the Prime Minister that Tarlochan Singh's going on leave was giving him a bad name and he should be allowed to come back and join his duty. Tarlochan Singh was allowed to join back a week before the expiry of his forced leave . But the trust between the Prime Minister and the President had completely been shaken and the Government was keeping a watchful eye on the happenings within the Rashtrapati Bhavan. Zail Singh was aware of it and he was waiting for another opportunity to hit back at Indira Gandhi. I found that every time Zail Singh called me to Rashtrapati Bhavan for any discussion, he was always apprehensive that the discussion might be recorded. He always tried to find a corner, which might not have been bugged and he would talk in a very low voice or he would take me out to the lawns and then talk. The gap between Indira Gandhi and Zail Singh had become quite wide and both of them did not trust each other.

Among the Akalis, the Government had its loyalists like Balwant Singh, former Finance Minister, in the Prakash Singh Badal Government. As I wrote earlier, among the Sikhs, three leaders— Jarnail Singh Bhindranwale, Giani Zail Singh and Balwant Singh—have been more responsible for damaging the Sikh cause and their interests than any other Sikh leader. Sikhs have always been respected in all parts of the country with the exception of Arya Samaj leaders of Punjab. Sikhs had made more sacrifices for the freedom struggle than any other community. Bhindranwale was incapable of understanding these things. He was only being exploited by the Congress leadership against the Akalis. Among the Akalis, Balwant Singh was a very shrewd man who never wanted any settlement between the Government and the Akalis. He was always playing double game giving the impression to the Government that he was the only Akali leader capable of finding a solution to the Punjab problem. He was in direct touch with Dr. P.C. Alexander, who was then Principal Secretary to the Prime Minister and known as the key administrator in the Indira Gandhi Government. Dr. Alexander had helped him in getting a loan of Rs. 6 crore from a public sector bank for his business. He did not want any settlement to take place between the Akalis and the Government of India. Many a times, the Akalis were prepared to come to some settlement and avert the situation further worsening but it was Balwant Singh who wanted this to continue. He was giving certain suggestions to the Government on how to handle Akalis and on the other side, he was further instigating the Akali leadership not to agree to any settlement. Even as late as February 1984, the Akalis had called a meeting of their *Jathedars* at Amritsar and they were feeling that their agitation, which had been hijacked by Bhindranwale, was doing more harm to the community now than helping it and they should withdraw it. They were mortally scared of Bhindranwale and were not prepared to criticize him for what he was doing. In fact, senior Akali leaders were so scared of Bhindranwale that they had started fearing threat to their lives. None of them had the courage to challenge Bhindranwale on the path he had adopted of indulging in violence. At the Akalis' meeting, many speakers expressed such views and wanted their agitation to be suspended or withdrawn as it was doing great harm to the Sikhs and Punjab. It was at this stage that Balwant Singh got up and made a very provocative speech saying that after making so many sacrifices, either suspension or withdrawal of agitation will be betrayal of Sikhs. He wanted the agitation to continue with greater vigour. His speech was so provocative that the Akalis were once again forced to rethink their stand and continue the agitation. After the meeting, Atma Singh, a senior Akali leader who was known as a sober person among the Akalis, rang up one of his friends in Rashtrapati Bhavan and told him that his impression was that the Government wanted the agitation to end but from Balwant Singh's speech at the Akali meeting, he got the impression that the Government did not want the agitation to stop. He narrated how the thinking among Akalis was that the agitation was now harming the Sikh cause and they should either suspend or withdraw it. But Balwant Singh's provocative speech had once again turned the tables to continue the agitation, which meant that the Government did not want the agitation to end. This was the role Balwant Singh was playing. But this certainly did not mean that the Government was instigating Balwant Singh to continue the agitation. In fact, at that stage the Government was extremely worried over the turn the situation had taken and was keen for some settlement. But Balwant Singh wanted the agitation to continue so that he could play a double role and remain in good books of the Government. He was not in India when *Operation Blue Star* took place and he had some hints of possible action. He had slipped away to London. During the Operation Blue Star, he spoke to me from London and wanted to know the development in Punjab. I remember having told him bluntly that he was also responsible for the action, the Government had to resort to and he was misleading the Government as its agent and also his own party. I had held him fully responsible for the development as I was aware about his role in the Akali Dal meeting in February in Amritsar where he had made a provocative speech to continue the agitation and also his relations with Dr. Alexander. After coming back from London, after *Operation Blue Star,* he came to see me and tried to explain that he had no role in continuing the agitation but I did not believe him at all and I had told him so right at his face. Even during the Rajiv Gandhi-Longowal accord and after the accord, he kept on playing the same role befooling the Akalis. After the Rajiv Gandhi-Longowal accord, when the Akalis came to power in Punjab in September 1985 with Surjit Singh Barnala as Chief Minister, Balwant Singh became the Deputy Chief Minister as he had helped the then Punjab Governor, Arjun Singh in arranging the Rajiv Gandhi–Longowal accord, which for Arjun Singh was a big achievement.

IV

1980s: Disastrous Period for Punjab

Though the foundations for extremism in Punjab were laid by the Congress leadership in Punjab, the Akalis were equally responsible for continuing agitations against the Central Government, despite knowing that their agitation had been hijacked by Jarnail Singh Bhindranwale and they were fully aware that their continuing agitation along with Bhindranwale was doing immense harm to the Sikh community. Unfortunately, the vision of the Akali leadership had been very narrow and they could not grow with the changing times. They were more interested in capturing power in the state than looking after the interests of the Sikh community or spreading the message of the Gurus. Whenever they came to power in the state after the reorganization of Punjab in 1966 they forgot all the demands, which they used to make as an opposition party in Punjab. It is a matter of record that they never raised any controversial issue with the Central Government, on which they were holding agitation, after coming to power. Even in 1978, when the Akalis were in power in Punjab, Parkash Singh Badal as Chief Minister and for the first time Akalis shared power in the Central Government headed by Morarji Desai, Surjit Singh Barnala joining as Agriculture Minister; they could have impressed upon their alliance partners to accept at least some of their demands. But there is not a single letter on the record of the Central Government, which Parkash Singh would have written to Morarji Desai on Punjab's demands or transfer of Chandigarh to Punjab and on the river waters distribution. For Punjab, river waters issue is more important than even the Chandigarh issue. Even Surjit Singh Barnala, as a Central Minister did nothing for Punjab. Whenever they got power, they forgot all the noises they used to make in the name of people of Punjab or the Sikh community. They never took up even the issue of setting any big industry in Punjab. But once they are out of power, they will again plan agitation and put forward many demands accusing the Centre of giving Punjab a step-motherly treatment. In this matter, Congress leadership was equally responsible for not being prepared to share power with Akalis. It was in 1950s only when as a result of Jawahar Lal Nehru—Master Tara Singh agreement that the Akalis joined the Congress and shared power for some time. Akali representatives—Giani Kartar Singh and Gian Singh Rareweala—were ministers in the Partap Singh Kairon Government for some time. But the Congress leadership of Jalandhar Division in Punjab sabotaged even this arrangement. Giani Kartar Singh was known as the brain of the Akali party. He was a selfless, most dedicated and honest politician unlike the present day Akali leaders. Unlike the present day ministers, Giani Kartar Singh whenever on official tour, used to carry some *atta* (wheat flour) with him in small bag for himself and his touring staff, would get some *chapattis* made from a road side *tandoor,* buy a plate of meat curry from a roadside *dhaba* and eat sitting in his car. Now even small politicians from every political party eat only in a posh-restaurant or a five-star hotel. Equally in the Congress party in Punjab, there used to be ministers who were scrupulously honest, simple and dedicated. The number of such ministers was plenty. But now one hardly finds such a minister. People used to respect ministers for their honesty and simplicity whereas now people hate politicians. Congress party in Punjab had ministers like Dr. Lehna Singh Sethi, Gian Chand Kharbanda and Ujjal Singh, who later became Governor of a State. Even for collection of funds for the party, no minister was ever known as a fund collector and even for any special occasion, the minister would never go alone for fund collection. I remember, at the time of AICC session in Amritsar in 1950s, S. Ujjal Singh was the industry minister. Congress needed funds for the party session. Punjab Congress deputed S. Ujjal Singh to approach the industry for donations. In Ludhiana, the biggest industrial town in the North, a message was sent to many industries giving date and approximate time that S. Ujjal will be coming to them personally to each one of them for donations. He was highly respected by all sections irrespective of political affiliations. He never went alone. He took the party treasurer with the receipt book in his hand and local district president with him. Every penny was received with a formal receipt. Lajpat Rai, a local RSS leader had started a "RITA" Sewing Machine factory in partnership with Mohan Lal. His factory also received a message about the visit of S. Ujjal Singh next day. This was told to me by none other than Mohan Lal himself, partner of Lajpat Rai. Mohan Lal informed Lajpat Rai about the message and asked him how much donation they should give. Lajpat Rai told him, "You sign a cheque and put it before S. Ujjal Singh and ask him to fill up the amount he would like his factory to donate. We have great respect for S. Ujjal and it will be our privilege that he will be visiting our factory." This is the respect the ministers used to enjoy those days. Mohan Lal did exactly as suggested by Lajpat Rai but S. Ujjal Singh very politely declined to accept the offer and told Mohan Lal to fill up whatever amount they wanted to donate. The treasure of the Punjab Congress who was accompanying S. Ujjal Singh, issued the formal receipt. Those days, party fund collections, that too only for the very special occasions used to be in small donations say a few thousand unlike the present day when these donations are in every party in crores and that too without any receipt. Ministers do not go to industrialists or businessmen as humble politicians but they call them to their houses and ask for donations. Nobody knows whether those donations reach the party at all in full or in part. Earlier, politics used to be public service but now for politicians, it is an industry without any investment and most rewarding. Values in politics have completely changed. Ministers in Punjab, whether they are from the Akali party or the Congress or the Akalis ally, BJP, they are no different from the politicians of other states.

The Akalis' main fight in Punjab against the Central Government or the Congress party has been more to share power than looking after the interests of Punjab or the Sikh community. Congress is not prepared to tolerate Akalis coming to power in Punjab and whenever the Akalis got power, the Congress did everything at its command to topple their Government. It was only with Sonia Gandhi as Congress President and Dr. Manmohan Singh as Prime Minister that the Central leadership of the Congress party decided not to allow the Punjab Congress leaders to topple the Parkash Singh Badal Government. The difference between the number of legislators in Punjab of the Akalis and the Congress party is not much and if the Central leadership of the Congress had allowed their Punjab leaders, they would have succeeded in toppling the Parkash Singh Badal Government.

VIOLENCE IN PUNJAB

There were simmering signs of violence taking roots in Punjab after the 1978 clash between the Nirankaris and the Sikh hard-liners of Damdami Taksal to which Bhindranwale belonged and the Akhand-Kirtni Jatha, a radical Sikh group of which 13 persons were killed, followed by the killing of Baba Gurbachan Singh, head of the Nirankari sect in Delhi in April 1980, soon after the Congress came to power at the Centre. The Nirankari-Akhand-Kirtni Jatha clash in Amritsar had taken place during the Akali regime in Punjab and this was considered a blot on the Parkash Singh Badal Government. When the Congress came to power at the Centre in 1980, it dismissed the Parkash Singh Badal Government. Akalis without power were feeling restless and had no political issue to fight the Centre or the Congress party. The River Water agreement between Punjab, Haryana and Rajasthan signed by the Chief Ministers of the three states in 31 December 1981 had given the Akalis an issue. It was well known that the then Punjab Chief Minister, Darbara Singh was not inclined to sign this agreement as he thought the agreement was against the interests of Punjab but the Central leadership had forced him to sign. It was almost under threat that he had to sign this agreement. The agreement was signed in the Prime Minister's office. The fact remains that Haryana had succeeded in lobbying with the Prime Minister and those around here were all helping Haryana. Darbara Singh could not muster much support and he was forced to fall in line. To carry the Haryana share in the river waters, Sutlej-Yamuna canal was to be built in some parts of Punjab as that canal had to pass through Punjab areas. The then Prime Minister, Indira Gandhi had to inaugurate the digging of the canal on 24 April 1982, which would carry Haryana's share in river waters to Haryana.

The Akalis announced their agitation against the digging of the canal from that day. The agitation was started but it flopped. The fact is that every agitation the Akalis started outside the Gurdwaras proved a failure and the agitation started from the Gurdwara premises especially from the Golden Temple complex, proved a success. Since thousands of devotees go to the Golden Temple every day for prayers, the Akalis could easily get *satyagrahis* for their agitation. It was for this reason that the Akalis shifted their agitation from Kapoori village to the Golden Temple complex in the name of "Dharam Yudh", on 4 August 1982. Jarnail Singh Bhindranwale had already shifted to the Golden Temple complex a few days earlier on 19 July 1982, fearing arrest. Bhindranwale had shifted to the Golden Temple complex because Bhai Amrik Singh, President of the All India Sikh Students Federation, who was very close to Bhindranwale, was arrested by the Amritsar Police and Bhindranwale started fearing that he might be arrested and he shifted to the Golden Temple Complex considering it a safe heaven. He had announced a *morcha* against the arrest of Bhai Amrik Singh. But when the Akalis started "Dharam Yudh" *morcha* from the Golden Temple Complex, he called off his *morcha* and joined hands with the Akalis. He knew that he did not have the support of Sikh masses and his *morcha* would flop. Therefore, he took the advantages of Akalis *morcha* and called off his own one. Ultimately, he took the advantage of Akali *morcha* and the Akalis, though opposed to him, did not have the courage to oppose Bhindranwale or his policies. They were mortally scared of him. During the agitation, differences had cropped up between Bhindranwale and Sant Harchand Singh Longowal over the style of Bhindranwale. While Bhindranwale was taking the agitation against the Centre on communal lines,

Sant Longowal was opposed to this trend. Bhindranwale had already tasted blood and created a fear psychosis among the Hindus and also among those Sikhs who were opposed to his thinking. The Akalis were realizing that this was doing great harm to the Sikh community and also to the state of Punjab but had no courage to take a stand against Bhindranwale. They started fearing that if they opposed Bhindranwale, they would lose votes in rural areas. As a result, the Akalis also started adopting more aggressive postures. Within their hearts they knew that they were doing a wrong thing. But still they were ultimately falling into Bhindranwale trap at least in taking a hardliner attitude towards the Central Government. Sikh Congress leadership in Punjab had succeeded in exploiting Bhindranwale against the Akalis during 1980 first Lok Sabha elections and then in the Assembly elections in which the Akalis had lost power in Punjab. Giani Zail Singh was the main sponsor of Jarnail Singh Bhindranwale and it was his policy with the knowledge of Sanjay Gandhi to put up Bhindranwale against the Akalis.

THE ROLE OF CONGRESS IN PUNJAB

The period from early 1980 onwards, when the Congress party came to power in Punjab and at the Centre, for Punjab it was the most disastrous period laying foundations of extremism and terrorism in Punjab and ultimately engulfing the entire country also. Right from the beginning of the Congress coming back to power at the Centre, Bhindranwale was emboldened and he started taking law into his own hands and considering himself as the uncrowned king of Punjab. He was making highly provocative statements affecting the communal harmony that existed in Punjab between Hindus and Sikhs.

His first victim was the Nirankari Guru Baba Gurbachan Singh, who was killed in April 1980. There was a report that Bhindranwale had announced at Jandua Bhimshah in Tehsil Fazilka that Bachna (Baba Gurbachan Singh) had killed 25 persons while he killed only three persons. He would kill 22 persons more. To compete with Bhindranwale, the extremist group of Akalis demanded in May 1980, a complete ban on the use of tobacco in Amritsar since it was the "holy" city of the Sikhs. They took out a procession in Amritsar city in which some provocative slogans were raised. Hindus Swarksha Samiti of Amritsar had opposed this move and had earlier taken out a procession opposing the move and raising slogans which did affect the communal situations in Punjab. Jagat Narain and a section of Congress leaders of Punjab were supporting the Hindu Swaraksha Samiti. This was the beginning of communal tensions in Punjab.

In the middle of March 1981, a Sikh educational conference was called by the Chief Khalsa Dewan at Chandigarh a non-political organization meant primarily to promote Sikh educational institutions. Ganga Singh Dhillon, a Sikh residing in USA, was asked to preside over it. There were at least three disgruntled leading Sikhs, one a doctor by profession, other a retired Chief Justice of the High Court and a doctor employed in the Health services of Punjab. They were the leading lights behind this conference. All the three had their own personal grievances against the Central Government concerning their own professional careers. Ganga Singh Dhillon was an unknown entity in the field of education but was known as close to the American administration and also the then Pakistan's military ruler, Zia-Ul-Haq. It was from this forum that for the first time, Ganga Singh Dhillon declared:

"Sikhs are a separate nation, and he moved a resolution demanding that the Sikhs be admitted to associate membership of the United Nations as they were not a part of the Hindu mainstream and had a separate identity." Before this conference, nobody had beard of Ganga Singh Dhillon. He had described himself as a businessman but nobody knew what business he was doing. But he was the spirit behind the Nankana Sahib Sikh Foundation, which ironically had its headquarters not in Pakistan but in Washington, and he often used to shuttle between the USA, Pakistan, UK and Canada. Ganga Singh Dhillon was always treated as personal guest of Pakistani military ruler, Zia. When a report on Ganga Singh Dhillon declaring Sikhs as a separate nation appeared next morning, Giani Zail Singh was the Home Minister of the country. I immediately realized that there was something much deeper in this resolution and this was an indication of the coming events. Those days, the budget session of Parliament was on and I went to Parliament House and went straight to the room of Home Minister, Giani Zail Singh. He was alone in his room. I bolted the room from inside and told Zail Singh about the implications of the resolution passed at the Sikh Educational Conference. Since Zail Singh himself was a semi-literate, he had not understood the implications of the resolution. I told him that he might not have realized it but my feeling was that this was an indication of some dangerous situations following it and he should do something about it. I suggested him that as a first step, he should ask the IB Director about the passport which Dhillon was carrying and if it was an Indian passport, he should impound it. In my presence, he spoke to T.V. Rajeshwar, the then Director of the Intelligence Bureau, later Governor of U.P., and asked him if Dhillon was having an Indian passport. Rajeshwar told him that Dhillon was having an American passport. Zail Singh suggested him to take some steps that he should leave the country. Two weeks later in the end of March, the SGPC met in Amritsar and passed a similar resolution moved by Sant Harchand Singh Longowal. This had created a commotion in Government circles and Zail Singh himself issued a statement criticizing the resolution moved by the SGPC as the role of the SGPC is only to look after the historic Sikh Gurdwaras and ensure spread of teachings of ten Sikh Gurus. SGPC had no political role. On both the occasions, at the time the resolution passed at the Sikh Educational Conference and the resolution passed by the SGPC, I had published reports in the *Indian Express* that the Government had taken serious view of the developments. There was a discussion in Parliament on this and A.B. Vajpayee had told Giani Zail Singh that Darbara Singh said that you had met Ganga Singh Dhillon in Karnal. While the situation in Punjab was deteriorating day by day because of the support the Congress leadership had given to Jarnail Singh Bhindranwale and the Akali leadership wittingly or unwittingly trying to compete with Bhindranwale in raising their demands against the Central Government and also occasionally extending support to Bhindranwale and ignoring the provocation and subversive acts of Bhindranwale, many anti national forces tried to take advantage of the situation to destabilize India. The intelligence agencies completely failed to caution the ruling Congress leadership about the trends towards the situation moving fast. Both RAW and the IB had not done their duty and they did not perform their job of assessing the situation and keeping the political leadership ruling the country fully briefed. Pakistan's ruling leadership in connivance with CIA had its own plans and this was their best opportunity in connivance with the CIA to plan some strategies against India. It was not a secret that the successive American administrations until the 9/11 had been working against India and were giving full support to Pakistan against India. Americans were particularly against the Nehru-Gandhi family, in particular against Indira Gandhi. The kind of hatred Americans had against Indira Gandhi can be imagined from the declassified documents of the White House of the period between 1969 and 1974 of the talks between the Chinese Premier Chou-En-Lai and Henry Kissinger, the then Advisor to US President Richard Nixon, that took place in Bejing on 10 July 1971. They were discussing the situation in Bangladesh, then East Pakistan. Even the language they used about Indira Gandhi was derogatory. Both the Americans and Chinese were all going out of their way to help Pakistan. So, the situation created by Bhindranwale and Akalis suited CIA and Pakistan to join hands against India. If Zia was scared of any international leader, it was Indira Gandhi only. In my article in the *Illustrated Weekly* of India dated 25 October 1981, I had written that the demand of Khalistan was a conspiracy hatched in America. Even the then Prime Minister, Indira Gandhi at her press conference on 10 July 1981 said: "So far, Khalistan existed only in Canada and perhaps in the USA also, but it does not mean that we would lower our guard or not exercise the utmost vigilance."

There was no doubt that the then SGPC President, Gurcharan Singh Tohra was a supporter of Jarnail Singh Bhindranwale and he had extremist views. Tohra and Sukhwinder Singh, another Akali leader with extremist views, had visited Singapore and soon after return, Tohra left for USA, ostensibly for medical treatment. Jathedar Gurdial Singh Ajnoha, Head of the Akal Takhat, was already in USA and they were followed by Rajinder Singh Bhatia, a General Secretary of the Akali Dal, who was also close to M.L. Fotedar, looking after the political work of Indira Gandhi. They had several meetings in that country with Ganga Singh Dhillon, Dr Jagjit Singh and Bhajan Yogi, who was running a big set up in USA and had close links with American administration. Bhajan Yogi was also very close to Giani Zail Singh and he along with his followers had been staying in Rashtrapati Bhawan as guest of Giani Zail Singh, the then President of India. The Akali leaders during their stay in the USA had set up a branch of the Akali Dal in the USA and resolutions were passed demanding a Sikh autonomous state on the grounds that the Sikhs were being discriminated against in India by the Hindu majority. Jagjit Singh Chauhan was in contact with Pakistan and the USA, especially CIA. During the 1971 Indo-Pak war, Pakistan was using Jagjit Singh Chauhan to appeal to the Sikhs in India to support Pakistan in the war.

PAKISTAN AND CIA'S STRATEGIES

Soon after the Nirankari-Akhand Kirtni Jatha clash in Amritsar in which Bhindranwale was supporting the Akhand Kirtni Jatha, in which over a dozen Akhand Kirtni followers were killed, the CIA and Pakistan had started planning its strategies against India. Zia had just taken over as Military Ruler of Pakistan. According to the reports then received by the Ministry of External Affairs from Pakistan, Zia had deputed Ch. Zahur Illahi, a Muslim League leader and a big landlord of Pakistani Punjab, to cultivate with important Sikhs living in Canada, USA and in some other countries, to bring them round to support a demand for a separate Khalistan. Zia himself had established personal contacts with Sikhs like Ganga Singh Dhillon and Jagjit Singh Chauhan. The ISI was given the task to prop up some fundamentalist Sikh organizations and to cultivate with Sikh youth to lure them to work for Khalistan and also give them financial support and arms supplies. Zahour Iliahi was killed in Pakistan by some persons in September 1981 and the task of cultivating with the Sikhs abroad was entrusted by Zia-Ul-Haq to Ch. Shujjat Hussain, his nephew, a Muslim League leader, and also to Parvez IIlahi, his son who later became Chief Minister of Pakistan Punjab. Even during the Morarji Desai regime in 1978, the Government had received reports from its Mission in Pakistan about Zia's plans and the task entrusted to Zahur IIlahi. But neither Morarji Desai as Prime Minister nor A. B. Vajpayee as Foreign Minister in the Morarji Desai Government took up this matter with Pakistan. When Indira Gandhi came to power in 1980, she had some reports about Pakistan sponsoring some extremist groups among the Sikhs in India and Pakistan's attempt to use these elements to destabilize India.

Pakistan and the CIA were concentrating more on hard-liner Sikhs in Punjab than the Jehadi elements in Jammu and Kashmir as they were hoping if they succeeded in motivating the hard-liner Sikhs to revolt against the Indian establishment in the name of a separate home land for Sikhs, it would pose a bigger threat to India than Pakistan's attempts in Jammu and Kashmir. Their strategy was to create bitterness among the Sikhs against the Central Government, which if succeeded could have affected the psychology of Sikhs in the armed forces of the country. Zia and the CIA had never realized that Hindus and Sikhs were so closely knit with each other that except for using a very small fringe of hard-liners, they could in no way succeed in their mission.

NAXALITES TAKE DEEP ROOTS IN PUNJAB

Along with Bhindranwale phenomenon, which was creating a poisonous communal climate in Punjab, there was another element raising its head in Punjab to disturb peace in Punjab and Bihar. The movement had taken its roots in Punjab in early 1960s but the then Punjab Chief Minister, Partap Singh Kairon, had crushed this movement with a strong hand. Now in early 1980, the Naxalites had once again become active in Punjab. I had published a report in the *Indian Express* on 3 June 1981 in which I had pointed out about the concentration of Naxals in Punjab and Bihar. In early 1981, the Naxalites were more active among students and teachers in Punjab and among tribal areas in Bihar, Andhra Pradesh and Assam and in the two left-ruled states of West Bengal and Kerala, the struggle was between the ruling groups of left and the Naxalites. In Punjab, apart from having cadres among teachers and students, nexalites had infiltrated into some Gurdwaras in the garb of *granthis* (preachers). Sangrur and Ferozepur districts of Punjab earlier used to be the centre of Naxal activities but in early 1980s, they shifted their headquarters to a village in Kapurthala district. The report which I had published in the *Indian Express* contained: 'The Naxalite strategy in Punjab is two-pronged: to instigate the extremist Akalis to intensify their agitation on the Anandpur Sahib resolution for greater autonomy and a separate Sikh nation, and to involve the student community in a confrontation with the government." Two groups of Naxalites were active in Punjab, one led by S.N. Singh and the other by C.P. Reddy. While the S.N. Singh group was involved with the extremist Akalis, the other group was concentrating on the students and farmers. Even the Home Ministry had reports which I had quoted in my report that "the Naxalites were also instigating farmers to refuse to return government loans and they were also suggesting to the hard-liners among Akalis to fight against the government on the issue of government's interference in the religious affairs of Sikhs." They also planned setting up of civil liberties organization and Kirti Kissan Cell. The then Punjab Chief Minister, Darbara Singh, had confirmed about the Naxal moves to this writer. The Naxals had those days succeeded in organizing students' strikes and the allies in various parts of the state. They were also trying to concentrate on the students of the Punjab Agricultural University at Ludhiana and organized a huge procession of students in Ludhiana town to monitor which, the then DIG, CID, Bhagwan Singh Danewalia, a Scotland Yard trained IPS Officer, had personally come to Ludhiana. Naxalites had also mingled in a procession taken out by Bhindranwale in Amritsar to ban tobacco in the city.

Through another plan, Pakistan was also concentrating on Sikh pilgrims visiting Sikh holy shrines in Pakistan including Nankana Sahib, the birth place of Guru Nanak and Gurdwara Panja Sahib. Pakistani leaders used to invite groups of Sikh pilgrims and try to cultivate with them by projecting Pakistan Government as pro-Sikh sentiments and old ties between Sikhs and Muslims before partition of 1947. The objective of the Pakistani establishment was to win over at least some of the pilgrims and create an impression that Pakistan was more sympathetic to them. But at the same time, Zia was worried and scared of Indira Gandhi. When Indira Gandhi made a statement in September 1983 supporting agitation in Sind

Province of Pakistan on restoration of democracy, Zia became extremely worried and called Ganga Singh Dhillon and Jagjit Singh Chauhan to Pakistan to have their assessment on Indira Gandhi's statement. The agitation for restoration of democracy was in whole of Pakistan but in the Sind province because of the death sentence to Z.A. Bhutto, who belonged to Sind, the agitation was more aggressive and pronounced. Ganga Singh Dhillon and Chauhan had told Zia that their assessment was that Indira Gandhi's statement supporting the agitation was her reaction to what Pakistan was doing in Punjab by sponsoring and supporting Sikh militants.

SUPPLY OF ARMS TO SIKH MILITANTS

There were reports with the Home Ministry that Pakistan was supplying arms to the Sikh militants and arms were smuggled into the Golden Temple complex through the trucks carrying wheat bags for the *langar*. G.S. Tohra was the President of the SGPC and he was known as a supporter of Bhindranwale and some other extremist groups also. Tohra was dominating the Akali leadership and no Akali leader including Sant Harchand Singh Longowal and Parkash Singh Badal had the courage to oppose Tohra or confront Tohra on his sympathies with Bhindranwale and other extremist groups. Instead, they would always toe Tohra's line fearing his wrath. Zia-Ul-Haq was so careful in dealing with India under Indira Gandhi regime that the Pakistan establishment was propping up Sikh militants in Punjab and Kashmiri militants in Jammu and Kashmir. Indira Gandhi never made statements like *Aar Paar Ki Ladai* if attacked again, as Vajpayee and L.K. Advani had been doing. She used to hit back in the same coin. If Pakistani agents did sabotage act and subversive activity anywhere in India, its reply used to be given within hours in Lahore and Karachi. If Pakistan's ISI was very powerful, India had created RAW, a counter-intelligence agency in 1960s, which was very effective having a free hand to deal with Pakistan. RAW had established extremely good contacts in Pakistan, who were very effective. This had always worried Zia-Ul-Haq. I remember, Jammu and Kashmir Liberation Front leader, Maqbool Bhatt was given death sentence for killing a senior Government official in Kashmir and Maqbool Bhatt was lodged in jail waiting for his execution. JKLF militants in 1983 kidnapped India's Counsel General in Birmingham (UK) Ravindra Mhatre, demanding release of Maqbool Bhatt. They set a deadline that if Maqbool Bhat was not freed by that deadline, they would kill him. Indira Gandhi refused to accept their demand and soon after the deadline fixed, the JKLF militants killed, Mhatre and his dead body was found. When the report on Mhatre's killing reached Indira Gandhi, she decided to act fast to reply to the militants that no mercy would be shown to the militants. She called an emergency meeting of her senior advisors including the RAW Chief and decided that Maqbool Bhatt must be hanged at the earliest, by next morning to give a befitting reply to the militants and their patron Pakistan. A team of officers led by P.P. Nayar, Special Secretary in the Home Ministry, which included I.B. Boss also, was flown to Jammu in a special plane with the instructions to complete all legal formalities before the sun set as the case against Maqbool Bhatt was decided in Jammu and to hang Maqbool Bhatt by early next morning. The team came back from Jammu by noon after the execution of Maqbool Bhatt. As a reaction, Pakistanis attacked the car of Indian Counsel General in Karachi, G. Parthasarathy and did some damage to the Building of the Indian Mission. When Zia heard about the attack, he was so scared of the reaction from Indians that he ordered the Chief Secretary of Sind Province in Karachi to personally go and meet the Indian Counsel General and apologize from him and assure that Pakistan will give full damage for the damaged car and also for the damage to the building. As compared to Indira Gandhi, during the Vajpayee Government's regime, when Indian Airlines plane was hijacked and taken to Kandhar in Afghanistan, the Pakistani hijackers demanded the release of three hard-core militants lodged in Indian jails in Jammu and Kashmir, the Vajpayee Government not only agreed to accept the demand, Jaswant Singh, Foreign Minister in Vajpayee Government personally escorted them to Kandhar in his plane and on the entire journey, Masood Azhar, a hardcore terrorist who later established a deadly terrorist organization, Jaishe-Mohammad in Pakistan, was giving choicest and filthiest abuses to Jaswant Singh on the entire journey from New Delhi to Kandhar. Not only this, Vajpayee had destroyed the premier counter-intelligence agency, RAW, by ordering it soon after his Lahore bus journey in early 1999, to stop all operations in Pakistan. It takes years and years for an intelligence agency to establish its contacts and sources of information in a foreign country and if the agency does not utilize those contacts, they dry up closing all options for the intelligence agency.

Knowing fully well that Pakistan was a hostile country supporting Sikh hard-liners, giving them arms, training and also financial help there was no law and order and people were not feeling safe. Bhindranwale and his supporters were targeting selectively Hindu bus passengers, some important individuals, RSS *Shakas* and Bhindranwale was giving them orders from the sacred premises of the Golden Temple. Many innocent had lost lives. Judiciary was almost non-functional and no lawyer was prepared to appear against Bhindranwale men. Police had become ineffective, still the Central Government under Indira Gandhi was watching the situation helplessly. If the Government had the will, it could have easily taken out Bhindranwale from the Golden Temple and put him in jail, which people would have appreciated and felt relieved. Right from 1980 onwards, till the Operation Blue Star, for more than four years, why was the Government giving such a long rope to Bhindranwale? The same Akalis who were demanding the release of Bhindranwale in the Jagat Narain murder case would have felt relieved as they were not his supporters; rather, they were scared of him and feeling threats to their lives. The fact is that while Indira Gandhi proved an iron lady and Pakistan and Americans were scared of her, her misfortune was that she was surrounded by a Kashmiri group led by her own relative Arun Nehru, who were misleading her and who had always in mind how to win elections by showing Centre's power to crush any powerful community whether they were Sikhs or Muslims. This group was responsible for deterioration of situation in Punjab and Jammu and Kashmir and in both the states, this group had played a negative role. This group was responsible for creating a wedge between Indira Gandhi and Dr. Farooq Abdullah and creating an uncertain situation in Jammu and Kashmir, and also misleading her totally on Punjab. Every time, she tried to have some settlement with Akalis in Punjab, it was this group which sabotaged any settlement.

One of the reasons for the Central leadership backing out on any understanding with Akalis in November 1982, just before the ASIAD was this Kashmiri group having influence over Indira Gandhi, to keep assembly elections in Haryana and Jammu and Kashmir in mind and creating an impression that the Centre was taking a tough line against the Akalis in Punjab. It paid off the Congress in Jammu region where the Congress did much better than before but in the Kashmir valley, National Conference led by Dr. Farooq Abdullah became victorious. But in Haryana, Congress lost to the National Lok Dal of Ch. Devi Lal. Arun Nehru and Makhan Lal Fotedar, two Kashmiri leaders very close to Indira Gandhi, were dead set against Dr. Farooq Abdulah. They were close to Mufti Mohammad Sayeed. Both Arun Nehru and Fotedar had started planning defections within the National Conference within a few months of the formation of the Farooq Abdullah Government and they succeeded in persuading Indira Gandhi to topple the Farooq Abdullah Government. This group was able to manage G.M. Shah, a brother-in-law of Dr. Farooq Abdullah, to defect from the National Conference and form his Government with the Congress support. G.M. Shah could muster the support of only 14 MLAs and 26 congress MLAs supported him. Even the State Governor, B.K. Nehru, a highly respected civil servant and a relation of Indira Gandhi, had to be transferred to Gujarat because he had refused to oblige the Central leadership to dismiss Dr. Farooq Abdullah Government. Jagmohan who was earlier Lt. Governor of Delhi and close to Sanjay Gandhi and Indira Gandhi, was sent as Governor of Jammu and Kashmir to topple Farooq Abdullah Government and install G.M. Shah as the State Chief Minister. This whole process took a few months and Farooq Abdullah Government was dismissed by the middle 1984.

Jagmohan as Governor of the State was sending very comprehensive monthly reports to the Centre. There were only two Governors who were sending detailed reports to the Centre. Jagmohan, Governor of Jammu and Kashmir, and former Army Chief, Retired General, Krishna Rao, who was Governor of Assam and who later succeeded Jagmohan in Jammu and Kashmir. While all the other Governors used to send their monthly reports mostly based on newspaper reports, these two Governors used to send detailed studies of the month, which used to comprise about 16 to 20 pages every month. Later on, the same Jagmohan who had installed G.M. Shah as Chief Minister, had sent reports during the Rajiv Gandhi regime quoting speeches of G.M. Shah delivered in some border areas, which were anti-Indian, and Jagmohan in his reports had frankly described these speeches as meant for consumption across the border. In the same report, he had praised Fraooq Abdullah for his pro-Indian speeches. The period of 1983-84 was the beginning of uncertain situation developing in Jammu and Kashmir, for which the country is paying a very heavy price, and none other than the Kashmiri group around Indira Gandhi was responsible for this situation. Mir Qasim, a former Chief Minister of Jammu and Kashmir, a highly respected Congress leader of the state, was extremely upset over these developments. He had told Indira Gandhi, "Do not push Farooq to the wall; this is a nationalist family, respected in the state." Mir Qasim himself had told me this.

Even on Punjab, this group was misleading Indira Gandhi. Arun Nehru was at that time known as having the confidence of Indira Gandhi. She trusted him fully as he was the main fund collector for the party. But she might not have realized that Arun Nehru had his own agenda and preferences. Then Haryana Chief Minister, Bhajan Lal was very close to M.L. Fotedar and Shiv Shankar and both of them were going all out in supporting him. I had been closely watching how this coterie had sabotaged every attempt first by Indira Gandhi and later by Rajiv Gandhi to reach any settlement with Akalis on Punjab issues. How even the Water Tribunal appointed to go into the dispute between Punjab, Haryana and Rajasthan was hampered from giving its decision or conducting proceedings fairly. In this game, M.L. Fotedar was more active than other members of the coterie. Fotedar at one point of time was looking after the Lok Sabha constituency of Indira Gandhi after Yash Kapur and Fotedar was considered close to Indira Gandhi. Many senior Congress leaders had complained to Indira Gandhi against Fotedar for his rude behaviour towards them. Although R.K. Dhawan, Private Secretary to Indira Gandhi, was known as one of her loyalists and her trusted aide but there was a vast difference between the style of functioning of Dhawan and Fotedar. Fotedar and Dhawan never saw eye to eye with each other and this was known to Indira Gandhi. Dhawan was close to Giani Zail Singh and he had helped Giani Zail Singh become President of India. Thakkar Commission appointed to go into assassination of Indira Gandhi, had pointed a finger of suspicion on R.K. Dhawan. But it was well known in the Government and political circles that the Thakkar Commission report was a manipulated report by Arun Nehru and his group and many fingers were pointed at Justice Thakkar himself for giving such a biased report. Even former Cabinet Secretary, B.G. Deshmukh had put a question mark. Arun Nehru dominated the Congress politics and the Government functioning till early 1986 when he and Rajiv Gandhi fell out and Rajiv Gandhi had confronted Arun Nehru on his dealing with Bofor Gun deal which had shocked Rajiv Gandhi. Even during his questioning by the CBI, he admitted having dealt with the Bofor Gun deal. The confrontation by Rajiv Gandhi on certain matters of Arun Nehru had given a serious setback to Arun Nehru and soon after this, during his visit to Srinagar, he suffered a heart attack and was in hospital for few days. He was then Minister of State in the Home Ministry looking after internal security. When he recovered from heart attack and returned to the capital, though he was retained in the Home Ministry, but important subjects on internal security were taken away from him and he was given a minor charge. When he pressed the then Home Minister, Buta Singh to give him back his original charge and he gave him a list of the subjects he wanted back, Buta Singh sent that list to Rajiv Gandhi, who sent him back a list of some insignificant minor departments to be given to Arun Nehru. Buta Singh accordingly issued an office order allocating some new subjects to Arun Nehru but none of the old important subjects were given back to Arun Nehru. He was told that since he had suffered a heart attack, he was being given a lighter charge. Arun Nehru went to Mumbai and got a medical certificate from a leading cardiologist declaring him absolutely fit. But Rajiv Gandhi refused to give him any important charge. A few weeks later, he went abroad and on the eve of his departure, he met Giani Zail Singh and gave him some documents against Rajiv Gandhi. Later on, relations between him and Rajiv Gandhi became more strained when he was hobnobbing with V.P. Singh on the Bofor issue and was trying to create a new front against Rajiv Gandhi with the help of V.P. Singh and Zail Singh. Rajiv Gandhi hit back and registered a corruption case against Arun Nehru and B.P. Singhal, who was an Additional Secretary in the Home Ministry under Arun Nehru and was brother of top VHP leader, under various sections for purchase of Czech Pistol for the Home Ministry. The CBI had prepared a very strong case but later on when Rajiv Gandhi lost Lok Sabha polls in 1989 and V.P. Singh became Prime Minister, he withdrew that case. Arun Nehru was appointed a Cabinet Minister by V.P. Singh even when the CBI case was still under investigations. The case against Arun Nehru was registered by the CBI on 10 March 1988 and the Czech Pistols were purchased in 1985.

Following is the copy of the CBI case, a copy of which was filed in the Court of Special Judge:

DELHI SPECIAL POLICE ESTABLISHMENT, ACU (II) BRANCH FIRST INFORMATION REPORT

(Recorded u/s 154 Cr. P.C.) 33

Crime No. RC. 1/88-ACU (II) Date and Time of Report 10.3.88, 1600 hours.

Place of occurrence with State	New Delhi (Union Territory of Delhi)
Date and time of occurrence	1985 to November 1987
Name of complainant or Informer with address	Source
Offence	U/s 120-B IPC r/w 5(3-A) r/w 5(1)(d) of the Prevention of Corruption Act 1947.
Name and Address of the	(1) Shri Arun Nehru, the then Minister of State (Internal Security), M.H.A., New Delhi (2) Shri B.P. Singhal, the then Addl. Secretary, Govt. of India, Min. of Home Affairs, New Delhi (3) and others
Action taken	Regular Case registered
Investigating Officer	Shri J.N. Prasad, Dy. Supdt. of Police, CBI, ACU(II)/New Delhi.

INFORMATION

A source information has been received that in 1985, the Ministry of Home Affairs, Govt. of India, New Delhi was considering placing a repeat order for the import of 18,319 Sturm-Ruger, .38 revolvers, a substantial quantity of which had been imported earlier, but the Ministry of Finance had advised fresh trade enquiries. As the Ministry of Defence was not in a position to meet the requirement of the police force till 1990, the Directors General of B.P.R & D. and C.R.P.F. had recommended that instead of .38 revolvers, 9 MM pistols should be purchased. Shri Rebeiro, the then Special Secretary, Ministry of Home Affairs, while endorsing the change in policy regarding the type of the weapon, suggested that the requirement should be reassessed and Army and other expert should be consulted to find out whether less costly 9.MM pistols than F. N. Browning were available. This was approved by the Home Secretary on 19.2.86 and the then Minister of State (Internal Security) on 21.2.86. On a letter dated 8.4.86 from the Weapons and Equipment Directorate, Army Headquarters, a note was recorded by Shri B.P. Singhal, Additional Secretary, MHA that the possibility of procuring the arms from the Rupee payment Area (R.P.A.) countries should be first explored in accordance with the directive of the Govt.

2. It is reliably learnt that even before the Ministry of Home Affairs could issue messages to the Indian Embassies in R.P.A. countries, a representative of Czechoslovakian Embassy in India had met Shri B.P. Singhal on 14.4.86 and told him that his country was in a position to supply 9.MM pistols. He was, therefore, asked to submit a written offer. On 17.4.86 the Trade Representative of the Embassy had presented personally to Shri B.P. Singhal, Additional Secretary, MHA, a letter dated

16.4.86 offering CZ-75, 9.MM pistols at a price equivalent to us $ 266.66 with a ten per cent discount if the order was for 20,000 pistols and above. A discount higher than 10% was offered if the order was for a much larger quantity. On this letter itself, Shri B.P. Singhal, Addl. Secretary had put an endorsement to form an Evaluation Committee and Negotiation Committee. On 21.4.86 Shri B.P. Singhal recorded a note to the effect that MOS (IS) had expressed his unhappiness at the slow progress in the matter.

3. The progress made in this regard by M.H.A. was reviewed by Shri B.P. Singhal, Addl. Secretary, who vide his note dated 21.5.86 to MOS(IS) recommended inclusion of ASIs for calculating the requirement of pistols and suggested that after technical evaluation by B.P.R.& D., the Evaluation Committee headed by D.G., C.R.P.F. should give a final report and that test reports of the Smith and Wesson, Beretta and Browning pistols already available with the army, should be examined by the Evaluation Committee. He had further suggested that 15.6.1986 should be the final date for receiving the offers. The file was returned by MOS(IS) for discussion.

4. As desired by the then M.O.S. (IS) Shri Arun Nehru, the subject of pistols was discussed on 22.5.86 after the meeting to review the working of B.P.R. & D. Shri Arun Nehru had then directed that the Czech pistol shall be purchased when replies were then still awaited from other RPA countries. In fact, this direction was given in the initial stages of process when the matter was still premature. He had further directed Shri B. P. Singhal, Addl. Secretary to conduct the test of the weapon himself along with the DsG., B.S.F., C.R.P.F. and B.P.R. & D. against the established norms. It is learnt that the aforesaid directions of the MOS (IS) were, however, not recorded in the

concerned file. Later, on 26.5.86 Shri B.P. Singhal, Addl. Secretary, had put up to the Home Secretary for approval, the draft Minutes of the meeting held on 22.5.86 by MOS (IS) to review the working of the B.P.R. & D. In the said draft minutes, no mention about the orders/decision of MOS(IS) regarding the pistols was made. When the file was returned by Home Secretary to Addl. Secretary Shri B.P. Singhal for finalization at his level, another para was added on 28.5.86 to the Minutes of the meeting mentioning therein the decision taken by MOS (IS) for purchase of Czech pistols and the tests to be conducted by the Additional Secretary along with the DsG., B.S.F., C.R.P.F. and B.P.R. & D. The aforesaid decision of the MOS (IS) was also recorded in the concerned file on 29.5.86 by Shri B.P. Singhal, Addl. Secretary, MHA.

5. On 11.6.86, the B.P.R. & D. was informed by Shri B.P. Singhal, Addl. Secretary that the Defence authorities were not to be associated with the evaluation of pistols and that the tests would be conducted by himself, the DsG, B.S.F., officers on 18.6.86 in course of which 65 rounds were fired from the Czech pistol, ten rounds from Browning and five rounds from the Steyr pistols. Even though defects/deficiencies in the Czech pistols were observed during tests by the officers, the Addl. Secretary Shri B.P. Singhal felt that the weapon in its existing form would be desirable. In this regard, Shri B.P. Singhal ignored the advice of the Evaluation Committee and accepted the explanation given by the representative of the Czech Embassy that the trigger mechanism of the pistol not locking when the magazine was taken out, was actually a facility and not a handicap.

6. On 18.7.86, the then Director (Provisioning), MHA, put up a note giving the sequence of events and in this the price of

the Czech pistol was mentioned as Rs.3,438 (equivalent to US $ 271.602). The fact that the Czech Embassy had earlier quoted US $ 266.66 with 10% discount for the pistol was not revealed in the said note. The said price was recommended by the Addl. Secretary. After the approval by M.C.S. (IS), the Negotiation Committee in their meeting held on 31.7.86 and 1.8.86, did not press for higher discount though more than 50,000 pistols were being purchased. Thus, the Negotiation Committee accepted the price of Rs.3,438 FOB of the firm without any objection. The total cost of 55,000 weapons was calculated at Rs.18,90,90,000 the total cost of spare parts at Rs.65,50,236, the cost of freight at Rs.1,95,64,023.60 and the grand total worked out to Rs.21,52,04,260, at which cost the MOS(IS) approved the purchase on 8.8.86. The administrative and financial approvals were then obtained for the purchase of CZ-75 pistols. Before the agreement was signed on 3.9.86, a telegram dated 14.8.86 was received from the Indian Embassy in Moscow, stating that the Soviet Govt. was willing to meet the requirements. However, this telegram was deliberately ignored.

7. The Contract was signed with M/s Merkuria of Czechoslovakia on 3.9.86 by Shri B.P. Singhal, Addl. Secretary on behalf of M.H.A, Govt. of India and not on behalf of the President of India as stipulated in the standard form. Furthermore, the contract was signed by the Addl. Secretary without getting it vetted by AL.A attached to M.H.A or by the Ministry of Law and Justice.

8. It is also learnt that while conveying their No Objection to the import of 9.MM pistols, the Ministry of Defence had agreed to take into account the requirement of the police forces from the year 1988-89 and had asked the Ministry of Home Affairs to indicate firm projection of demand to enable the

Ordnance Factories to augment their production capacity. Inspite of the fact that the Czech Embassy had given their delivery schedule vide their letter dated 2.8.1986 that out of 55,000 pistols, only 35,000 would be supplied by 1988 and the balance by June 1989, the quantity to be imported was not reduced and the Ministry of Defence was not informed about meeting the demand of the police forces from 1988 onwards.

9. One of the terms of the contract was that out of the 4 samples of the pistols supplied by Merkuria for testing and that the future supplies of pistols would conform to the specifications of the test samples thus retained. When B.P.R.G.D. took some time to organize the trials with the help of the Army authorities, Shri B.P. Singhal, Addl. Secretary, M.H.A had expressed considerable annoyance over the delay and pressurized them to have the tests completed without the help of army authorities. The firing/trials were conducted at Bhondsai Range of B.S.F. on 18.12.86 and the Committee Report incorporating the results and the defects noticed was sent by the D.G., B.P.R. & D. to the Govt. In fact, the trials had been done at Delhi instead of at the Controllerate of Inspection (Small Arms), Ichapur without associating army experts as per the specific directions of Shri B. P. Singhal, Additional Secretary, who had tried to ensure that a mere formality of tests were done hurriedly.

10. In January 1987, out of the Czech pistols received in four consignments, 9 pistols were picked up for test. Out of them only two pistols fired flawlessly and hence in a meeting convened by the Home Secretary, it was decided to reject the whole consignment. Out of the consignment received in April'87, 130 pistols were tested and most of them were found unsatisfactory. In view of this, the Govt. of India was compelled

to cancel the agreement with M/s Merkuria of Czechoslovakia in Nov. 1987. Consequently, though cost-price was subsequently returned by the firm, the air freight, storage and bank commission charges etc. to the tune of Rs.25 lakhs approx. had been incurred as loss by the Govt. of India on account of the above deal for purchase of Czech pistols.

11. In view of the facts stated above, there are reasons to believe that Shri Arun Nehru, the then Minister of State (Internal Security), Min. of Home Affairs, Govt. of India, New Delhi had entered into a criminal conspiracy with Shri B.P. Singhal, Addl. Secretary, MHA and others to cause wrongful loss to the Govt. of India in the matter of purchase of CZ-75, 9.MM pistols. The main grounds for this belief are as under:

(i) While processing the suitability and requirement of pistols for the police forces in India, Shri Arun Nehru, the then M.O.S. (IS) together with Addl. Secretary, MHA Shri B.P. Singhal, abused their official positions while working as public servants and caused undue favours to be shown in the award of contract for supplying Czech CZ-75, 9.MM pistols by M/s Merkuria.

(ii) Shri Arun Nehru, the then MOS (IS) directed that instead of the weapons being evaluated as per established norms (by a Technical Committee of the B.P.R & D. set up earlier for this very purpose) these should be tested by the Additional Secretary personally along with the Ds.G.B.S.F., C.RP.F. and B.P.R & D. (without associating the army authorities).

(iii) M/s Merkuria of Czechoslovakia was blantly favoured by S/Shri B.P. Singhal, the then Addl. Secretary, MHA and Arun Nehru, the then MOS (I) in the matter of placing an order for 55,000 CZ-75 pistols at a price of Rs.3438 per piece which was equivalent to US $ 272.12 (as on 31.7.86), when the firm had earlier offered in writing a rate even lower than US $ 240 per piece if the quantity purchased was over 20,000 pieces. Thus, M/s Merkuria was clearly favoured to the tune of over US $ 32 per piece aggregating to Rs.2.20 crores.

(iv) Shri B.P. Singhal, the then Addl. Secretary, MHA also abused his official position in conducting grossly inadequate firing tests of pistols and ultimately recommended purchase of a substandard weapon, consignments of which had to be rejected and finally cancelled, thereby resulting in infructuous expenditure of air-freight, storage and bank commission charges incurred by the Govt. of India, and thereby caused a loss of about Rs.25 lakhs to the Govt. of India.

(v) The then Minister of State (IS) Shri Arun Nehru and Shri B.P. Singhal, Addl. Secretary, MHA failed to record in writing the decision/orders of the MOS (IS) regarding the pistols on 22.5.86 in the file when they ought to have been recorded, and the fact that Shri B.P. Singhal, Addl. Secretary chose to record the decisions belatedly with the Minutes of the B.P.R & D., and in the concerned file, reveal malafide intensions behind the decisions to purchase the CZ-75 pistols and resultant transactions.

(vi) The Negotiation Committee headed by Shri B.P. Singhal, Addl. Secretary, MHA, held meetings with the Trade Representatives of Czechoslovakia and even though a large number of pistols were to be purchased, they did not ask for the discount and accepted the price of Rs.3438 i.e. US $ 272.12 per piece, without any objection.

(vii) Shri B.P. Singhal, Addl. Secretary signed an agreement with M/s Merkuria of Czechoslovakia on behalf of MHA and not on behalf of the President of India as stipulated in the standard form, and without getting it vetted by the legal advisers.

The above facts disclose commission of offences under section 120-B IPC r/w 5(3-A) r/w 5(1)(d) of the P.C. Act by Shri Arun Nehru, the then Minister of State (Internal Security), Ministry of Home Affairs, Govt. of India, Shri B.P. Singhal, Addl. Secretary, M.H.A and others.

A Regular Case is, therefore, registered and entrusted to Shri J.N. Prasad, Dy. Supdt. of Police, CBI, SPE, ACU (1I)/New Delhi for investigation.

Sd/- 10/3/88
(YASHVANT MALHOTRA)
SUPERINTENDENT OF POLICE, CBI, SPE,
ACU (II)/NEW DELHI

No. 891 to 896/3/1/83-AC.I/ACU(II) Dated: 10.3.1988

Copy forwarded to:

1. The Special Judge, Delhi.
2. Shri J.K. Dutt, Dy. Inspr. Gen!. Of Police, AC.I, CBI/New Delhi.
3. Mrs. C.R. Chibber, Dy. Secy (Vigilance) DP&T, North Block, New Delhi.
4. Sh. P.K. Mallick, Special Secretary, Home Ministry, orth Block, New Delhi.
5. Shri AK. Garde, Secretary, Central Vigilance Commission, 3 Rajendra Prashad Road, New Delhi.
6. Sh. J.N. Prasad, Dy. SP, CBI, ACU (11)/New Delhi.

Sd/- 10/3/88
(YASHVANT MALHOTRA)

V

Giani Zail Singh's Rise and Fight with Indira Gandhi

As I mentioned earlier, the role of Giani Zail Singh, as Home Minister and later even as President, was most destructive and he had started feeling that as President of the country, he was the most powerful politician and was superior even to the Prime Minister, Indira Gandhi. The man who before becoming the President of India had declared that he was prepared to sweep the floor on orders from Indira Gandhi, wanted to rule the country as a Monarch and enjoy powers more than even the Prime Minister. Giani Zail Singh, though semi-literate, was much shrewder than other politicians. For the first time, it was during Zail Singh's tenure that Rashtrapati Bhawan became a centre of intrigues and conspiracies first against the then Prime Minister, Indira Gandhi and after her assassination, against Rajiv Gandhi and most unscruplous persons, even undesirable persons, had a free access to Rashtrapati Bhawan. He wanted that Punjab should be ruled indirectly by him as President of the country. I have known him very intimately for 40 years and I had found that he was the biggest political manipulator. A semi-literate man, how he first became the Home Minister of the country in 1980 through Sanjay Gandhi and later became the President of the country with the help of R.K. Dhawan is a fascinating story. What had in fact clinched the issue was delegations of some southern politicians organised by Zail Singh on advice of Dhawan, to impress upon Indira Gandhi to select Giani Zail Singh for the post of President of the country. Dhawan, occupying the important position as her personal secretary, used to be in a position to get appointments to those delegations to meet Indira Gandhi. Soon after his election as President of India, I had said in my article in the *Illustrated Weekly* of India dated 25 July 1982, that "To say that Zail Singh will be a 'Rubber-stamp' President" will be to underestimate him. He does believe in giving unstinted loyalty to the leader. But, in Rashtrapati Bhawan, he will be his own leader and will have full freedom to act within the constraints imposed by the Constitution and convention. See copy of the article as annexure.

A BRIEF HISTORY OF ZAIL SINGH

Born in a mud-house in an artisan (carpenter) family, and starting his life as a preacher in a gurdwara in the Faridkot State, (then Faridkot was a princely state, the district to which Sant Jarnail Singh Bhindranwale had belonged, and reaching to the position of the President of the country, is a very big achievement for a semi-literate man, which shows his political understanding. How he was arrested by the Maharaja of Faridkot on charges of embezzlement of Gurdwara funds, which he could project as a freedom fighter, only a shrewd brain could do that. He never pardoned the Faridkot Maharaja for this arrest throughout his life and never missed any opportunity to harm the Maharaja through his political connections even as late as 1960s when he met the then Home Minister, Gulzari Lal Nanda, and levelled false charges against the Maharaja that he was supporting the Akali agitation then launched by the Akalis, against the Central Government and he had pleaded with Gulzari Lal Nanda to stop his princely pension. The file had moved but luck saved the Maharaja. When I learnt about this episode, I confronted Zail Singh, and he sheepishly avoided answering my question.

The relations between Giani Zail Singh and Indira Gandhi had started turning sour right from the day Zail Singh occupied Rashtrapati Bhawan. Perhaps, Zail Singh was waiting for this day and he started exerting pressure on the Government to act on his advice at least in the matter of Punjab, which for Indira Gandhi was very difficult. There is a tradition that whenever the President goes on a foreign tour, the Prime Minister goes to the airport to see off the President and timings for arrival of President and the Prime Minister are fixed keeping in view that the Prime Minister does not have to wait for the President to arrive, for long, not more than five minutes or so. But in the case of Zail Singh, he started arriving at the airport late deliberately everytime he had to go out of the country, so that the Prime Minister would keep waiting for him. This was very irritating for Indira Gandhi and she knew that Zail Singh was doing it deliberately. Even during their meetings at the airport, many a times, Zail Singh used to make it a point to show a cold shoulder to Indira Gandhi. As Dr. P.C. Alexander, her then Principal Secretary, has mentioned in his book "Through Corridors of Power," an incident noticed by many including Dr. Alexander of 22 October 1984, when Zail Singh was going to Mauritious, only nine days before her assassination. Indira Gandhi had broached the subject with Zail Singh about his changed attitude and she wanted to discuss with him, to which Zail Singh had said he too was unhappy which he would like to discuss with her if "I come back alive." This only shows the height of the differences which the two had reached, for which Zail Singh was more responsible than Indira Gandhi.

Soon after Operation Blue Star, one day Giani Zail Singh rang me up and asked me to see him urgently. In fact, for some time, I had been avoiding him because the way he was destroying Punjab and encouraging all sorts of elements. I was reluctant to go but on his pleadings, I went to the Rashtrapati Bhawan to meet him. I was escorted to the first floor of his family suites, where we had a long chat. He was very apprehensive for his personal security. I told him as President of the country, he had plenty of security cordon for himself and nobody can come near the Rashtrapati Bhawan. Moreover, he was the Supreme Commander of the Army and he is protected by the army also. He was again and again looking towards the fan, fearing the room might be bugged, which in fact was and I came to know of it only later that day. I told him that he was made President of the country by Indira Gandhi ignoring all the opposition. So why was he fighting with her? I said that if he thought by pressuring her, he could have a deal with her to have second term, he was mistaken. He will not get that because he had already become very controversial. I advised him to have good relations with her and seek her help in getting some land for a farm house, where he should settle down and all the politicians will come to him to seek his advice. He will become an elder-statesman. Those days I was writing for the *Indian Express* and I used to go to the PMO and meet Dr. P.C. Alexander, almost once a week. I never went to anybody else's room. I used to ring up Dr. Alexander's PA and fix the time for the meeting before going I had never gone there without appointment. When I returned from the Rashtrapati

Bhawan, a little later I got a call from Dr. Alexander's office and he spoke to me and said: "How is it that we have not met for a long time? I said we met just two days ago, his reply was, "That is too long a period; why don't you come today at 3 p.m. for a cup of tea with me?" I agreed and the moment I entered his room, he stood up and said: "Hats off to the man who can talk to the President of India in this language. He said, "You are a friend and I would not hide: I want to tell you that I have full tape of your conversation with the President." He said nobody had ever talked to the President in this language, and asked what prompted me to talk like this. I was taken aback and I understood that Rashtrapati Bhawan is bugged and whatever the denials by the Government, every Government keeps an eye on the functioning of the Rashtrapati Bhawan and most of the staff at junior level for service, etc. is always from the Intelligence Bureau. Zail Singh as Home Minister knew all this and then IB Director, TV Rajeshwar, was his trusted man. Since those days, I was writing on sensitive matters, like terrorism and the Home Ministry, I knew that for a long time my own telephone was put under observation and I used to be very careful in talking on the phone, especially more to protect my sources of information in the Home Ministry and at other political level. Initially, Dr. Alexander's disclosure that he had full report of my talk with the President had shocked me but later on I realised that every government has been doing this. Even Zail Singh was always apprehensive that his rooms were bugged and generally, he would talk on sensitive issues either in a corner of his study or take the visitor to the gardens. I had noticed this a number of times.

Every President, with the exception of Zail Singh, had maintained the sanctity of the office of the Rashtrapati and

Rashtrapati Bhawan was always kept away from intrigues and conspiracies. But during Zail Singh tenure as President, all these traditions were forgotten. How a lot of intrigues were taking place within the premises of the Rashtrapati Bhawan is disclosed in an affidavit filed by one Gurcharan Singh, before the CBI, in an enquiry ordered by the Supreme Court in a Cofeposa case. Even the Supreme Court had expressed 'deep concern' over the 'fall in standards' in the Rashtrapati Bhawan Secretariat. It was in the Habes Corpus petition by Pushpa Devi Jatia, wife of Mohan Lal Jatia, that the Supreme Court discovered some mutilations in the Rashtrapati Bhawan records with regard to the entry of Mohan Lal Jatia's petition to the President. The Supreme Court on 30 April 1987, directed the CBI to hold an enquiry into this matter, and the Apex Court had observed lack of security and vigilance at the President's secretariat. Giani Zail Singh was the President. This was a very interesting case and glaring example of misuse of the Secretariat of Rashtrapati Bhawan by criminals. Pushpawati Jatia, wife of a detenue Mohan Lal Jatia, for the release of her husband had approached Supreme Court as the Government had not replied to the petition filed by her husband through the Rashtrapati Bhawan, which never reached the Government. When the Supreme Court examined the records of the Rashtrapati Bhawan, it found some mutilations and some portions of the page having this entry torn. The Supreme Court had ordered an enquiry by the CBI, and the CBI, consequently, had registered a case. The Supreme Court had detected that entry of Jatia's application in the receipt register of Rashtrapati Bhawan bore the date of 15 April. On that day, there were two entries—19 and 20—made by the same person. In between another entry was converted into 20A and it was done by a different person. The CBI had been summoning some staff members of Rashtrapati Bhawan and one employee of the Bhawan and the person who had carried the letter to the Bhawan were arrested by the CBI. It was during this investigation that Gurcharan Singh, a member of personal staff made disclosures. The affidavit was affirmed before an SDM of Delhi.

Some of the portions of the Affidavit are given below.

"A lot of activities detimental (detrimental), to the national interest are going on the seclusive environment of Rashtrapati Bhawan. We the employees have no option but to watch silently and obey. Hence the necessity to bring some of the glaring facts to your kind notice. So many persons of doubtful integrity are visiting Rashtrapati Bhawan clandestinely. For example, Chandraswami, a man of uncertain morals. The officers not connected with President's secretariat like Bagla and Bindra have easy access to files and freely give their advice regularly. Both K.C. Singh and Bagla had been working in USA before being posted in India. These officers try to influence the day to day working of the President and thereby destablize the country.

"Many other undesirable persons have free access to Rashtrapati Bhawan. Quite a few of these persons were contacts from the past. (Many names are given).

"Some pro-Khalistani elements and supporter of terrorism from abroad also visited Rashtrapati Bhawan. Deedar Singh Bains and Harbhajan Singh Jogi were two such persons.

A photo copy of the Affidavit is as an annexure.

Even the Horse-buggy of Rashtrapati Bhawan, used by the President for the solemn occasion of addressing Parliament session, was being used by a Deputy Secretary to send his children to school. I had myself noticed this and questioned Giani Zail Singh about it. As a result the Deputy Secretary shifted his house and got accommodation elsewhere within a week, so that I could not notice such activities in future. This was the state of affairs happening in Rashtrapati Bhawan.

GROWING HOSTILITY BETWEEN RAJIV GANDHI AND ZAIL SINGH

This particular incident happened during the term of Rajiv Gandhi as Prime Minister and Zail Singh was equally hostile to Rajiv Gandhi, as he was with Indira Gandhi. I had published full text of the affidavit in the *Pioneer,* Lucknow, as I was writing for that paper also.

When Jagat Narain, who was a rabid Arya Samajist and anti-Sikh, was killed on 9 September 1981, near Ludhiana, Jarnail Singh Bhindranwale was a suspect in the murder and warrants were issued for his arrest. He was in Chandonkalan, in Hissar District of Haryana. It was announced in the evening radio news about the arrest warrant. Zail Singh was at that time Home Minister of the country, and Bhajan Lal was Chief Minister of Haryana. When the news of his arrest warrant was announced, Bhindranwale immediately left for his Ashram in Amritsar, a distance of about 300 kilometers, by road. It was Zail Singh who spoke to Bhajan Lal and asked him not to arrest Bhindranwale within his state, but let Darbara Singh deal with it. There were a number of check-posts on the way from Chandokalan to his Ashram and it was not a difficult task for Haryana Police to arrest him. Zail Singh had told Bhajan Lal, "Aap is mein kayon phanstey Ho, Darbara Singh ko phasne do? (Why do you get entagled in this, let Darbara Singh face the situation). And it happened as it was suggested by Zail Singh and Bhindranwale could reach Chowk Mehta, in Amritsar, without any check on the way despite many check-posts. Darbara Singh himself had complained to Indira Gandhi about it. But, Zail Singh's then trusted man, T.V. Rajeshwar, who was Director of the IB, had put the blame on Darbara Singh, for not arresting Bhindranwale during his journey from Chandokalan to Chowk Mehta. Rajeshwar could not mention a bigger lie than this. Everybody knew that it was Zail Singh who advised Bhajan Lal not to arrest Bhindranwale in his state. Even P.C. Alexander has admitted in his book that Darbara Singh had complained to Indira Gandhi that Zail Singh had stopped Bhajan Lal from arresting Bhindranwale in his state. Darbara Singh, as Chief Minister, must have been having some contracts with some senior Akali leaders. But he was incapable of conspiracies and maneouvers like Zail Singh. I have known both of them very intimately for decades and I know that Darbara Singh was no match to Zail Singh in such matters. Moreover, Darbara Singh was a Congressman from his heart unlike Zail Singh. Rajeshwar's narration of events on Punjab shows that he had no real assessment of the situation and had no political estimation that a Director of the IB should have. There was rivallary between Zail Singh and Darbara Singh, and sitting in Delhi, as Home Minister of the country, Zail Singh was using every opportunity to corner Darbara Singh and get him removed as Cheif Minister. His plan was to get Amrinder Singh, who was very close to him, become Chief Minister of Punjab and for this purpose, both of them were prepared to go to any extent. While Zail Singh himself was dealing with Indira Gandhi on Punjab, directly or through R.K. Dhawan, and he had put Amrinder Singh on the job to concentrate on Rajiv

Gandhi and Arun Nehru, who was the main culprit alongwith his gang to sabotage every effort for any settlement with the Akalis in Punjab. It was Arun Nehru alongwith M.L. Fotedar, a Kashmiri lobbyist, who was responsible for destroying peace in the country. Then Haryana Chief Minister, Bhajan Lal, was very close to them and it suited Bhajan Lal to act on their advice. Even the agreement for settlement of the issues between the Cabinet Committee as negotiated by Swaran Singh and the Akalis, on 3 November 1982, was sabotaged by this gang led by Arun Nehru, at around 11 p.m. that night convincing Indira Gandhi that this would have an adverse effect on upcoming Haryana Assembly elections. Dr. Alexander has also admitted in his book how another settlement between the Centre and Akalis on 18 November 1982, when the then Home Secretary, T.N. Chaturvedi, had to go to Amritsar in a special plane at night to get approval of the Akali leaders, was sabotaged at the last minute, and the visit of T.N. Chaturvedi to Amritsar, was cancelled at the last moment. This agreement was arrived at a meeting of the Cabinet Committee held at the residence of Dr. Alexander and the Akalis were prepared to accept the terms. Amrinder Singh, Ravi Inder Singh and Rajinder Singh Bhatia were to accompany Chaturvedi to Amritsar. I have given a detailed account about it in earlier chapters. But Amrinder Singh, Ravi Inder Singh and Rajinder Singh Bhatis, still were sent by special plane. But the Akali leadership even refused to meet them. This was their credibility with the Akalis. Zail Singh had thus succeeded in sabotaging every agreement with the Akalis arrived at without involving him, whether through Amrinder Singh or by using Amrinder Singh, through Arun Nehru and M.L. Fotedar. Arun Nehru was related to Indira Gandhi and Fotedar as her aide dealing with political matters and sitting at 1, Akbar Road, the residence of Indira Gandhi, both had great evil influence on Indira Gandhi and were in a position to know all the developments taking place and then planning their moves to sabotage every effort to solve the issues with the Akalis.

SOARING DIFFERENCES BETWEEN RAJIV AND ZAIL SINGH

After Indira Gandhi's assassination, Zail Singh thought since he had given him oath, as Prime Minister, Rajiv Gandhi will be under his thumb. But Rajiv knew how Zail Singh was treating his mother and he did not attach any importance to him. The differences between the two were more open than what was between Indira Gandhi and Zail Singh. Zail Singh started creating hurdles at every point in the functioning of Rajiv Gandhi. In 1986, when Arun Nehru was Minister of State for Home Affairs in-charge of internal security, differences between Rajiv and Arun Nehru had become an open secret and it was well-known that Rajiv had confronted Arun Nehru on taking money in some deals, and had told him: "I feel ashamed calling you my cousin." This was a great set back for Arun Nehru who had enjoyed all the power during the lifetime of Indira Gandhi. Arun Nehru had been exposed by then. He went to Srinagar on tour where he got a heart-attack. He was in the hospital there. Rajiv did not go to Srinagar to enquire about his health. Zail Singh, as a very shrewd politician, rushed to Srinagar, just to meet Arun Nehru and enquire about his health. Zail Singh met Arun Nehru in Srinagar, through the bath-room door. According to reports then in circulation, Zail Singh told him he did not consider Rajiv from the real Nehru family but Arun

Nehru, and he will be with him in future in staking his claim. Arun Nehru, when he returned from Srinagar, was not given the same charge and a few weeks later he left for London but on the eve of his departure, he met Zail Singh in Rashtrapati Bhawan and handed him over certain documents against Rajiv Gandhi. By this time, the differences between Zail Singh and Rajiv Gandhi had further escalated and Zail Singh was always threatening to strike at Rajiv Gandhi. He was sending messages to Rajiv Gandhi threatening that he was planning to dismiss Rajiv Gandhi as Prime Minister. I was getting all kinds of reports about the conspiracies and other manipulations taking place in Rashtrapati Bhawan from people who were very close to Zail Singh and who were in touch with the developments. Sant Ram Singla, a former aide of Zail Singh, who was still very close to Zail Singh, came to see me at my house and asked me as to why I was not meeting Zail Singh those days. I told him that in my view, the activities of Zail Singh were anti-national and he was hell-bent on destroying the system and the country. I told him that with three-fourth majority in Lok Sabha, the Congress Party could impeach him accusing him of his anti-national activities and in that case, nobody would be able to help him and he would be on the road, condemned by all. Later, I learnt that when these messages for dismissal were coming to Rajiv Gandhi, the then Cabinet Secretary, B.G. Deshmukh, who was very straight-forward and apolitical, conveyed to Zail Singh that since any such decision will have to be implemented through the Cabinet Secretary only, he will refuse to implement it, and he could be impeached also by Parliament. But those around him, whose list is mentioned in the Affidavit by the staffer, Gurcharan Singh, were still egging him on to fight against Rajiv Gandhi. It was only after the Supreme Court directions to the CBI in the Mohan Lal Jatia's case to investigate the matter and the Supreme Court's observations expressing deep concern over the falling standards in Rashtrapati Bhawan, when a number of staff members of the Rashtrapati Bhawan close to Zail Singh were being summoned by the CBI for investigation that Zail Singh realised that his game was over and now instead of creating problems for Rajiv Gandhi, he himself would land in trouble as he knew that the CBI would not only be enquiring into this particular case but about the security aspect also because of the observations made by the Apex Court on the security matter. He used his old contacts with Buta Singh, then Home Minister, and conveyed to Rajiv Gandhi that he was upset over his staff being summoned by the CBI, and he was prepared for a compromise that neither he would create any problem for the Government nor the Government should harass his staff. It was during this period that his staff member, Gurcharan Singh, had filed an affidavit before the CBI, giving details of the goings on within the Rashtrapati Bhawan premises.

The Affidavit was revealing and further investigations would have put a black spot on Zail Singh for ever and no politician irrespective of his party affiliation would have supported Zail Singh. But still the CBI had to complete its task as the investigation was on the directions of the Supreme Court. However, this brought a brief thaw and Zail Singh became a little careful though secret parlays continued within the premises of Rashtrapati Bhawan for the second term of Zail Singh as President of the country.

Since the Presidential election was due in early July 1987 as the first term of Zail Singh was coming to an end, the next few weeks were most crucial for all the political parties, especially for Zail Singh and the then Prime Minister Rajiv Gandhi, and this period was an unprecedented period of planning strategies, conspiracies and manipulations for politicians, in particular the period from 15 to 25 June 1987 when a final decision on the next President was to be taken and Zail Singh himself was the Centre of all controversies. I had written an article for *Telegraph*, Calcutta in its issue of 28 June 1987. The article discloses all the details about what was going on during those crucial days.

VI

Role of Kashmiri Group

The role of the Kashmiri group led by Arun Nehru around Indira Gandhi and later around Rajiv Gandhi, was highly reprehensible in sabotaging any settlement on the Punjab problems. Indira Gandhi was almost playing into the hands of this group: Arun Nehru, as a relation of Indira Gandhi, and M.L. Fotedar, sitting at Akbar Road dealing with political matters, as her secretary. For sometime, Vijay Dhar, son of DP Dhar, also used to sit at 1 Akbar Road, and was a part of this group. Their main interests were in the northern states, especially the states of Jammu and Kashmir, Punjab, Haryana and U.P. In Jammu and Kashmir, this group was strongly opposed to Dr. Farooq Abdullah and his family, and Mufti Mohammad Sayeed was a part of Arun Nehru-Fotedar group. In 1983, when Dr. Farooq Abdullah had invited non-Congress Chief Ministers for a conference in Srinagar, this group had poisoned Indira Gandhi's mind against him. There was a move to overthrow Dr. Abdullah. Mir Qasim, a respected Congress leader from Kashmir who had been Chief Minister of the State, met Indira Gandhi and told her: "Do not push Farooq Abdullah to the wall. This is a nationalist family, people around you are misleading you." Mir Qasim himself had told me this, soon after meeting Indira Gandhi. he was a good friend of mine and often used to visit me when he was staying in Delhi.

CREATION OF UNREST IN PUNJAB

During the Assembly elections in Jammu and Kashmir, for the first time, Congress put up candidates, especially in Jammu region, on communal basis, which helped the Congress to gain more seats in the Jammu region. Even at that time, it was analyzed that this experiment will be repeated in Punjab also, where the Congress will play a divisive role and use of Sant Jarnail Singh Bhindranwale was a part of that plan. How this group had sabotaged every effort first by Indira Gandhi and later by Rajiv Gandhi to settle the Punjab issue is a horrific story, and how Punjab had to face bloodshed. Indira Gandhi was completely in the clutches of this "gang" and ultimately she lost her life, and the country was brought to a situation of unrest and terrorism. Rajiv Gandhi had realized this much later in 1986 when he started taking steps to retrieve the situation and get rid of this "gang." Everyone knows that during Indira Gandhi's time and later for sometime during Rajiv Gandhi's regime, Arun Nehru was extremely powerful, and even senior Cabinet Ministers used to be scared of him and used to address him as "sir." He was the man who twice scuttled the settlement with Akalis on the pleas that if the Government accepted Akalis' demands, Congress will lose Haryana Assembly elections. This happened twice in November 1982 itself at the last moment and even P.C. Alexander, who was Principal Secretary to the then Prime Minister, and was a part of the negotiations with the Akalis, has mentioned in his book how at the last moment the programme to send then Home Secretary, T.N. Chaturvedi, to Amritsar with the formula by a special plane, to meet the Akalis and announce it on TV, was cancelled by Indira Gandhi herself and this had done great harm.

Alexander himself was present in that official Cabinet Committee meeting held at his residence where the formula was agreed to and Akalis had also agreed to accept it, only an official announcement was to be made. This, she had done under pressures and persuasion from Arun Nehru and Fotedar, etc.

Fotedar sitting at 1 Akbar Road knew every development taking place and he immediately used to inform the then Haryana Chief Minister, Bhajan Lal. Bhajan Lal was acting on his advice only. This group had succeeded in persuading Rajiv Gandhi to induct Mufti Sayeed in his ministry as a minister, so that Dr. Farooq Abdullah could be kept at a distance. Arun Nehru in 1985 and early 1986 was behaving like a Mughal ruler. He managed to get the locks of Babri Masjid opened in early 1986. For this VHP, RSS and BJP had always been praising him. From his heart he was closer to RSS-BJP than being a Congressman. After the 1984 Sikh massacre following Indira Gandhi's assassination, once I asked BJP leader A.B. Vajpayee, with whom, I had good relations, that why don't they take up in Parliament the role of Arun Nehru and Bhajan Lal in organizing the anti-Sikh riots? He said: "We will not attack Arun Nehru but we will take up Bhajan Lal's role." This was the clout Arun Nehru had with BJP leaders because Arun Nehru was a hardliner, pro-BJP-RSS or the *Saffron Parivar.* Arun Nehru was equally very close to the VHP top man, Ashok Singal, whose younger brother, an IPS officer, B.P. Singal, was Additional Secretary in the Home Ministry under Arun Nehru as Minister of State for Internal Security, and later B.P. Singal was named as co-accused in the Check-pistol corruption case against Arun Nehru. There was a strong nexus between Arun

Nehru, Fotedar, Shiv Shankar, then Law Minister, and Gopi Arora, a senior bureaucrat about whom Rajiv Gandhi discovered much later and had even refused to meet him when Gopi had come from the World Bank on leave and was waiting for an appointment for one month. As Fotedar had disclosed in his book, Rajiv Gandhi's Presidential speech for the Bombay session of the Congress in December 1985, where Rajiv had talked about power-brokers, was drafted by Gopi Arora. Even Rajiv Gandhi's infamous remark at the Boat Club rally which has been a black-spot on Rajiv Gandhi, where he had said: "Jab Bada Ped Girta Hai to Dharti hilti hai" (when some big tree falls, the earth shakes), was also got written in Urdu by Gopi Arora from a Muslim lyric writer. Gopi Arora, though professed to be a leftist, was in fact a fellow traveller like Arun Nehru and Fotedar.

There was an understanding that T.N. Chaturvedi will replace Krishnaswami Rao Saheb as Cabinet Secretary but Arun Nehru and Fotedar group manipulated in such a way that T.N. Chaturvedi was appointed as CAG and P.K. Kaul, a Kashmiri was brought as Cabinet Secretary. M.M. Wali, another Kashmiri was brought as Home Secretary. This was the hold Arun Nehru-Fotedar combination was having. After the assassination of Indira Gandhi, this "Gang" had complete hold on the administrative setup.

MANIPULATIONS BY ARUN NEHRU

Arun Nehru had complete hold, as Minister of state for Internal Security, on the intelligence agencies and he also started controlling State Governors. All the intelligence reports used to be filtered through Arun Nehru to the Prime Minister whereas there was a time when the Director of the Intelligence Bureau used to walk straight to the room of the Prime Minister and the Home Minister. It was a tradition from the times of Jawahar Lal Nehru and Sardar Patel. But Rajiv Gandhi was getting filtered reports and Arun Nehru had started deciding what should be given to the Prime Minister. This was a very dangerous game plan. When an attack took place at an RSS *Shakha* in Daresi ground, Ludhiana and many persons were killed, Arun Nehru rushed to Ludhiana, along with Bombay Police Commissioner Reberio, and posted him in Punjab. Narsimha Rao was the Home Minister at that time and Arun Nehru had gone to Punjab even without informing Narsimha Rao. In the evening, Rao spoke to me and said: "Chawlaji, I was not even informed by Arun Nehru that he was going to Ludhiana." Rao was a highly competent Home Minister. He was shifted to Human Resources Development Ministry in September 1985 and for a few months, S.B. Chavan was appointed as Home Minister. Chavan was a good human being and non-controversial. A few months later, he was shifted and Buta Singh was brought in as Home Minister. When Buta Singh was appointed as Home Minister he was in London looking after the treatment of his wife. Arun Nehru had rung him up and informed him about his shifting to the Home Ministry. Although Buta Singh was a senior minister, he used to address Arun Nehru who was his junior as "sir." R.D. Pardhan, who belonged to Maharashtra cadre, was the Home Secretary and he was more loyal to Rajiv Gandhi than Arun Nehru. He was an efficient Home Secretary. Arun Nehru, having full control over the intelligence agencies, was manipulating everything in the administration.

After the installation of the Akali Government in Punjab led by Surjit Singh Barnala in September 1985, Arun Nehru had started dictating to Barnala. At the Northern Zonal Council Chief Ministers meeting held in Manali at the end of 1985, Arun Nehru had a meeting with Akali Minister Balwant Singh who was known as the Central Government's man, in a Manali Hotel, where Arun Nehru impressed upon Balwant Singh not to elect G.S. Tohra as SGPC President at the next annual general body meeting of the SGPC. But Balwant Singh expressed his inability as Barnala-Balwant Singh group did not have a majority in the SGPC and election of Tohra was certain. When Arun Nehru spoke to Balwant Singh, Amrinder Singh and Ravi Inder Singh, who had also gone to Manali, were sitting in another corner of the hall. After the meeting when Balwant Singh came to Delhi on his next visit, he told me accordingly and I published a report in the *Indian Express.*

Arun Nehru was also in touch with some militants through the intelligence agencies. A few militants, known to be hard-core, were sneaked into the *Golden Temple* in April 1986, and they were called as "Panthic Committee." On 29 April 1986, Gurbachan Singh Manochal, a leader of the Panthic Committee, declared establishment of Khalistan from the *Golden Temple.* Surjit Singh Barnala was in Delhi. Arun Nehru forced him to send Police to the Golden Temple to capture the members of the Panthic Committee next day itself. Only one person was found in the *Golden Temple.* It was well known in Punjab and Delhi circles that the whole episode has been manipulated by Arun Nehru to justify *Operation Blue Star.* In fact, Arun Nehru was against the installation of the Barnala Government and he was trying hard that his close friend

Amrinder Singh, who had by then joined the Akali Dal, should be the Chief Minister. Even at that time the Akalis opposed to Barnala had openly alleged that Manochahal was sent inside the Temple and his statement as leader of the Panthic Committee was at the behest of Intelligence Bureau. It was alleged that IB was in touch with Panthic Committee and Manochahal and some other extremist groups also. While Barnala was forced by Arun Nehru to send police inside the *Golden Temple* to justify *Operation Blue Star,* Amrinder Singh, who had joined the Akali Dal and was a Minister in the Barnala Government, resigned from the ministry on this issue. It was to weaken Barnala within his own party and bring out Amrinder Singh as the real representative of the Sikhs.

Even the Punjab accord signed by Rajiv Gandhi with Sant Harchand Singh Longowal on 24 July 1985, was sabotaged by this "gang" led by Arun Nehru. Amrinder Singh had even gone to the constituency of Arun Nehru in the 1991 Lok Sabha polls to campaign for him. He was there for four days. But Arun Nehru lost the election.

After the force was sent inside the Golden Temple, Parkash Singh Badal, G.S. Tohra and some other senior Akali leaders left the Longowal Akali Dal alongwith 27 legislators and the Barnala Government had survived with the support of the Congress Party but was removed in May 1987 and Punjab was brought under the Central rule, just before the Haryana Assembly Polls.

Just a few weeks before the *Operation Blue Star* in February 1984 there were three communal incidents in Haryana, at Panipat where a Gurdwara was attacked and some Sikhs were targeted at Karnal and Jind. This was well known that all the three incidents were created to show communal polarisation as a result of Punjab situation and all these were sponsored by Bhajan Lal sitting in Haryana Bhawan in Delhi, on indication from his supporters around Indira Gandhi. Preparations for the extreme step of *Blue Star* were being made much before the actual date of the *Operation Blue Star.* Indira Gandhi was almost like a prisoner in the hands of the "gang" led by Arun Nehru. Even Arun Singh had equal share in advising extreme step in Amritsar. But there are many questions why was the situation allowed to reach this point? Why the Government was not using its power to bring out Bhindranwale and other militants from the Golden Temple complex when it was very easy a task. The fact is that while Indira Gandhi was being pressurised by this "gang" for the extreme step, she was still reluctant to go all out. She had become suddenly so confused that she did not know what to do. Ultimately, the surrounding evil designs could influence her. I had known her a little bit and had seen her functioning, and I can say that she was not at all communal.

Rajiv Gandhi had started realising the game this "gang" was playing after tension in Sirsa area adjoining Punjab in middle of January 1986, as a reaction to the provocative statements made by Bhajan Lal at the AICC Bombay session and later, and counter-statements by Surjit Singh Barnala and he had decided to cut this "gang" to size. In early 1986, he also learnt how Arun Nehru had been collecting funds in the name of the party. He also realised that this gang was sabotaging the implementation of Rajiv-Longowal accord, on both the important issues, territorial as well as the water issue. Law Minister Shiv Shankar, was completely with Arun Nehru and Fotedar and was acting according to their plans. On some pretext, the hearing of the water tribunal was postponed that the judge could not get seat on the plane to reach Delhi.

Rajiv Gandhi had in the Longowal Accord promised to transfer Chandigarh to Punjab. First it was to be done on 26 January 1986. A territorial commission, Venkataramiah Commission, was appointed to recommend the areas to be transferred to Haryana in lieu of Chandigarh. Shah Commission had given award in favour of Haryana. This award was under the influence of the then Home Minister, Gulzari Lal Nanda, who had leanings towards Jan Sangh and wanted to enter politics in Haryana, though he was known as a Gandhian, a Congressman. Second time, date for transfer was fixed as 21 June 1986, and third time, transfer of Chandigarh was fixed for 15 July 1986. But the gang of Arun Nehru was not allowing it on one side and on the other was Balwant Singh who was number two with Barnala to create hurdles in any accord on Punjab. Balwant Singh's survival was based on playing mischiefs to ensure that there is no settlement of the Punjab problem. But Rajiv Gandhi was very keen that he should fulfil his assurance on Chandigarh.

Rajiv had, in the accord, promised to transfer Chandigarh to Punjab on 26 January 1986. He was extremely worried that he will not be able to show his face if he does not fulfil his promise. He asked me to meet Barnala, who was in the capital, and ask him to seek an appointment with him and come alone and not with Balwant Singh and offer his resignation if Chandigarh is not transferred to Punjab. Buta Singh was aware of this but none else. I went to Punjab Bhawan, met Barnala, bolted his room from inside and conveyed Rajiv's message. We were still talking on this when his door was knocked and in came Balwant Singh. I stopped talking and in a minute or so,

Charanjit Singh of Coca Cola, also came in and I left his room and came back. Barnala did seek appointment but he went to meet Rajiv Gandhi along with Balwant Singh and he did not threaten or offer his resignation if Chandigarh was not transferred to Punjab, fearing that if it does not materialise, his ministry will go and he will be again out of job. Barnala was completely in the clutches of Balwant Singh as Balwant Singh had won over Barnala's family members.

ARUN NEHRU SNUBBED BY RAJIV GANDHI

Rajiv Gandhi was so much upset that he called Arun Nehru and snubbed him saying: "I feel ashamed of calling you my cousin. You never told me that you were doing all this and collecting huge sums of money." Arun Nehru was so much upset with words he had never heard that he went to Srinagar on tour where he got a heart-attack. Ultimately, Arun Nehru was dropped from the Ministry in the next reshuffle in October, after Arun Nehru returned from abroad. P.K. Kaul, Cabinet Secretary, was sent to USA as Indian Ambassador, and a few months later, Fotedar was included in the Cabinet. The object was to remove his presence from the Prime Minister's house. Haryana Chief Minister, Bhajan Lal who was a villain, and was sabotaging every possible step for settlement of the Punjab problem, was also removed. Arjun Singh who was the architect of the Rajiv-Longowal accord, had suggested to Rajiv Gandhi to change the leadership in Haryana as he was sabotaging every effort. Fotedar tried his best to save Bhajan Lal and pleaded with Rajiv Gandhi not to shift him but Rajiv Gandhi insisted you take his resignation immediately, which Rajiv Gandhi accepted without wasting even one minute. However, Gopi

Arora, another member of this gang managed to escape and he had assured that he was loyal to him. But later on Rajiv Gandhi found out that Gopi was too clever a man and he had kept his contacts with Arun Nehru even after Arun's ouster from the Cabinet. Rajiv Gandhi came to know about it much later. This way he had thrown out all conspirators and saboteurs out of his residence and key positions. M.L. Fotedar was a very important member of this gang.

If Rajiv Gandhi would have appointed a high-level commission to go into the causes of sabotaging, this gang would have been exposed thoroughly and their place would have been somewhere else. But that would have given a very bad name to the Congress Party embarrassing it further. All these actions amounted to anti-national activities as these actions had bearing on the national security.

I wrote an article in *The Pioneer*, Lucknow, dated 14 April 1989, under the caption: "Suspicion of Leakage on Arun Nehru." This was on leakage of The Thakkar Commission report on Assassination of Indira Gandhi, indicting R.K. Dhawan. Since the report was with Arun Nehru when he was Minister incharge of internal Security, and it was leaked through Arif Mohammad Khan, a right-hand man of Arun Nehru. About the Thakkar Commission and the Ranganath Commission which went into the anti-Sikh riots in Delhi and elsewhere, less said better as disclosed by B.G. Deshmukh former Cabinet Secretary about both the Judges, how pliable these two judges were and how they were ringing up Deshmukh to inform the Prime Minister how they were working. Deshmukh himself has cast doubts on the functioning of both the Judges of the Supreme Court. Unfortunately, Justice Ranganath Mishra was later promoted as Chief Justice of the

Country. Both the Judges had given a serious set back to the credibility of the highest judicial forum.

When my article appeared, the IB got a copy of the article on fax from Lucknow. M.K. Narayanan, who was then Director of the IB, took a copy of the article with him when he met Rajiv Gandhi in the evening. G. Parthasarthy, who retired as Indian Ambassador to Pakistan, was posted with Rajiv Gandhi as his Press Secretary, and was sitting with the Prime Minister when Narayanan met Rajiv Gandhi. Narayanan took out copy of the article and gave it to Rajiv Gandhi and said: "Sir, this is what G.S. Chawla has written in today's *Pioneer.*" Rajiv Gandhi went through the article and gave it back to Narayanan and remarked: "Narayanan, don't you appreciate only G.S. Chawla can write this." Soon after this briefing session, Parthasarthy went to his room and rang me up. "Chawla Sahib, I am coming to your house in the evening for a drink, give me good whisky," he said: I told him whatever I have I will offer you. He came around 8.30 p.m. and told me exactly what had transpired. Unless he had told me, I would not know what had happened.

Some portions of the article are given below:

"But in the Home Ministry, Arun Nehru was more open as a hawk and was opposed to the installation of the Barnala Government and he was always keen to bring in his close friend among Akalis, Capt. Amrinder Singh, as the Chief Minister and for that he was prepared to go to any length. In April 1986, when Gurbachan Singh Manochahal of the Panthic Committee announced creation of Khalistan from the Golden Temple, and Barnala was forced by Arun Nehru to send police force into the Golden Temple complex on 29 April 1986, otherwise to face a sack, some Akali leaders had alleged that the Government through the Intelligence Bureau was behind the announcement of Manochahal to force the Barnala Government to send police into the Temple to justify *Operation Blue Star*. It was alleged at that time that the IB was in touch with the Panthic Committee members and some other extremist organisations. On one side Barnala was forced to send police inside the Temple, and on the other side Arun Nehru's friend Capt. Amrinder Singh, on this issue left the Barnala Government. It was a double-edged weapon to weaken Barnala within his own party and bring out Amrinder Singh, as the real representative of Sikhs."

"In 1985, it was well known in the political circles in the capital that a gang of four headed by Arun Nehru was ruling the country. Other members of the gang were M.L. Fotedar, then Cabinet Secretary P.K. Kaul, and G.K. Arora, then in the Prime Minister's Secretariat." In the beginning of the article quoting then Home Minister Buta Singh's statement in Lok Sabha, it was written: "Buta Singh has also alleged in the Lok Sabha that Arun Nehru and Arun Singh were largely responsible for the "rivers of blood that has been flowing in Punjab."

Rajiv Gandhi's remarks to the Director of the IB, M.K. Narayanan, when he showed him my article, shows how much he was mentally disturbed with the activities of this gang. It is certainly difficult to get rid of persons who have been inside your establishment for years together, fearing that they knew too much and even a false allegation by them will be happily picked up by the opposition. It is for this reason that Rajiv Gandhi took some time to cleanse his stable. Sonia Gandhi is also facing the same problem. She cannot throw out V. George, her Private Secretary because he has been there for more than three decades and he could put the family into difficulty. She knows how rich George has become, still she cannot remove him. Rajiv Gandhi had stopped trusting V. George, and he had a very frank talk with me. One day, in 1990, while I was sitting with him, he got a fax message from Calcutta. The Fax machine was installed in his room. He got up to pick up the Fax message and found an envelop lying near the Fax. This envelop contained an urgent and important information, which Rajiv Gandhi had given to George to deliver it personally to that person. When he found that envelop, he was shocked and called George inside the room in my presence. He asked him, "George, I had given you a letter yesterday and asked you to deliver it personally. What have you done with that letter?" George said: "I have done it yesterday." Rajiv was surprised at the reply and showed him the letter and asked him from where has it come? It shook up George completely. In anger, Rajiv sent him out, and told me: "Chawlaji , have you seen this? How can I trust such persons? That is why I want you to have a Fax machine at your house, so that both of us could have direct contact." Those days, fax machine used to cost Rs. 70,000 as it had just been introduced in the market and I told him that I will install it later. It took me about one year to procure a fax machine but by that time Rajiv Gandhi was not in this world.

How much Rajiv Gandhi was feeling disturbed over the activities of Arun Nehru and his gang, is evident from the speech of Rajiv Gandhi in Parliament on the leakage of the Thakkar Commission report. While intervening in the discussion on the Thakkar Commission report in Lok Sabha on 10 April 1989 he said: "The friends of the conspirators could, if they wished, leak the portion of the report relating to the large conspiracy. Why did they deliberately restrict themselves to publication of only portions related to Dhawan?" Next day, the then Home Minister, Buta Singh replying to the debate pointing his accusing fingers at Arun Nehru for the leakage, said that he had kept the report in his house for six months without even showing it to his senior Minister. This was a grave charge against Arun Nehru.

Arun Nehru and Fotedar had the impression that Arun Nehru was dropped from the Ministry at the behest of Sonia Gandhi and Capt. Satish Sharma and this is indicated in Fotedar's book also. That is why when Arun Nehru was questioned by the CBI in the Bofor gun case, in his statement repeatedly he pointed fingers at Sonia Gandhi and asked the CBI to question Sonia Gandhi on these issues. In fact, Arun Nehru should have been an accused in the Bofor case but as I said earlier, BJP never wanted to touch him as he was toeing their line more than even the RSS-VHP. The bitterness between Arun Nehru and Rajiv Gandhi was more on the dangerous role this gang had played in unsettling the Punjab situation which amounted to an anti-national act, and also indulging in other activities collecting huge sums of money. A few years before his death, Arun Nehru had patched up with Sonia Gandhi through some family relations, and in the last days when Nehru fell ill, arrangements for his hospitalisation were made by the 10 Janpath, Sonia Gandhi had always been scared of him. She knew to what extent Arun Nehru could become a ruthless person.

My object of writing all this is to show that the gang of Arun Nehru which included M.L. Fotedar also, had played a major role in destroying Punjab and creating blood-shed in that state. This gang is responsible for destroying the Gandhi family and doing immense damage to the country.

VII

Akali and Misuse of SGPC

Sant Jarnail Singh Bhindranwale was originally a simple preacher, who attracted rural youth through his religious preaching. He was dragged into politics by the Congress Party to fight the Akalis. But in the first fight against the Akalis in the SGPC elections in early 1970s, he lost to the Akalis in a big way though the Congress Party had supported him. It is well known that in the 1980 Lok Sabha polls, he had supported Gurdial Singh Dhillon and R.L. Bhatia, Congress candidates. While Bhindranwale was gaining ground in rural areas, Akalis were slipping gradually and they often adopted Bhindranwale. Jathedar G.S. Tohra, who was President of the SGPC for over 27 years, was the supporter of Bhindranwale. The SGPC is a religious body, meant to preach Sikh religion through teachings of the ten Gurus. It has a huge budget and controls all Gurdwaras in Punjab and Himachal Pradesh. Earlier, Gurdwaras in Haryana were also within its control. But the Akalis used the SGPC platform for political purposes rather than preaching teachings of the ten Sikh gurus.

The Akali leadership, especially Parkash Singh Badal, have been fully exploiting the SGPC and the supreme religious authority of the Sikh religion, the *Akal Takhat*. The edict of the Jathedar of the *Akal Takhat* used to be like Law for the Sikh community. The *Akal Takhat* Jathedar's word used to be a final word. It is well known in Sikh history that the *Akal Takhat*

Jathedar had even ordered lashes to Maharaja Ranjit Singh, the great Sikh ruler and the Maharaja had bowed before the verdict and had prepared to face the punishment. This used to be the respect the *Akal Takhat* used to command. Even Mater Tara Sigh, the great Akali Leader, who led the Akali dal for more than four decades, had to face the verdict of the *Akal Takhat* and clean utensils in the Gurdwara Langer. But now the Akali leadership, in particular the Badal family, has misused the *Akal Takhat* against opponents so much that within the Sikh community itself there is criticism of the *Akal Takhat* decisions. After the assassination of Giani Partap Singh, former Jathedar of the *Akal Takhat,* who had criticised the militants, no *Akal Takhat* Jathedar had the courage to voice against militancy and mostly those were appointed as *Akal Takhat* Jathedars who were pliable by the Akali Leadership or who had close links with Sant Jarnail Singh Bhindranwale. Parkash Singh Badal had even marginalized stalwarts like Jathedar G.S. Tohra.

Bhai Ranjit Singh, who was serving jail term in a murder case for killing Nirankari Chief, was appointed *Akal Takhat* Jathedar. Badal and some other Akalis had pressurized the then Prime Minister, I.K. Gujral, for early release of Bhai Ranjit Singh whom they wanted to appoint as the Akal Takhat Jathedar. Gujral was initially reluctant to accept this demand. He spoke to A.B. Vajpaee and sought his views. Vajpayee had no objection to the Akali demand, and Gujral released Bhai Ranjit Singh who was soon after appointed Jathedar of the *Akal Takhat.* Earlier, on 4 March, 1988, over three dozen important prisoners, including Jasbir Singh Rode, nephew of Sant Jarnail Singh Bhindranwale, were released as a deal between the Intelligence Bureau and the militants and Jasbir Singh Rode was appointed as Jathedar of the *Akal Takhat*. This experiment of the IB proved again a disaster and a new phase of militancy started. Only two months later, another Operation had to be launched against the militants in the Golden Temple complex, by the NSG, headed by Ved Marwaha, a distinguished police officer with the help of the Punjab Police.

THE ROLE OF PARKASH SINGH BADAL

All historic gurdwaras in Punjab are in the control of the SGPC ruled by the Badal group. Personally, Parkash Singh Badal has been known as a weak but clever leader who moves according to the situation. He used to be mortally scared of the militants and during the Governor's rule in Punjab when S.S. Ray was the Governor, Badal was in a jail and he preferred to remain there rather than coming out as he was afraid of being attacked by militants.

As Chief Minister of Punjab in 1978, when Parkash Singh Badal headed the Akali Government in Punjab, there is not even one letter on record which he would have written to the Central Government, either on the Chandigarh issue or river waters, Punjab's main demands. He has been taking up these issues only when he was out of power. Therefore, they used to resort to agitations to gain power, for self-service more than public service. For peace in Punjab, Akalis have to be kept busy, otherwise they resort to agitations even if these affect nation al security. This politics has ruined the state which was built up by leaders like Partap Singh Kairon, who was the architect of development and industrialization of the state. Industrial estates in Ludhiana and other districts of Punjab and conversion of Faridabad, as a major centre of big industries was the effort of Partap Singh Kairon. Badal cannot claim having done anything worthwhile for the state for which people of Punjab could be proud of him.

No doubt, Punjab has only two tallest leaders, Parkash Singh Badal and in the Congress Party, Amrinder Singh. Neither Badal nor the Congress has allowed another leader to grow bigger than their present size. In the political fight, Amrinder Singh is much more aggressive than Badal. Amrinder Singh is more courageous also. There have been reports in Punjab that both these leaders have been having links with ultras. Both, Amrinder Singh and Sukhbir Singh Badal, son of Parkash Singh Badal, after bitter fights against each other and launching corruption cases, a few years ago, they had reached some tacit understanding in Dubai through some mediators, to stop fighting at a very personal level and resorting to launching cases against each other, but to fight only at the political level. After this understanding, Badal is not persuing much the cases filed against Amrinder Singh and it is more than 8 years since the case against Amrinder Singh and his other friends was filed in the Ludhiana Sessions court. The progress is so slow in the Sessions Court that even charges have not yet been framed in the case. In a way this is a healthy sign that they are fighting only at the political level but not at the personal level.

People of Punjab, in general, are peaceful and hard-working. At one point of time, Punjab had become number one state in the country in the matter of development and industry. Punjab had succeeded in bringing green revolution in the country for which Punjab Agricultural University which had been having leading lights as its Vice-Chancellors and Agricultural scientists produced by this University are highly respected in countries like USA and other developed countries. But the political leadership of Punjab has let down the people of the state and its position from number one state of the country has considerably come down, and position has come to this state that many a times, the state Government does not have enough funds to pay salaries to the staff on time and the state is mortgaging its properties. While the state is starving of funds, politicians are becoming richer day by day. This can result in unrest among people. A large number of farmers are committing suicides and they are under heavy debts. They are resorting to agitations. These politicians have ruined the state. There is serious dearth of honest and sincere leadership. Industry in the state is in a very bad shape. In such a situation, unemployment will increase which will give impetus to militancy. Already, clouds of such situation are becoming visible. For this situation, Akali leadership, in particular the Badal family, is held responsible.

The first Akali Chief Minister, Justice Gurnam Singh had commanded the respect of people of the state as well as the Central Government. Only he had the courage to write to Indira Gandhi in 1969 when Sant Fateh Singh went on fast unto death, on the Chandigarh issue, that "Your Home Minister is very communal." Gulzari Lal Nanda was the Home Minister. He had also written: "Do you want Punjab to secede?" Indira Gandhi had respected him and when he was no more the Chief Minister, he was appointed as an Ambassador. Whereas Badal on one telephone from Morarji Desai was prepared to bend and do anything.

Akalis are also as responsible for the bloodshed in Punjab as the Bhindranwale or the Congress party because though they were opposed to the policies of Bhindranwale, whenever they found that he had hijacked their agitation, they followed his militant posture. They had no courage to oppose him or his policies. Rather, they used to start following his policies. Had they stuck to their original policy of peaceful agitation, the situation could not have reached the point it had reached. As the law and order situation in the state was worsening and Bhindranwale's authority was being established over even state administration, he was becoming emboldened and Akalis were gradually withdrawing from the scene, except for passing some resolutions in their meetings where they started indirectly supporting Bhindranwale. While G.S. Tohra had sympathies with Bhindranwale, Badal and Sant Longowal were too meek and had no courage to face the situation. Therefore, while conspirators and saboteurs around Indira Gandhi and Rashtrapati Bhawan were busy playing their destructive role and misguiding Indira Gandhi, the Akalis were meekly withdrawing and hiding themselves. They were realising that their agitation was now harming the cause of the Sikh community and the situation was going out of control, as the speeches at their meeting of District Jathedars held in Amritsar in February 1984 indicated, and at one point of time they were thinking of suspending their agitation. If they had done that, Punjab would still have been saved much of the bloodshed and the Centre would have to deal with its own creation-Bhindrawale, directly.

In the Akali Party, there are many stalwarts who have been loyal to the party for four or even five decades but Parkash Singh Badal has not allowed any other Akali leader to match him. He is very vindictive also. He cannot forget that in 1985, after the Rajiv-Longowal accord, when Assembly elections were held in Punjab and Surjit Singh Barnala government was formed, he was offered a position in the Ministry much below his status. He was prepared to be number-two to Barnala, though earlier Barnala was a Minister under Badal. But Barnala insisted that Balwant Singh will be number—two and Badal could join as number—3 which was humiliating for Badal. Badal was not only senior to Barnala, but to Balwant Singh also and in the earlier Akali Government, Balwant Singh was in the Badal Government as a Minister. Badal had suggested a way out that their status should be according to Alphabetic order. But Barnala and the congress party did not agree on this saying there was a commitment with Balwant Singh to make him the Deputy Chief Minister. Badal had a talk with me also on this issue in Central Hall of Parliament. Since then Badal has been the strongest critic of the Congress Party.

DR. MANMOHAN SINGH AT THE HELM OF AFFAIRS

In 2004, when UPA came to power at the Centre, Dr. Manmohan Singh became the Prime Minister. He was the first Sikh Prime Minister of the country having good reputation at the international level as an economist and also as a very clean person. The SGPC was celebrating 300 years of some Sikh religious festivity. Parkash Singh Badal, as Akali Dal Chief having indirect control over the SGPC, did not invite Dr. Manmohan Singh but invited President Abdul Kalam. Dr. Manmohan Singh is a devout Sikh and respected by the community. In fact, he should have been honoured by the SGPC, as it was a pride for the Sikh community that a learned Sikh was the Prime Minister of the country. Badal insisted he will not invite Dr. Manmohan Singh. A senior Akali leader took up this matter and strongly pleaded with Badal to invite Dr. Manmohan Singh. When Badal still refused to agree, it was suggested that district Jathedars should be consulted. A meeting was called where majority was of the view that Dr. Manmohan Singh should be invited. Badal agreed to invite but put the condition that he will not receive him at the airport. The senior Akali leader said he will go and receive him as a representative of the party. Amrinder Singh was Chief Minister of Punjab and when he learnt that Manmohan Singh will be attending the S.G.P.C. ceremony, he also arranged a separate independent function at the same time in Amritsar and invited Dr. Manmohan Singh for that. It was difficult for Manmohan Singh to ignore a Congress Chief Minister and attend the SGPC function. Ultimately, Mrs Sonia Gandhi sent a word to Amrinder Singh to cancel his function and then SGPC sent an invitation to Amrinder Singh also for its function and Amrinder Singh also attended it. This only shows how vindictive is Parkash Singh Badal and how much rivalry existed between Badal and Amrinder Singh.

Parkash Singh Badal is quite happy with the BJP leadership but BJP leadership are feeling suffocated with Badal. BJP leaders, including its Prime Minister, Narendra Modi, have been taunting the Congress leadership on 1984 anti-Sikh riots. But even the Akali-Dal ally, BJP, has not passed any resolution in Parliament or otherwise, to condemn 1984 riots. When the first NDA Government, led by the BJP, was formed in 1998, Madan Lal Khurana, who was known as the most popular leader of the party in the capital, had given a notice for a resolution in Lok Sabha, to condemn 1984 riots expressing sympathy with the victims, he was forced by L.K. Advani to withdraw that resolution. Khurana was an honest and popular BJP Chief Minister of Delhi and he was especially very popular among the Sikh community. After Khurana's exit as Chief Minister of Delhi, BJP could not come to power. Khurana was a victim of L. K. Advani. Khurana had refused to sign a file to sanction a power plant to Ambanis, which was later signed by Sahib Singh Varma who succeeded Khurana.

As compared to Parkash Singh Badal, his son Deputy Chief Minister, Sukhbir Singh Badal, is a ruthless person and can adopt any means to achieve his goal. Therefore, ultimately, political fight between Congress and Akalis in Punjab will remain confined to the fight between Sukhbir Badal and Amrinder Singh. Sukhbir Badal has come up as a leader of the Akali Party only a few years ago, but during the peak militancy main players in active politics were Parkash Singh Badal in the Akali Dal, and Beant Singh and Amrinder Singh, in the Congress Party. Beant Singh had kept the Congress flag up in Punjab. As Punjab Congress President, he remained very active and attended the *bhog* ceremonies of all those killed by the militants despite the fact that he had no personal security arrangement. Still he remained in the field during the peak period of military. Punjab Congress has survived because of his untiring work and sacrifice, though Amrinder Singh has been shuttling between Congress and Akali Dal. P.V. Narsimha Rao was not happy with Beant Singh and Rao was using Maninderjit Singh Bitta, then Youth Congress President, against Beant Singh. Beant Singh still survived but was gunned down by militants in Chandigarh Secretariat. Unlike others, Beant Singh was not playing any hidden game with the militants.

VIII
Intelligence Agencies' Gamble

The role of the Intelligence agencies, RAW and IB in the entire Punjab's dark days, is necessary to be probed. Both the agencies have been keeping track of militancy which is its normal job. But their role has been more than keeping track. The RAW and IB had to have contacts with militant organisation directly or indirectly to know their plans but by going the extra mile to cultivate with them, had proved as encouragement. For instance, when A.S. Atwal, DIG, Jalandhar range, was killed at the foot-steps of the Golden Temple, by Bhindranwale's men, it was later learnt that a senior RAW officer, a particular Brigadier, had called Atwal to Amritsar and had told him that he was sent by the Central Government, as Bhindranwale was very angry that his men going to Chok Mehta were checked by the Police and encounter had taken place, and the Centre wanted Atwal to apologise to Bhindranwale. Atwal had refused. The Government owes an explanation to the nation why did it want to pacify Bhindranwale even if his men were checked and encounter had taken place. When Atwal was killed, this Brigadier was sitting with Bhindranwale. Indira Gandhi was extremely upset over Atwal's killing. She had sent J.S. Bawa, then Director of the CBI, for an on-the-spot study of the situation. Bawa had personally briefed Indira Gandhi and had told her that Atwal was killed by Bhindranwale men and the culprits were still within the Golden Temple Complex. Despite this information, from head of the CBI who had visited the spot, why did not the Central Government take steps to get the men, including Bhindranwale, arrested from the temple complex which was much easier than the *Operation Blue Star* a year later, when Bhindranwale had fortified his positions within the temple complex and why were the arms allowed to be taken inside the temple? What were these intelligence agencies doing at that time?

In 1986, the IB was fully in touch with the Panthic Committee and it was at the behest of the IB that Gurbachan Singh Manochahal of the Panthic Committee had announced establishment of *Khalistan* to force Surjit Singh Barnala to send Police force inside the Golden Temple to justify the *Operation Blue Star*. Why was the Central Government playing such games? It was Arun Nehru who had done it as Minister of State, but still the Central Government was responsible as Arun Nehru was Minister of State for Internal Security.

In 1988, again, the IB got released Jasbir Singh Rode, nephew of Sant Jarnail Singh Bhindranwale, and many others, provided them with some arms and Jasbir Singh Rode was installed as Jathedar of the Akal Takhat why even after the *Operation Blue Star,* the Central Government could not come out of the clutches of Bhindranwale family, even after his death during the *Operation Blue Star*? These are some very pertinent questions which need to be answered by the Government.

It is well known that riots in Delhi and elsewhere were not spontaneous but organised ones. Who had organised these riots? Was this the work of the gang around Indira Gandhi or some other organisation? Soon after the formation of the Rajiv Gandhi Government after the elections in 1985, V.P. Singh had become Finance Minister. V.P. Singh had asked his Ministry's then DPIO, Mrs Deepak Sandhu, who retired as Chief Information Commissioner, to give him a list of journalists whom he could invite for talks with him one by one. She had given him a list of about two dozen journalists who were covering the Economic Ministries. At the end of the list she had included my name. V.P. Singh selected my name first to talk to me. Though Mrs Sandhu told him that I was not an economic journalist, he insisted that he would meet me first. When I met him, he started talking about the political situation and I said let us start from the riots. I asked him his views on the riots. At the time of riots, he was living somewhere in Greater Kailash or around that area which he mentioned but I am forgetting it. He said when he got down from his flat to catch a flight for Lucknow, he found crowds with kerosine tins and iron rods in their hands, indulging in riots. When he reached Lucknow, he found the same pattern. I asked him: " Don't you think these were organised riots?" He said: "Yes, I think so." We were on this when Raghuramiah, a former Minister and at that time a Governor in a state entered his room and they started talking. I got up and said that both of you will take sometime, so we will meet sometime later. I did not meet him again so long as he was the Finance Minister. But even at that time the view was that the riots were an organised affair, and nobody else than the gang around Indira Gandhi could have done it. The three violent incidents in Haryana in February 1984, were also the handiwork of the gang through Bhajan Lal who had no scruples in such matters.

In the Delhi Sikh Gurdawara Committee Act, there was a provision that President of the Committee should at least be a matriculate. The first thing that the Central Government did in

1980 after coming to power was to amend the Act and remove the clause of educational qualification to enable Jathedar Santokh Singh to become President of the Committee, Jathedar Santokh Singh was very close to the then Government and he was instrumental in delivering a very provocative speech at Chowk Mehta on 20 September 1981, when Police had gone to arrest Sant Jarnail Singh Bhindranwale in the Jagat Narain murder case, and six persons were killed in the police firing. When Indira Gandhi had gone to Chandigarh for an all-party meeting just before leaving on a foreign tour, Parkash Singh Badal had pointed out the speech given by Jathedar Santokh Singh, a Congress Supporter.

Sant Jarnail Singh had visited Delhi, on the invitation of Jathedar Santokh Singh, in the first week of April 1982, and was in the capital for a week. He used to move around with almost one hundred armed supporters sitting even on the roof-top of the buses, holding arms in their hands. Why was the Central Government a silent spectator at that time? It was said at that time that Giani Zail Singh had met Sant Bhindranwale at the residence of Jathedar Santokh Singh. Only three months later in 1982, Akalis had supported Giani Zail Singh in the presidential election. Knowing all this what was happening in Punjab and how Bhindranwale's men were becoming law upto themselves, why was the Central Government not checking the movement of Bhindranwale in the capital? There should have been a Commission of Enquiry after the *Operation Blue Star* headed by a sitting judge of the Supreme Court (not a judge like Ranganath Mishra or Justice Thakkar who are a blot on the highest judiciary), and the real facts would have come out. Delhi had never seen such threatening scenes of armed men sitting on the roof-tops of the buses, moving on New Delhi roads. It used to be the scenes as Delhi was raided by armed men during the Mughal period. If it was not with the connivance of the Central Government, then what else it could be?

BHINDRANWALE'S ARREST PLAN SABOTAGED

When Bhindranwale was moving about in the capital with his armed men on his bus roof-top, the Union Home Ministry and the Delhi administration felt seriously concerned and the Liet. Governor of Delhi, S.L. Khurana who was in touch with the Home Secretary, T.N. Chaturvedi, brought this to the notice of Prime Minister Indira Gandhi, and its repercussions that will arise. Indira Gandhi herself had also seen pictures of Bhindranwale moving in bus-loads with armed men on roof-top, on the Delhi roads. Khurana was also in touch with the Director of the IB, TV Rajeshwar, who was a confident of Zail Singh. Khurana was planning to arrest Bhindranwale in Delhi itself. He personally discussed this matter with Indira Gandhi who asked him many questions on the arrangements for the arrest and if any untoward thing happened, what will be the consequences. Khurana had explained to her the strategy the Administration will adopt and felt that since Bhindranwale himself used to sit inside the bus, even in an unfortunate situation, nothing will happen to him. But even if as a last resort, something very unfortunate, the government will be able to handle it. Khurana spoke with full confidence. This convinced Indira Gandhi who gave her consent for Bhindranwale's arrest in the capital. As this information reached Bhindranwale, he immediately shifted to Gurdwara Majnu Ka Tilla, near Yamuna river, in the outskirts of Delhi. Khurana got information that there was a sabotage of the plan to arrest Bhindranwale, by two sources, Zail Singh and another Sikh Minister close to Indira Gandhi, who conveyed this information to Bhindranwale. This was a serious set back to the Government Strategy to arrest Bhindranwale in the capital. Had the Government succeeded in its plans, stock of Indira Gandhi would have gone sky-high in the world and everybody including akalis in Punjab would have felt relieved. The surroundings of the Gandhi family have proved to be disastrous for the country and the Gandhi family itself. Though Indira Gandhi had agreed to the arrest of Bhindranwale in the capital, still not arresting him had created an impression in the country that Bhindranwale was not arrested because he was the protege of the Congress leadership. The then Home Secretary, T.N. Chaturvedi and the Delhi L.G., S.L. Khurana, were both disappointed that a sabotage had taken place and their plan to arrest Bhindranwale had not materialised. Who had leaked this information to Zail Singh and the other Sikh Minister, is known to the IB, and it was conveyed to the Prime Minister also.

When Rajiv Gandhi became Prime Minister, initially, Arun Nehru and M.L. Fotedar and Gopi Arora, another hard-liner in the PMO were guiding him on Punjab. Buta Singh was brought in as Home Minister, a little later. But Rajiv Gandhi's Punjab policy was not working smoothly and he started distancing away from the Kashmiri lobby. But Gopi Arora still managed to remain at the helm of affairs in the PMO. Rajiv Gandhi started relying more on his Director of the Intelligence Bureau, M.K. Narayanan, than even Buta Singh though Buta Singh was close to him. Narayanan had differences with Buta Singh on the approach on Punjab and he used to brief Rajiv Gandhi directly rather than through the Home Minister. The IB had its own views on Buta Singh, one of the retired Joint Director of the IB who was dealing with the subject, has hinted in his book three years ago. Buta Singh is a well-educated politician unlike Zail Singh he had a great weakness for his two sons who did not bring him glory as a politician as they were actively meddling in his official work which attracted a lot of criticism in newspapers.

When Giani Zail Singh became Home Minister, after the elections in 1980, he stayed in Kapurthala House, a Punjab Government Guest House, in New Delhi, for a short time till he was allotted a house on the Race Course Road. Kapurthala House was about 250 meters from my House on Shah Jehan Road. Giani Zail Singh rang me up in the evening after his return from Home Ministry, and asked me to come to Kapurthala House for a chat. It was around 7.30 p.m. I was sitting with him when I found a man coming with a file in his hand and Giani Zail Singh indicated him to sit on the dining table, in a small cabin-like room. We went on talking for an hour or so and the man waiting in the dining room was called after I left. Next day also, it was the same situation. When I noticed this man coming on my third visit and Giani Zail Singh asked him to wait in the dining room, I told Giani Zail Singh: "Gianiji, aggar tussi is admi da kam karna hai to karo, Ise rose rose kayon bullato Ho" (if you want to do his work, do it, why are you calling him again and again). He said: "He is not a businessman but Director of the IB." I replied: "Gianiji is this the way to treat the Director of the IB? Do you know, Director of the IB is such a busy man that his every minute is valuable and I know during Pandit Nehru's time, Director of the IB used to walk straight into the room of the Prime Minister, brief him and come back. I said Director of the IB is supposed to be the head of the security set up, and why are you wasting his time daily? Later on, I found out it was TV Rajeshwar, who was Director of the IB, who used to spend more time with the SA of the Home Minister than the Home Minister. He was shifted as Director before the completion of his tenure and sent as a Governor, as he was a Gandhi family loyalist. He was the first Police officer to be appointed as a Governor and the IPS faternity was quite happy that an IPS officer had been appointed as Governor.

When T.N. Chaturvedi was Home Secretary and Giani Zail Singh was the Home Minister, both were not pulling on well as Chaturvedi was not happy on seeing what was happening. Chaturvedi was a very straight-forward Home Secretary. But Giani Zail Singh did not like him. Giani Zail Singh started campaign against Chaturvedi describing him as a hawk and poisoning Indira Gandhi against him. He had involved Amrinder Singh and G.S. Tohra also to campaign against Chaturvedi. Ultimately, P.P. Nayyar a senior IAS officer of Bihar Cadre who was at that time posted as additional Chief Secretary, Bihar, was brought in the Home Ministry, as a Special Secretary to handle Punjab affairs exclusively. The Home Ministry was fully aware how arms were being smuggled into the Golden Temple in the foodgrain bags meant for the Langar. This was based on the IB reports. Despite these reports, why the Cental Government was not taking steps to ensure that the arms are not smuggled in the foodgrain bags into the temple premises? Even Darbara Singh as Chief Minister of State had told Punjab M.Ps in the capital that arms were being manufactured within the complex. There are not one but many unanswered questions which the Government could not explain.

What an irony of fate? Sant Jarnail Singh Bhindranwale, a simple religious preacher of rural areas, picked up by the Congress Party, Giani Zail Singh, as President of the Punjab Congress in 1970s, coaxed in to fight the Akalis, his sentiments aroused, projected first as a messiah, used him politically, given him a very long rope to bring communal disharmony and disturb peace in the state, and then ultimately kill the same person. Only criminal minds can plan such things, at the cost of national security. There are many questions, whether Bhindranwale died fighting or he was captured and tortured by the forces and then killed. There are many doubts which will never be cleared. This poisonous flame lit by unscrupulous and unprincipled politicians has done unimaginable damage to the unity and integrity of the country.

Similarly, Dal Khalsa was created by the Punjab Congress headed by Giani Zail Singh on 13 April 1978, and payment for its first press conference on that day was made by Hans Raj Sharma, then General Secretary of the Punjab Congress and next day all Punjab newspapers had reported about the payment made by the Punjab Congress. The same Dal Khalsa hijacked an Indian Airlines plane to Lahore on 29 September 1981 and on 1 May 1982, the same organisation was banned by the Government. It had established contacts in Canada and some other foreign countries and came out to be a dangerous organisation. The Almighty may give peace to restless souls of the Sabotiers, who are no more in a position to destroy the country and those who are still in this world, should be dealt with according to the law. Will politicians of all hues learn any lesson from the past?

In this book, I have not gone into the details of the Akali-government meetings, what happened within the Golden

Temple Complex as a lot has already been written on this. My sole object of writing this was to give details how this situation was created and with what purpose. During the peak days of militancy, I had written extensively in the Indian Express and some other newspapers also and I was following the developments very closely. It was very necessary to bring out all the facts before the country without any bias or prejudice.

Annexures

Accord on demands of Akalis likely to be announced today

By G. S. CHAWLA
Express News Service

NEW DELHI, Nov 3.

The Akali Dal and the Government are understood to have reached an accord on most of the Akali demands after hectic political activity and consultations between the special cabinet committee and Mr Swaran Singh on one side, and the Akalis on the other.

The Home Minister, Mr P. C. Sethi, is expected to make a statement in both Houses of Parliament on Thursday on the accord. According to knowledgeable sources, Mr Sethi may not spell out details of the accord except that some of the demands have been accepted and talks are progressing well on the remaining demands. He may also appeal to the Akalis to withdraw or suspend their agitation and reciprocate the Government's efforts.

A final decision on the Punjab situation was taken on Wednesday evening after a meeting of the special cabinet committee in the room of the External Affairs Minister, Mr P. B. Narasimha Rao. Besides the four senior cabinet ministers, the cabinet secretary, Mr Krishnaswami Rao Saheb, home secretary, Mr T. N. Chaturvedi, and special secretary, Home Ministry, looking after Punjab affairs, Mr P. P. Nayyar, were present.

Mr Swaran Singh had two meetings with the committee. He was present in the evening meeting at which a final shape was given to the accord. He was also in touch with the Akalis in Amritsar.

The CPM leader, Mr Harkishan Singh Surjeet, was in touch with the Akalis and the Finance Minister, Mr Pranab Mukherjee.

Of the four Akali leaders who had come to the Capital on Tuesday morning, Mr G. S. Tohra and Mr Jagdev Singh Talwandi left for Amritsar early on Wednesday morning. Mr Parkash Singh Badal and Mr Balwant Singh left for Amritsar by the 11.30 a.m. flight. Before Mr Badal and Mr Balwant Singh left, they hinted that some decision was likely to be taken on Wednesday and they should preferably postpone their meeting till evening. Therefore the meeting was held at 5 p.m.

Earlier after the first meeting between Mr Swaran Singh and the special cabinet committee, Mrs Gandhi consulted her four cabinet colleagues. This was followed by another meeting between Mr Swaran Singh and the committee in the evening.

Earlier indication was that an announcement about the accord might be made on Wednesday. But then it was decided that since Parliament was in session, it would be proper to inform both Houses first.

It is understood that the Government has agreed to accept all religious demands of the Akalis. They are relay of gurbani from Golden Temple, enactment of an All-India Gurdwara Act, carrying of kirpan of a small size in internal flights of the country's air-

continued from p 1 col 8

lines and closure of tobacco, meat and liquor shops up to a particular area in the walled city of Amritsar.

There is reported to be an agreement on political demands also. But still certain modalities have to be discussed with the Akalis. Other states have also to be consulted.

On the Chandigarh issue, there is no dispute. But there will be no declaration till Haryana is satisfied. According to informed sources, in the 1970 award, it was stated that Haryana will be given Rs 10 crore as aid and another Rs 10 crore to build its new capital. But Haryana leaders have claimed over Rs 100 crore, both as aid and loan. Haryana might be given Rs 60 crore, half as loan and half as compensation.

Another issue to be sorted out is on Fazilka and Abohar. This might be tagged to the proposed commission to settle the question of areas claimed by both the states.

The Akalis will be satisfied if a committee is appointed to go into the Centre-state relations within the framework of the Constitution. There is reportedly some understanding on river waters also which may be acceptable to Haryana and Rajasthan.

The Punjab Chief Minister, Mr Darbara Singh, met the Prime Minister and told her that he was not opposed to the acceptance of religious demands of the Akalis except with some reservation on the All-India Gurdwara Act. But no political demand should be accepted which should encourage devisive forces.

He was against the acceptance of the Anandpur Sahib resolution. On the Akalis' insistance for the release of 41 extremists and supporters of Sant Bhindranwale, he said those arrested on serious charges like murder or violence should not be released. However, he offered that the Home Ministry could examine all these cases and take a decision.

He pleaded that Chandigarh should be given to Punjab without

linking Fazilka and Abohar areas with it. He said this was the demand of all the Punjabis and not Akalis alone.

Mr Darbara Singh had a one-hour meeting with three of the four Union ministers looking after the Punjab situation on Tuesday night.

Mr Darbara Singh and the Haryana Chief Minister, Mr Bhajan Lal, met on Wednesday afternoon in the room of the Lok Sabha Speaker, Mr Balram Jakhar, and exchanged views on their respective stands.

Mr Bhajan Lal is understood to have suggested to Mr Darbara Singh to take a stiff stand towards the Akalis.

A 15-member deputation of the Punjab BJP led by Mr Baldev Parkash met the Home Minister, Mr P. C. Sethi, and suggested that a round table conference of all interests should be called to defuse the situation.

In a memorandum the deputation warned the Government that in its attempt to defuse the situation, any submission before the separatist and communal demands under the pressure of violent and terrorist activities will be disastrous for the country, the state and Punjab as a whole. It will invite vehement opposition from all sections of the people.

Indian Express, New Delhi.
Dated Nov.4,1982.

Suo moto statement to be made by Shri P.C. Sethi, Minister of Home Affairs on 4.11.1982, in Lok Sabha/ Rajya Sabha, regarding situation in Punjab.

Sir,

Government has been deeply distressed over the situation in Punjab. The Prime Minister and senior members of the Cabinet have met delegations of the Akalis several times. The Prime Minister has indicated to them that practically all religious demands could be accepted subject to details being worked out but this could not be finalised because of their other demands.

During the recent agitation, Government made further efforts to resolve the crisis and has been considering the demands conveyed recently by the 5-member committee of Akali leaders through Sardar Swaran Singh. Certain areas of agreement have been identified in respect of some demands. The others concern various States also. Therefore consultations have to be held with the Punjab and other concerned Governments and also with representatives of other communities before a decision can be taken. This process of consultation has been initiated and I have been in touch with the respective Chief Ministers and others, including leaders of Opposition parties and Members of Parliament. It is likely that this process will take some more time.

In taking any decision the Government cannot ignore the overall interest of national unity, integrity and the welfare of all sections of the people.

Government hopes and trusts that representatives of the Akali Dal will look at their problems in the larger context. We repeat our invitation to them to come for further discussions and to create the right atmosphere for this by calling off or suspending their agitation. I hope that in the present circumstances nothing will be done which may escalate tension or give rise to violence and suffering. I appeal to all parties to extend their cooperation.

THE PIONEER, LUCKNOW, dated April 14, 1989.

Thakkar Commission Report

Suspicion Of Leakage On Arun Nehru

By G.S. Chawla

THE Prime Minister, Mr. Rajiv Gandhi, while intervening in the discussion on the Thakkar Commission Report in the Lok Sabha on April 10 said: "The friends of the conspirators could, if they wished, leak the portions of the report relating to the larger conspiracy. Why did they deliberately restrict themselves to publications of only portions related to Dhawan? Was it not a ruse to divert the attention of the nation"? He continued: "We do not have definite answers. What we do have is a stackful of needles all quivering on the magnetic field of suspicion that points to the conspirators, to their political peers, to their friends and to their accomplices". Home Minister, Mr. Buta Singh replying to the debate in the Lok Sabha on April 11 pointing his accusing fingers at the former Internal Security Minister, Mr. Arun Nehru, said that he had kept the report in his house for six months without even showing it to his senior minister. "We will definitely find out who is responsible for the leak". Taken the two statements together, it is beyond any doubt that the Government's suspicion for the leakage is on Mr. Arun Nehru and the Prime Minister has described those who leaked that report as "friends of the conspirators". This is the gravest charge that could be levelled against any politician and it is much more serious charge than against those who have been detained under the NSA. Mr. Buta Singh has also alleged in the Lok Sabha that Mr. Arun Nehru and Mr. Arun Singh were largely responsible for the "rivers of blood that has been flowing in Punjab"

MOVE POWERFUL THAN P.M.

Nobody, even Mr. Rajiv Gandhi himself, can deny that as Minister of State for Internal Security, Mr. Arun Nehru had become more powerful than even the Prime Minister himself. Arun Nehru could not have become so powerful unless he had the tacit backing of the Prime Minister who had complete faith in his cousin. Nehru family or for that matter any ruler, always had weakness for close friends and relations. During late Indira Gandhi's time when Arun Nehru was acting as extra-constitutional authority and was the main fund collector in the name of the party, many senior Congress leaders had complained to her but she was not prepared to listen to anybody. After the assassination of Mrs. Gandhi, when Mr. Rajiv Gandhi became the Prime Minister, Arun Nehru became more powerful and ultimately a stage reached when he was known as the super Prime Minister. He had arrogated himself so much that he used to bully even the senior ministers and behaved like a gangster running his own empire.

In the Home Ministry, none of the three Home Ministers, Mr. S.B. Chavan, Mr. P.V. Narsimha Rao and Mr. Buta Singh, had the courage to challenge the authority of Arun Nehru who was their junior as minister of state. The Intelligence Bureau was under the charge of Arun Nehru and he used it fully to get reports on politicians and journalists. There has been practice in the Home Ministry that all intelligence reports used to be sent to the Home Minister as well as to the Prime Minister. It used to be the duty of the Director of Intelligence Bureau to fully brief the Home Minister every evening about the situation in the country. During Jawaharlal Nehru's time, the Director of the Intelligence Bureau, considered as the senior-most police officer in the country, used to walk straight to the Prime Minister's room for any discussions. But the standard of the Director of Intelligence Bureau came down when Mr. T. Rajeshwar took over as the head of the intelligence agency and Mr. Rajeshwar used to spend more time with the personal staff of then Home Minister, Giani Zail Singh than the Home Minister himself. When Arun Nehru became the Minister of State for Internal Security, he saw to it that all IB reports were routed through him, and later on he became so powerful that he issued instructions to the IB not to send any report either to the Prime Minister or to the Home Minister and only he would decide what should be sent to them. Arun Nehru misused his position so much to keep a tag on all politicians. Those journalists who never saw eye to eye with him, were threatened that their entry to the Home Ministry would banned and in some cases Arun Nehru asked the IB to keep them under surveillance.

Arun Nehru was in the Home Ministry from September 25, 1985 to October 22, 1986, when he was dropped from the Ministry. As far as Punjab is concerned, Arun Nehru and Arun Singh were dabbling in it even before that 'Operation Bluestar' and if the reports are correct, Mrs. Gandhi would not have gone to the extent of 'Operation Bluestar' if Arun Nehru and Arun Singh were not in the picture and the only person who can throw light on this is Mr. R.K. Dhawan who was close to Mrs. Gandhi and knew the forces advising Mrs. Gandhi for the extreme action.

But in the Home Ministry, Arun Nehru was more open as a hawk and was opposed to the installation of the Barnala Government and he was always keen to bring in his close firend among the Akalis, Capt. Amrinder Singh, as the Chief Minister and for that he was prepared to go to any length. In April 1986, when Gurbachan Singh Manochahl of the Panthic Committee announced creation of Khalistan from the Golden Temple, and Mr. Barnala was forced by Arun Nehru to send police force into the Golden Temple Complex on April 29, 1986, otherwise to face a sack, some Akali leaders had alleged that the Government through the Intelligence Bureau was behind the announcement of Manochahl to force the Barnala Government to send police into the Temple to justify the Operation Blue Star. It was alleged at that time that the IB was in touch with the panthic committee members and some other extremist organisations. On one side, Mr. Barnala was forced to send poice inside the Temple, and on the other side Arun Nehru's friend, Capt. Amrider Singh, on this issue left the Barnala Government. It was a double-edged weapon, to weaken Mr. Barnala within his own party and bring out Mr. Amrinder Singh as the real representative of the Sikhs. The Northern Zonal Council meeting was held at Manali where the Chief Ministers of the northern states were meeting. The Home Minister and Arun Nehru were also in Manali to attend the meeting. Mr. Barnala and his Finance Minister, Mr. Balwant Singh were representing the Punjab Government. Curiously, Capt. Amrinder Singh and Mr. Ravi Inder Singh had also gone all the way to Manali for consultations with Arun Nehru.

In 985, it was known in the political circles in the Capital that a gang of four headed by Arun Nehru was ruling the country. Other members were Mr. M.L. Fotedar, then Cabinet Secretary, Mr. P.K. Kaul and Mr. G.K. Arora, then in the Prime Minister's secretariat was later sent to Washington as Am-bassador before even the expiry of his term as Cabinet Secretary and when Mr. Fotedar and Mr. Gopi Arora found in May, 1986 that the Prime Minister was annoyed with Arun Nehru, they also started distancing away from him. They are known as the great survivors, who could again be the trusted men of the Prime Minister. I am definite that the Punjab Accord signed by the Prime Minister with late Sant Longowal was sabotaged by this coteries. The accord was signed on July 24, 1985, around 3 p.m. in Parliament House. On the next day, July 25, 1985, at 10 a.m. a senior South Indian journalist who was working in a national news agency and used to report to Mr. Fotedar every evening about the reactions on political matters, came to may house. This was a surprise visit and the journalist himself was little surprised over the events. He told me that privious night he had rung up Mr. Fotedar around 11.30 p.m. and told him that the reaction to the accord was not good as people felt that it was a surrender to the Akalis. According to the journalist, Mr. Fotedar told him not to worry as the Akalis will neither get Chandigarh nor any thing will be done on river waters. The Journalist expressed surprise over this policy. It was not later but on July 25, 1985, that I knew that somebody around the Prime Minister will sabotage this accord and the result is by now known to everybody. Since then I had told this story to Many people including the CPI(M) leader, Mr. Harkishan Singh Surjeet. Once I suggested to Mr. Gopi Arora that the Prime Minister should call me and this South Indian Journalist and I would confront him in his presence. But he kept quiet.

THE QUERY

The question is that the man who had become so powerful, how suddenly in May-June 1986, the two cousins started distancing away from each other. According to the grapewine, in early May, 1986, the Prime Minister had discovered many things about the doings of his cousin and had personally confronted him on some matter before Arun Nehru left for Srinagar in May 1986, where he got heart-attack and after which he could never get back his same position. What had the Prime Minister discovered about his cousin that forced him to clip his wings? This is a big question mark and only the Prime Minister or Arun Nehru can throw light on it. It was in Srinagar during Arun Nehru's illness that Giani Zail Singh as President visited him in the hospital and told him that his own cousin could not come to Srinagar to inquire about his health whereas he could fly to Bombay to meet Amitabh Bachchan when he was ill. Giani Zail Singh had also given him the idea that he considered him only from the real Nehru family and not Mr. Rajiv Gandhi. A few months later, when Arun Nehru went to London in September, he spent more than three hours with Giani Zail Singh in Rashtrapati Bhawan before leaving for abroad.

When Arun Nehru came back to the Home Ministry in 1986, he tried his best to get back his old charge, and one day he wrote a list of the charge he wanted and asked Mr. Buta Singh to issue the order on the spot. Mr. Buta Singh took the list from him and sent it to the Prime Minister for his instructions and on the same evening, a different list giving some minor charge to Arun Nehru was issued He was told that his health did not permit heavy load of work. He went to Bombay for medical check up and the doctor issued a statement saying that Arun Nehru was absolutely fit. Still, he was not given the charge he wanted and later, he was dropped from the Government.

In 1987, when the Government found that he was hobnobbing with the opposition and was activily involved against the Prime Minister, the Government took advantage of a Special mention in the Rajya Sabha by a Congress (I) M.P., on the Czech pistol deal case, which was approved by Arun Nehru, and decided to hand over that enquiry to the CBI.

In March 1987 when Indian Express had published Giani Zail Singh's controversial letter to the Prime Minister, the next day the rest house of the newspaper where Ramnath Goenka, 'chairman of the organisation, was staying was raided by the C.B.I. But in the case of Arun Nehru, though pointing a needle of suspicion on him, the Government avoided either raiding his house or arresting him despite the grave allegations the Prime Minister has indirectly mentioned. If what the Prime Minister has said in Parliament is correct and he suspects Arun Nehru for the leak and a ruse to divert the attention of the nation, the law should have been allowed to take its own course and there was equally a graver charge of sheltering the conspirations as entering into the conspiracy. The Prime Minister owes an explanation to the nation on this.

Active US interest in Indian politics

From G C. Chwala

NEW DELHI, Aug. 4—The Bush administration seems to be increasingly involving itself or at least seems to be showing greater interest in Indian affairs in the recent past. This is indicated from some of the recent statements given by the Bush administration and some other leading Americans, especially former CIA specialists on Indian affairs during the recent two major internacriseis the VP Singh government faced. The administration's full support to the Prime Minister was obvious from some of the press statements.

On the other hand, the USSR is having doubts about the stability of the VP Singh government as was evident from a recent article in a government-owned Moscow eveninger. It expressed doubts that by the time President Gorbachyov decides to visit India would Mr. VP Singh still be the Prime Minister.

Besides the statements from Washington and some other places in the US predicting that Mr. VP Singh will come out victorious in both the crises, the US Ambassador in India, Mr. William Clark, is paying a four-day visit to Punjab next week for an on-the-spot study of the situation in the trouble-torn state. This is the first time that any American Ambassador is personally going to Punjab to meet some leading personalities of the State including some Akali leaders.

PERSONALLY IN TOUCH

According to highly placed sources, President Bush has been personally keeping himself in touch with both the crises in the Janata Dal, first on the Chautala issue leading to Mr. VP Singh's resignation offer and the second on the issue of the Prime Minister's forged letter forwarded to him by Mr. Devi Lal, then Deputy Prime Minister.

Mr. VP Singh had full assurance from the Bush administration that they were fully supporting him. In fact, the night Mr. Devi Lal was dismissed when everybody was expecting some patch up formula, the American Ambassador in New Delhi knew by the evening that "something will happen tonight". This remark was made by the American Ambassador to a journalist at a cocktail party given by the Ambassador himself to a few journalists.

Mr. Paul Kreisberg, described by the ANI (Asian News International) as a top South Asia expert at the reputed Carneg Endowment (who in fact is a known CIA expert on India), told the ANI: "Mr. VP Singh demonstrated courage and sound political judgement. The Indian Prime Minister was fair and considerate to Mr. Devi Lal". During the first crises also, Mr. Kreisberg had predicted that Mr. VP Singh would overcome the crises.

Earlier, Mr. Walter Anderson, a counsellor with the American Embassy in New Delhi, another American diplomat and an expert on Indian affairs known for his background in the US administration, has been a regular visitor to Punjab. Mr. Anderson has been meeting different shades of people of Punjab including a large number of Akali leaders and he knows each Deputy Commissioner of Punjab by name.

Mr. Anderson once stayed in Mr. Amrinder Singh's house also. He has written a book "The Brotherhood in Saffron" on the Rashtriya Swayamsevak Sangh and Hindu revivalism, with Shridhar D. Damle as coauthor. The book is a revealing study of the RSS and no other scholar has undertaken such a venture. This shows the deep study he has about the Indian situation.

AMERICAN INTERESTS

What are American administrations interests in India will be

US interest

Continued from Page 1

revealed from the background of all those.

Only recently, the VP Singh government has taken a decision under pressure from the American Congress to lift ban on the Amnesty International to visit sensitive areas in Kashmir and Punjab. President Bush is said to be under heavy pressure from American businessmen to pay an early visit to India and finalise certain deals.

Soviets are perhaps aware of the American interests in the VP Singh government and it was possibly for this reason that "Izvestia", Government-owned eveninger from Moscow had raised the question of the possibility of a new leader heading the government in Delhi by the time President Gorbachyov travels to India next year.

The trouble in Punjab was ascribed to the CIA by the Late Indira Gandhi and it was well known that all anti-Indian forces on the Punjab issue were getting support is the US and Canada. In this background, American interest in Punjab when there is spurt in violence is worth watching. Ambassador William Clark's Punjab programme has been organised by Mr. Anderson.

THE PIONEER, Lucknow, Aug.5,90.

Will the US allow Cong. to survive?

From G.S. Chawla

NEW DELHI, April 30

DESPITE optimism to form the new government after the Lok Sabha poll, there is lurking fear in the Congress (I) leadership in the international perspective if the most powerful nation that has emerged now, the US, would allow the Congress (I) Government to survive unless the Americans are convinced that the new Congress (I) Government will be as friendly towards the US as the previous V.P. Singh Government and the Chandra Shekhar Government have been.

During the discussions which the party president, Mr. Rajiv Gandhi, had with his core group on election prospects in the country and the post-election scenario, this matter s believed to have figured and the arty leadership had a detailed iscussion.

The core group also went into e foreign policy implemented during the Congress (I) rule in late 1980s and the subsequent developments of the policies followed by the V.P. Singh Government and now by the Shekhar Government. It is realised by the Congress (I) leadership that while the VP Singh Government and now Shekhar Government have been quietly following the signals from US, the Congress (I) leadership has been going out of its way to attack the US on the Gulf issue and had even threatened to demolish the present Government on the issue of refuelling of American military aircraft.

This had irked the US administration and President Bush had to say publicly that they did not want to embarrass Mr. Chandra Shekhar and so they have decided to withdraw their planes from Indian soil.

One view during the discussion was that the party should have continued giving statements condemning the Government for

Continued on page 12 Col. 1

Continued

permitting American military planes to have refuelling facilities in India, the party should not have gone to the extent of threatening to withdraw its support on this issue. The protests on refuelling should have been up to a limited point and only for the consumption of Iraq and other Middle East countries which had stood by India on the Kashmir issue.

The Congress (I) leadership is fully aware that during the 1989 Lok Sabha elections, the Americans had shown a great interests and a lot of anti-Congress (I) materials had been flooded to India via Nepal. The American Embassy in New Delhi had organised some press parties of UP and some other important places in the country which was very unusual. Americans are again showing keen interest in the present elections and the Bush Administration had deputed a number of poll sruvey teams, either as research scholars or tourists for the poll assessment Americans are predicting a weak and disunited India after the poll.

THE PIONEER, Lucknow. 1.5.91.

Renewing ties with USA task for Cong

From G.S. Chawla

NEW DELHI, May 2: Despite optimism to form the new government after the Lok Sabha poll, there is lurking fear in the Congress(I) leadership in the international perspective if the most powerful nation that has emerged now, the USA, would allow the Congress(I) government to survive unless the Americans are convinced that the new Congress(I) government will be as friendly towards to the USA as the previous V.P. Singh government and now as Chandra Shekhar government have been.

During the discussions which the party president, Mr Rajiv Gandhi, had with his core group on elections prospects in the country and the post election scenario, this matter is believed to have figured and the party leadership had a detailed discussion. The core group also went into the foreign policy implemented during the Congress(I) rule in late 1980s and the subsequent developments, the policies followed by the V.P. Singh government and now by the Chandra Shekhar government. Lately, it is realised by the Congress(I) leadership that while the V.P. Singh government and now Chandra Shekhar government have been quietly following the signals from USA, the Congress(I) leadership has been going out of its way to attack USA on the Gulf issue and had even threatened to demolish the Chandra Shekhar government on the issue of refuelling of American military aircrafts from the Indian soil during the Gulf war. This had irked the US administration and President Bush had to say publicaly that they did not want to embarrass Mr Chandra Shekhar and they have decided to withdraw their planes from India soil.

One view during the discussion was that the party should have continued giving statements condemning the Chandra Shekhar government for permitting American military planes to have refuelling facilities in India, the party should not have gone to the extent of threatening to withdraw its support on this issue. The protests on refuelling should have been upto a limited point and only for the consumption of Iraq and other West Asian countries which had stood by India on the Kashmir issue.

The Congress(I) leadership is fully aware that during the 1989 Lok Sabha elections, Americans had shown a great interest and a lot of anti-Congress(I) material had been flooded to India via Nepal. The American Embassy in New Delhi had organised some Press parties to UP and some other important places in the country which was very unusual. Americans are again showing keen interest in the present elections and the Bush administration had deputed a number of poll survey teams, either as research scholars or tourists for the poll assessment. Americans are predicting a week and disunited India after the poll.

The Congress(I) leadership feels that with the stance the party has been taking on foreign policy, Americans will not be happy if the Congress(I) forms the next government at the Centre. How the Americans should be convinced that the Congress(I) will not be hostile to its policies in this region, is the question worrying the party's brain-trust. If Americans can help, their first preference will be for BJP, and then Mr V.P. Singh or Mr Chandra Shekhar. Americans by now know that both, Mr V.P. Singh and Mr Chandra Shekhar have no chance to come back.

Perhaps, it is because of this lurking fear that Mr Rajiv Gandhi refuses to say anything on the pressures that are forcing Mr Chandra Shekhar to hold elections in Punjab and Assam. Though, in the core group meetings it has been said that Americans are pressurising Mr Chandra Shekhar for elections in Punjab and Assam. This is exactly the same view which CPI(M) leaders, Mr Harkishan Singh Surjeet and West Bengal Chief Minister Mr Jyoti Basu, hold. Even in the meeting between Mr Rajiv Gandhi and Mr Jyoti Basu and Mr Surjeet sometime back, the reason for insistance on Punjab elections by Mr Chandra Shekhar was mentioned as American pressure.

Both the Congress(I) and the CPI(M), have apprehensions that American plan is first to have elections in Punjab and bring militants to power and then get a resolution passed in the state assembly for severing ties with India and a similar situation to be created in Assam. If Americans succeed in this game, this will be the beginning of disintegration of India.

The Congress(I) president has given the same reason for boycotting the Punjab elections without making any reference to American plans. But in their brain-trust meetings, they freely mention about American intentions.

The apprehensions in the Congress(I) leadership are that with the Soviet Union on the verge of disintegration and facing a disastrous economic situation and Americans proving their superiority in the world after the Gulf war and humiliating President Saddam, their next target may be India. Americans may concentrate on this region now.*

LOKMAT TIMES, AURANGABAD. DATED May 3, 1991.

'Hidden hand' may never be known

From G.S. Chawla

NEW DELHI, May 29—WHO got Rajiv Gandhi killed? Though the Government has appointed a commission headed by a Supreme Court judge and also a special investigating team (SIT) has been set up, the experience in the past political assassinations all over the world shows that the hidden hand may never be known.

The Congress (I) leaders in general, straightaway talk of CIA's involvement in the conspiracy for the meticulously planned brutal assassination. The same view is shared by some Janata Dal and Left parties leaders. Whichever agency, group or individual is responsible for the killing it has a powerful backing, is the general view. Politicians talk about the hidden hand but in a hushed voice, even the Left leaders talk about it in a low voice ruling out nothing, indicating a scare: Who may be the next target.

Rajiv Gandhi has been having a feeling that the Americans would not allow his Government to survive, though he was confident of getting a majority, and forming the next Government. His stand on the Gulf, and more particularly on the Chandra Shekhar Government's permission for refuelling American aircraft on Indian soil during the Gulf war and his mission to Moscow and some Middle East countries on the Gulf, had irked the American administration and Rajiv Gandhi was having some apprehensions.

In such a well-planned assassination the special investigating team may find some clue about the 'assassor in'assassins but to know about deep-rooted conspiracy may be a difficult task. The accusing finger towards CIA is only on the basis of certain circumstance and apprehensions but who actually may be behind the conspiracy is a big question mark.

If one goes by the terms of the commission, it is to go into only the security aspect of Rajiv Gandhi. The commission is to find out if there were any security lapses or dereliction of duty on part of any body connected with the security, any deficiency in the security set up and suggest corrective measures. The issue of any conspiracy behind the assassination is beyond the purview of the commission. Moreover, the commission gives its views only on the basis of the material provided to it by the special investigating team and other agencies.

The experience in the Thakkar Commission which went into the assassination of Mrs. Indira Gandhi discloses how in effective the special investigating teams can be. Justice Thakkar in his lengthy report, wrote a chapter on the role of Mr. R.K. Dhawan, then special assistant to Mrs. Indira Gandhi and now a member of the Rajya Sabha pointing needle of suspicion at his complicity or involvement. This chapter came to light in early 1989 when Mr. Dhawan was appointed as OSD in the Cabinet Secretariat and the matter had figured in Parliament. What just Thakkar had written about Mr. Dhawan's role in the assassination was based on the material supplied to him by the special investigating team headed by Mr. Anandaram who was considered as a very upright officer. When the Government was attacked in Parliament over the appointment of Mr. Dhawan as OSD, the same Anandaram overnight changed him role and gave a letter to the then Home Mimister saying that he had gone into the matter and Mr. Dhawan had no role to

Continued on Page 12 Col. 3

'Hidden hand'

Continued from Page 1

play. The appointment of Mr. Dhawan showed that even the Government had not agreed with the findings of Justice Thakkar. Though the special investigating team had questioned and tortured a large number of Sikhs even those who attended AISSF camps many years earlier, the SIT could not go beyond two securitymen and two accomplices of whom one was hanged and the other acquitted and the conspiracy behind the assassination remained a mystery. Late Mrs. Indira Gandhi had publicly expressed threats to India's unity and integrity from some big powers, but the hidden hand behind her assassination could never see the light of the day.

What happened in the Kennedy assassination? Despite the Warren Commission, the hidden hand could never be known. The same thing happened in the case of Pakistan's President Gen. Zia-ul-Haq.

THE PIONEER, Lucknow, May 30, 1991

Rajiv flays US presence in Bangla

From G.S. Chawla

NEW DELHI, May 16—

EVEN before American marines landed in Bangladesh on the pretext of relief operations for the cyclone-hit people there and creating a piquant situation in the sub-continent, Congress chief Rajiv Gandhi had written a few days ago to Prime Minister Chandra Shekhar, pointing out the possibility of a new American-led military and strategic concept emerging in this area and the need for India to take some advance action.

It was after his meeting with Soviet leader Gorbachyov during the last days of the Gulf war that Rajiv Gandhi took up this issue with the Government. He took it up also with President R. Venkataraman. He gave a note to him, detailing the various threat factors, particularly from the American-backed Pakistan. He drew the attention of the President to the ensuing nuclear threat from Pakistan.

Despite the hectic election canvassing, Rajiv Gandhi took time to raise this matter with the Prime Minister. According to him, the Gulf war had radically changed the defence concept and that India should quickly alter the strategy. He had pointed out in his letter that the unipolar regime of the United States would put countries like India and others in a difficult and helpless position. India should not surrender the right to develop her own missile and nuclear technology. It was noted that while political uncertainties haunted India, Pakistan was going ahead with the fabrication of bombs, getting technology and assistance from China and other western countries.

Observers here pointed out that the sudden landing of over four thousand American marines in Bangladesh was more than humanitarian operation. This is the First time time that such a large number of American troops, well equipped and backed up with air-borne systems and naval carriers, had landed in a country in the Indian sub-continent. The full task force of the American would include 4600 marines and about three thousand sail rs. Most of them have come from the American bases in the Philippines.

During the 1971 war, the American navy came very close to Chittagong with a view to entering the conflict. But somehow, the war came to an abrupt end. Ever since, the United States was having an eye on the port facilities in Chittagong, observers fear that the Bangladesh Government may ultimately provide some base facilities for the Americans in Chittagong. With its hold in Pakistan and now Bangladesh coming on the line, the American military machine would be in a comfortable position in this sub-continent. And this would definitely pose a threat to this country, according to military experts here.

DPA adds: U.S. marines launched relief efforts on Bangladesh's cyclone-ravaged offshore island on Thursday amid protests from opposition political parties and student groups.

Militant students battled with police, protesting the U.S. military presence & demanding that the American froces leave, eyewitnesses said.

About 8,000 marines reached the southern port city of Chittagong on Wednesday night aboard eight ships led by the USS Tarania, bringing in badly needed helicopters, amphibious vehicles and relief supplies.

Maj. Gen. Henry Stackpole,

Continued on Page 12 Col. 3

THE PIONEER, Lucknow, May 17, 1991.

Giani Zail Singh's broadcast to the Nation on June 17,1984.

Shed Hatred

WHILE TALKING TO you my heart is full of sorrow and anguish. For quite some time, reports about some events in Punjab had been coming. The Gurdwaras which are centres of spiritual peace and human brotherhood are meant for all. Unfortunately, some aberrations occurred in recent times. The Gurdwaras came under the control of extremists and even office-bearers responsible for management of Gurdwaras seemed helpless before the extremists. The holy places became the refuge for extremists and misguided elements. As a consequence extremists indulged in murder, loot and arson. They brought misery to Punjab. The victims were both Hindus and Sikhs. These included prominent journalists, religious preachers, scholars, political leaders even farmers and workers. Extremism went to the extent of claiming the life of a great scholar like Singh Saheb, Giani Pratap Singh, former Jathedar of Shri Akal Takht. He was an eminent personality of the 20th century. He was also an acknowledged writer, thinker and minister of the Guru's Gospel. His life was taken, because his ideas did not conform to those of extremists. Those in-charge of the administration of Punjab cannot be absolved of responsibility in this matter. The Government had most reluctantly to send the security forces. Two religious and political leaders surrendered themselves to the security forces in the interest of maintaining the sanctity of the holy places. If extremists had also surrendered, the sanctity of the religious places would not have been disturbed and the subsequent sad events could have been avoided.

I say it with anguish in my heart that we should follow the correct path in the face of these sad events. A nation is sometimes beset with such circumstances when its patience, statesmanship and its courage are on trial. I appeal not only to Sikhs but all my countrymen to consider these sad events and see that never in future unlawful arms and items not sanctioned by Sikh tradition enter the Gurdwaras. It is a matter of satisfaction to me

---

Broadcast to the Nation, New Delhi, June 17, 1984

that the structure and sanctity of Shri Harmandir Saheb remained intact. I have been told by the officers and men of the security forces that they had vowed not to fire in the direction of Shri Harmandir Saheb, even in the face of certain death. In the operations some people have been killed including the officers and men of the security forces. Patience and far-sightedness are the needs of the hour. We have also to ensure that such a sad situation never occurs again.

We have to maintain the unity and integrity of the country. We have also to endeavour to maintain friendly and harmonious relations between our people. My agony is all the more, because I am the representative of the whole nation. I am grateful to all my countrymen for having reposed this trust in me. It is my duty to look after all the States and territories of the country and to share the sorrow with the people wherever such events take place.

I specially want to remind the Punjabis that they have common traditions, heritage and a common history. They have been sharing the same food, the same air and have common joys and sorrows. We have to fill the breaches in our minds and have to march together. We shall have to look after the interests of the whole country and nation. I am confident that all of us, Government as well as the people, will make sincere efforts in this direction. Never again should we allow such circumstances to develop which create disunity among us. We have to strengthen the unity of our people.

The Holy Book, Guru Granth Saheb, teaches compassion, service, sacrifice and universal brotherhood. We have to foster mutual love and affection. Not only Sikhs but people professing other religions also have faith in Gurbani. The Sikh Gurus thought of the country as a whole. They travelled to each and every part of the country. Every inch of this country belongs to all of us, whether we are Sikhs, Christians, Muslims, Jains, Buddhists, Hindus and others. We have to heal the wounds and maintain the sanctity of all religious places. We must remember the teachings of Guru Gobind Singh that one who loves humanity, loves God.

AFFIDEVIT

I Gurcharan Singh s/o Shri Bishan Singh resident of 29,Kali Bari Apartments,New Delhi do hereby affirm and declare as under:-

1. That I am working in the Personal Cell of the President of India since September 1982. Earlier too when he was the Home Minister I was attached to his personal staff. Working so long a time with the personal staff,I was able to win their confidence.

2. Now I am being falsely imlicated in a CBI case by the senior officers of the Rashtrapati Bhawan. They are trying to make me a sacrificial goat fot their own selfish ends. I am being asked to repent for their own sins and for considerations best known to them.

3. The actual position is that the petition in question was got incerted at the intance of the senior officers and thereafter I was asked to put my initials in token of having received it. I was also asked to keep the same for a few days. After some time I tried to hand it over to Shri K.C.Singh,Dy.Secy.to the President, but he put off the matter on one or the other pretext. Knowing fully well the facts,he went even to the extent of submitting fals affidevit to the effect that no visitor can deliver the dak at the Central Registry Counter without getting a pass.and that no letter had been received in the Central Registry of Rashtrapati Bhawan. The purpose thereof,it appears to me,was to fix me up for the false confidence reposed in me.

4. A lot of activities detimental to the national interest are going on the seclusive environment of Rashtrapati Bhawan. we the employees have no option but to watch silently and obey. Hence the necessity to bring some of the glaring facts to your kind notice. So many persons of doubtful integrity are visiting Rashtrapati Bhawan calendstinely. For example,Shri Chanderaswami,a man of uncertain morals and having a dubious distiction of being a power broker,visited Rashtrapti Bhawan under some false name in the

Minister is said to have been leaked by this man.) The officers not connected with the President's Secretariat like Shri Bagla and Shri Bindera have easy access to files and freely give their advice regularly. Both Shri K.C.Singh and Shri Bagla had been working in USA before their posting in India. These officers try to influence the day-to-day working of the Present and thereby destabelise the country.

5. Many other undesirable persons have free access to Rashtrapati Bhawan. Quite a few of these persons were contacts from the past. Among these that I can recall Shri Ranjit Singh Rana and Mohinder Singh Baghi who were connected with the Dal Khalsa. One Inderjit Singh Sekhon,a lawyer of Faridkot who was general secretary of the United Akali Dal,was also very close to and a visitor to Rashtrapati Bhawan. I came to understand that Sekhon has a close relationship with Baba Joginder Singh. Similarly Giani Mohinder Singh who was one time secretary of the SGPC and Satbir Singh has access to Rashtrapati Bhawab. In side Rashtrapati Bhawan It was being mentioned that these persons were connedted to Shri G.S.Tohra.

6. Afrequent visitor to Rashtrapati Bhawan was Parminder Singh @ Pinki of Ferozepur who was referred to as an extremist. Another person who used to visit Rashtrapati Bhawan was Nihal Singh Harianbel-anwale who was reported to leading a criminal Nihang gang in Punjab. Yet another visitor was one 'Kuku' of Faridkot who had repo-tedly links with some top terrorists in Punjab.

7. Some pro-Khalistani elements and supporter of terrorism from abroad also visited Rashtrapati Bhawan. Shri Deedar Singh Bains and Harbhajan Singh Jogi were two such persons.

8. Quite a few political leaders like Yashpal Kapoor,Vikaram Mahajan,Mohinder Singh Gill and Charanjit Singh use to visit Rashtrapati Bhawan regularly and calendestinely. Among journalists Kuldip Nayar,Prem Bhatia,Arun Shourie seldom faloowed the normal procedure intended for visitor to Rashtrapati Bhawan. Keeping these meetings secret,the security staff was asked to withdraw from the Ist and 2nd floor of the Family Wing.

9. Many dissident ministers including Shri Arun Nehru and Shri V.P.Singh had secret parleys with the Presidents. The President met Shri Arun Nehru through a bathroom door at Srinagar. Shri Nehru also has a long parley with the President secretly without any record before his departure for London. Shri V.P. Singh also met the President many times. During these parleys some papers have also changed hands

was sent to the President for his approval. Mr. Ramaswamy sent one Shri P.Ratnavellu of Madras as a contact man to Rashtrapati Bhawan. Shri Ramaswamy also maintained contact with Shri S.Bala Subramanian, Addl.P.S.to President. I donot know for what considrration on one or the other pretext. It was sent to the Law Ministry on the suggesti of Shri P.Ratnavellu.

11. As for the much publicised President's letter to the Hon'ble Prime Minister, to my knowledge there appear to be three versions of it. The one which contained the request to be laid on the tables of the Parliament was the brain-child of Shri K.C.Singh. May be some jounalist was also invloved. Shri K.C.Singh leaked it to the Press under the impression that the President had signed it. The other was a modified form of Shri K.C.Singh's draft and I was asked to modify it and to make milder in tone. The same was leaked by Shri Wasu and Chanderaswami.

12. These are a few of the facts which I felt was my duty to inform your goodself as the silence could prove desastous to my country. The nation should not suffer on account of the whims of some perverted minds.

13. Keeping in view the above cicumstances, I humbly pray to your goodself to take pity on my family as I have not done anything wrong on my own. I have committed but one sin and that is my continued silence. I should have come out with the facts much earlier. But as they say it is never too late to mend.

Deponant 14/5/87

Verification:-

I above named deponant do hereby verify that the content of my above affidevit are true to the best of my knowledge and belief.

Deponant 14/5/87

Before me

14/5/87

Sub Divisional Magistrate

Sub-Divisional Magistrate, New Delhi

INSIGHT

The night of the coup...

...and the morning after

INDIAN EXPRESS, NEW DELHI dated June 3, 1981.

Naxalites concentrate on Punjab, Bihar

By G. S. CHAWLA

Express News Service

NEW DELHI, June 2.

The Naxalites have intensified their activities, concentrating mainly on Bihar and Punjab.

The Naxalites are more active among students and teachers in Punjab and among tribals in Bihar, Andhra Pradesh and Assam. In West Bengal and Kerala, the two CPM-ruled states, the struggle is between the ruling groups and the Naxalites.

The number of extremists in Punjab, according to a source, has increased considerably in the last three years. Apart from having cadres among teachers and students, the extremists are reported to have infiltrated into some gurdwaras in the garb of "paranthis".

Sangrur and Ferozepur districts used to be the centres of extremist activity. But the extremists have now moved their headquarters to a village in Kapurthala district.

The Naxalites' strategy in Punjab is two-pronged; to instigate the extremist Akalis to intensify their agitation on the Anandpur Sahib resolution for greater autonomy and a separate Sikh nation; and to involve the student community in a confrontation with the Government.

There are two groups of Naxalites active in Punjab — one led by S. N. Singh and the other by C. P. Reddy. While the Singh group is involved with the extremist Akalis, the other group is concentrating on the students and the Kisans.

The agitation against the rise in bus fares early this year was the handiwork of the extremists The Punjab Government was aware of this and dealt with the agitation firmly. Ultimately, the agitation had to be withdrawn.

The Naxalities are now planning to start an agitation to demand the release of their party workers arrested during the agitation. The object is to sustain the students opposition to the Government.

According to reports here, the Naxalites are trying to pressurise the extremist Akalis into starting an agitation for greater autonomy to the state. One of the suggestion being considered is to ask the farmers to refuse to return government loans Another suggestion is to take up the issue of the Government's "interference" in the religious affairs of the Sikhs.

The extremists are also thinking of setting up a civil liberties organisation. The Kirti Kisan cell, a similar oranisation, has not been able to make any headway.

The Punjab Chief Minister, Mr Darbara Singh, told ENS that the Government was "fully alive to the situation" and was keeping a close watch on the extremists' activities.

He said steps had been taken to ensure that there was no law and order problem. The Government would be firm.

In Bihar, the activities of the extremists have been on the increase, involving murder, looting and gherao. The state has a fairly large tribal population on whom the Naxalities are concentrating. They are stated to have recently sponsored an organisation of Adivasis called the Jharkhand Kranti Dal, to demand a separate Jharkhand state. Their main effort is to incite the tribals to violence. In tribal areas, the extremists have succeeded.

According to reports, there are several extremist organisations in the state. Most of them are concentrating on the student unrest in the universities. According to reports, the extremist-sponsored organisation attempt to create conditions of violent confrontation between the students and the authorities. In fact, the extremists are trying to take advantage of every available opportunity, including the Biharsharif riots, to use it against the Government.

In West Bengal, the CPI, Government has arrested a number of extremistss and recovered arms from them. There have been clashes between CPM workers and the extremists.

INDIAN EXPRESS, New Delhi dated June 3, 1981.

Punjab: Another Assam?

It is almost 18 months since extremists in Punjab first demanded a "Khalistan". About a dozen murders, several blasts in banks, three hijackings, four attempts on Chief Minister Darbara Singh's life and horrendous acts of sacrilege at both Hindu and Sikh shrines have made life in the State very insecure. Will Punjab go the way of Assam? Yes, says the author, unless the Congress (I) learns from the past and agrees to share power with the moderate Akalis.

by G. S. Chawla

BUSING PROBLEM? Armed supporters of Sant Bhindranwale stand guard on top of a Delhi bus carrying their leader. The Sant was in the capital in the first week of April at the invitation of the SGPC.

THE border State of Punjab is fast becoming another Assam, thanks to the weak-kneed and indecisive policy of the Government. The situation is confused, complicated and explosive. No solution is in sight.

It is almost 18 months since the extremists have been demanding a "Khalistan", and the Government has not been able to contain them. Indeed, the secessionists have increasingly taken to violence.

SANT HARCHAND SINGH LONGOWAL, President of the Akali Dal.

GURCHARAN SINGH TOHRA, President of the Shiromani Gurdwara Prabandhak Committee.

About a dozen incidents of killings in various towns of Punjab have occurred during the last one year, besides some bank-blast cases in which the extremists were alleged to be involved. Early this year, horrendous acts of sacrilege were committed by both Hindu and Sikh miscreants at the shrines. Thrice Indian aircraft have been hijacked in the last 12 months by the Sikh extremists—twice in August alone. And there have been as many as four attempts on the life of Punjab's Chief Minister, Darbara Singh.

No wonder the people are feeling insecure. Industry and trade have been hit hard. Entrepreneurs are buying land around Delhi to secure a more peaceful haven.

The Akalis belonging to the Longowal group have been staging a morcha at the Golden Temple, Amritsar, since August 4 to press their demands. Originally, the morcha was started at the village of Kapuri in the Patiala district against the digging of the Sutlej-Yamuna canal meant to carry the Ravi-Beas waters to Haryana. It was an abysmal failure. The Akalis then decided to shift to Amritsar to give their agitation a religious twist.

Earlier, the militant Sikh leader, Sant Jarnail Singh Bhindranwale, had started a morcha from the same place against the arrests of some of his close associates, including Amrik Singh, President of the Sikh Students Federation, and Thara Singh, the man in charge of Gurdwara Gurdarshan Prakash, the headquarters of Sant Bhindranwale. This morcha had also not picked up the momentum the Sant had expected.

The Akali Dal's decision to shift its morcha to Amritsar, however, came as a shot in the arm for Sant Bhindranwale. He promptly claimed that the Akalis had "adopted" his morcha, announced that he himself would not send any more Jathas to court arrest. Though the Longowal group repeatedly asserted that it had not "adopted" Sant Bhindranwale's morcha, it unwittingly fell into his trap.

Following the arrests of his supporters and apprehending his own arrest, Sant Bhindranwale had moved into the Golden Temple premises on July 19 and, since then, he has been taking shelter there. For over a year now, he has been brazenly defying the authorities. A few months ago, the Punjab Government had asked him to ensure that his men surrendered their arms. He publicly refused to do so. The Government did nothing. Later, the Sant came to Delhi (in the first week of April) at the invitation of the Congress (I)-dominated Gurdwara Prabandhak Committee. For a full week, he was seen moving about in the capital, surrounded and escorted by nearly 100 supporters armed with sophisticated automatic weapons. Even on the top of the bus in which the Sant used to travel in the capital, his armed supporters took positions, with their fingers on the trigger. The Union Home Ministry remained a silent spectator.

DARBARA SINGH, Chief Minister of Punjab, who has been the victim of four assassination attempts.

The Punjab Government has been complaining for over a year that some of the extremists and persons wanted for murder are hiding in the Gurdwara premises. It made repeated appeals to the SGPC, controlling the management of historic Sikh gurdwaras, to cooperate with it and turn out the absconders. Punjab Chief Minister Darbara Singh even wrote to the SGPC President, G. S. Tohra, in this connection and gave him the list of persons who, according to the State Government's information, were hiding in the Gurdwara. The SGPC, as usual, denied that any extremist was taking shelter in the gurdwara. And that was that.

But not quite. On July 24, Darbara Singh told a group of Punjab MPs in Delhi that, according to the State Government's information, not only extremists were hiding in the Gurdwara but even arms were being manufactured on the fourth floor of Nanak Niwas, adjoining the Golden Temple. Still no action. Later, Darbara Singh made public statements accusing Sant Bhindranwale of conniving in the attempt on the Chief Minister's life in the village of Rahon on August 20, but again there was no follow-up.

The moderate Akalis are feeling embarrassed by the Sant's presence in the Gurdwara and they have recently been suggesting to him to leave it and carry on his morcha from outside. But the Sant refuses to oblige. He has the support of the SGPC President, G. S. Tohra. In any case, he is now more important than any other Akali leader.

The moderate Akalis thus dare not oppose the Sant. Some 15,000 Jathedars have already courted arrest. Nor does the Government allow the police to enter the Gurdwara to arrest wanted persons. In fact, the repeated statements of its leaders that the police will not enter the Gurdwara has made the situation a lot worse by virtually inviting criminals to seek a safe haven in the shrine.

Failure Of Nerve

All this only underscores the failure of nerve at the highest political level. It is argued that the police is not allowed to enter the Gurdwara out of respect for its sanctity. By the same token, temples, mosques and synagogues should also be declared sanctuaries for murderers, gangsters, smugglers and other fugitives from the law. Where will the Government draw the line?

The problem would not have arisen at all if the SGPC had behaved responsibly. Unfortunately, it is in the grip of extremists. For the first time in its history, this statutory body, constituted under the Act to look after the management of the Sikh gurdwaras, passed a resolution in March last year declaring the Sikhs as a separate nation!

Giani Zail Singh, in a pamphlet entitled *Sikhism Today—A Perspective*, issued before he took over as President, lamented that the SGPC thought of passing the resolution because, "for them, religion and politics are inseparable".

The Government, no doubt, has been firm of late in dealing with the extremists outside the gurdwaras, but the Congress (I) has done nothing to educate the masses about the dangers they pose. Its leaders have mostly confined themselves to press statements and holding closed-door meetings occasionally.

Soon after Jagat Narain's murder in September 1981, the Government had tried to isolate the extremists from the Akalis by inviting the Akalis for talks on their grievances. But, unfortunately, the talks failed (in April 1982) and were not revived, largely because the Haryana Assembly elections were on the cards and the Akalis had raked up the settled Ravi-Beas waters dispute. Subsequently, the Akalis supported Giani Zail Singh, the Congress (I) candidate, for Presidentship and later Mrs Gandhi made a statement that the doors were open for talks with the Akalis. But, by that time, the hawks among the Akalis were dominant and the moderates had been pushed to the wall.

The moderate Akalis still feel that the only way to restore peace in Punjab is to settle their grievances through negotiations. Some spadework is reportedly under way. The Akalis had originally given a list of 45 demands to the Government and later submitted a "priority list" of 15 demands. These fell into three categories: religious, political and economic.

During the talks in April, the Government had agreed to accept some of the religious demands, like the supremacy of the SGPC in sending pilgrims to gurdwaras in Pakistan, carrying a *kirpan* on internal flights, and banning the sale of tobacco, meat and liquor in the area around the Golden Temple. Though the Government did not announce its decisions right away in view of the Haryana poll, it has publicly done so since.

Among the pending Akali demands, the reopening of the Ravi-Beas waters issue and the inclusion of Chandigarh and other Punjabi-speaking areas in Punjab are the most important. Since the Chief Ministers of Punjab, Haryana and Rajasthan had entered into an agreement on the Ravi-Beas waters on December 31, 1981, and that, too, after prolonged deliberations, it is simply not possible for the Government to unscramble this particular egg. It can, however, still appoint a commission to go into territorial claims of Punjab, Haryana and Himachal Pradesh. This would certainly give some satisfaction to the moderate Akalis.

The Government was also ready, in April, to partially accept the Akalis' demand for live broadcasts of the *Gurbani* from the Golden Temple by increasing the time of relay. This proposal needs to be discussed further. As for the implementation of the Anandpur Sahib resolution seeking more autonomy for Punjab, even the Akalis had not talked much about it during their meetings with Mrs Gandhi. Obviously, they were aware that the Government would not agree to that demand, though the rival Akali Dal President, Jagdev Singh Talwandi, has been carrying on another morcha in the capital for over 16 months to press it.

The Akalis When In Power

Incidentally, the Akalis were in power in Punjab for three years during the Janata regime at the Centre, but there is not a single letter on record to show that they were agitated over any of the issues they are now raking up. The Anandpur resolution was passed in 1973 and ratified by the party in 1978. Obviously, the Akalis in power had a healthy respect for the Government at the Centre. It is, therefore, argued that if they again start sharing power with the Congress (I) in Punjab they will forget their demands. Already the possibility of forging a Congress (I)-Akali partnership in Punjab is being furtively explored. ■

AN ARMED FOLLOWING. Sant Jarnail Singh Bhindranwale with his supporters.

INDIAN EXPRESS, NEW DELHI dated Nov.5,1981.

'Punjab may become another Nagaland'

By G. S. CHAWLA
Express News Service

PARIDKOT, Nov 4.

Once the slogan of Khalistan has been raised it is bound to materialise one day, may be after 10 years: this is the feeling of non-Sikhs in Punjab after the recent violent happenings in the state. Unless the Prime Minister, Mrs Indira Gandhi, herself pays immediate attention to this problem and takes a firm stand it is feared Punjab may turn into another Nagaland or Mizoram.

It is not the state government alone which is responsible for the present situation. The Congress (I) leadership at the Centre is equally responsible.

Though the situation in the urban areas is calm, there is an undercurrent of tension and a sense of insecurity among the people. Trade and industry have received a setback and the services are demoralised.

Businessmen and industrialists complain that after the incidents of the last few weeks, buyers are not coming from other states and they are not placing orders for future production. For a number of industrial products, traders from other parts of the country used to place orders months in advance and this would keep the industries busy.

A number of groups of big industries which were planning to start their projects have decided to delay them.

Most of the officers, including police officers, want to be posted outside the state on deputation.

Shake-up in Punjab imminent — p 7

The law enforcing agencies fear that if they act firmly they may have to face some judicial inquiry later on and then no political leader would be prepared to protect them. They are also not sure about political decisions taken by the Centre.

The arrest and release of Sant Jarnail Singh Bhindranwale in the Jagat Narain murder case is a classic example. Sant Bhindranwale's arrest and release were political decisions taken at the highest level. The decision to arrest the Sant was taken after careful consideration of the evidence with the police. Even now Sant Bhindranwale has not been "acquitted" of the charge against him. His name still figures in the Jagat Narain murder case and the authorities, if permitted, can still call him for interrogation.

After Sant Bhindranwale's release most of the senior police officers are apprehensive about their future. After the three incidents — the murder of Nirankari Baba last year, the murder of Jagat Narain recently and the shoot-out at the Punjab Secretariat in Chandigarh — they are afraid that similar incidents might happen again. Punjab is being ruled by the Sant and not by the Congress (I), they feel.

During his interrogation by half a dozen Sikh police officers (he had laid down the condition that he could be questioned only by Sikh officers), the Sant had denied any link with the incidents. But when he was asked to swear by touching "gutka", he declined to do so on the plea that it was against Sikh tenets to swear. He was also asked about the "saropa" he had presented to relatives of Ranjit Singh and Kabul Singh, both wanted in the Nirankari Baba murder case. He told the interrogators that he had done this because of their services to the Panth.

There is so much fear among officers that on the day that Sant Bhindranwale left Chando Kalan in Haryana to avoid arrest, senior police officers of two adjoining districts did not arrest him despite being alerted earlier.

The state Chief Minister, Mr Darbara Singh, as well as central leaders, including the Prime Minister, have been saying that security measures have been tightened to ensure strict maintenance of law and order. However, one sees nothing in the state which would indicate that the Government was really concerned

continued on p 7 col 3

INDIAN EXPRESS, New Delhi, dated Nov.5,1981.

Punjab

continued from p 1 col 1

about the situation. Even administrative officers could not point out any concrete step taken in this direction.

Whatever the Akalis might say about their attitude towards Sant Bhindranwale, the fact remains that senior Akali leaders are afraid of him. In their private meetings they have been discussing ways to contain the Sant but publicly they seem to be supporting him.

The people, particularly the non-Akalis, are of the view that Mrs Gandhi should visit Punjab again. She must assure the people that the Government means business and would handle the situation firmly. Along with this, the state administrative set-up should be revamped and officers should be assured that the politi-

THE WRITING ON THE WALL. Balvir Singh Sandhu (left), the self-styled Secretary-General of the Republic of Khalistan at his "headquarters" in Nanak Niwas in the Golden Temple complex at Amritsar. With him is Ujagar Singh who crossed the Indian border with a "Khalistani passport" last April and on his return from Pakistan, addressed a press conference.

Khalistan: A Conspiracy Hatched In America

by G.S. Chawla

"Khalistan" is the new cry for a secessionist State. This sort of factionalism bodes no good for our nation. The hijacking of an IA Boeing to Lahore by these extremists was the culmination of their agitation. Has the Centre dealt strongly enough with this movement?

PUNJAB is in turmoil today due to the misguided actions of a small number of extremist Akali young men demanding "Khalistan". Their organisation, the Dal Khalsa, is led by Dr Jagjit Singh, a former Finance Minister of Punjab, and Mr Ganga Singh Dhillon, an American citizen, having close links with foreign powers, notably Pakistan.

The Punjab Government as well as the Centre are equally responsible for the present situation in the State. If they had heeded the numerous warnings that they had received and taken timely action, they could have easily avoided the current crisis.

The Punjab Government's mishandling of the arrest of Sant Jarnail Singh Bhindranwale in the Jagat Narain murder case provided an opportunity to the protagonists of Khalistan to fish in troubled waters. Until his release on October 15, Sant Bhindranwale himself reportedly did not have any link with the Dal Khalsa or sympathy for its demand; his main domain was the preaching of Sikh religion. But the Punjab Government's ineptitude in dealing with him gave the extremists a convenient excuse to generate communal strife. It also led to a series of sabotage attempts in Punjab on the railways and to the hijacking of the Indian Airlines Boeing to Lahore.

The Akali Dal led by Master Tara Singh had started an agitation soon after the first general elections in 1952 for a Sikh-dominated Punjabi Suba. As a result the so-called regional formula was evolved in 1957 under which the State was divided into two.

Agitation

The Akali Party revived its agitation for a Punjabi Suba in 1960— till the outbreak of the war with the Pakistan in 1965. In 1966, when Mrs Gandhi came to power, Punjab was reorganised and Haryana was carved out of it and some portions of the adjoining Himachal Pradesh were added to that State.

The Real Danger

Though a vulnerable border State, Punjab has never been an outpost but an integral part of the Indian heartland. This is at once a measure of and a tribute to the valour, prowess and patriotism of Punjabis, both Sikh and Hindu. They have demonstrated these qualities up to the hilt during the three wars with Pakistan and in the pursuit of the arts of peace in between. What is more, Hindu-Sikh relations have been, until recently, a model of communal harmony. It is grimly ironical, therefore, that secessionist forces should be raising their head in the State just when its citizens are in a better position than ever to garner the fruits of their cooperative endeavours. To be sure, the campaign for securing an "independent Khalistan" is inspired and financed by foreign conspirators. Even headquarters of the organisation spearheading it is in the USA and that of the "Khalistan government in exile" is planned to be established at Nankana Sahib in Pakistan. But this does not mean that the small number of its activists have no support at home. For the first time in the history of post-independence Punjab, they have been able to stir up savage communal riots, set up not-so-secret cells and collect arms.

It would be simplistic to suggest that their movement feeds only on religious fanaticism, Sikh and Hindu. Without a shadow of doubt it prospers more on the calculated politicking of the leaders at the top—both in government and outside it. The situation—and the danger it implies—is familiar. In almost all areas on the country's periphery—Nagaland, Mizoram, Assam and Kashmir, for example—even the patriotic elements have developed a sort of vested interest in keeping insurgency alive. "Who would care for the loyalists," so goes their argument, "if there were no rebels?" Punjab is much too closely integrated with the rest of the country, however, to go the same way without impairing its own development and, eventually, ruining itself. But this may not prevent selfish and scheming politicians from trying.

—EDITOR

26 THE ILLUSTRATED WEEKLY OF INDIA, OCTOBER 25, 1981

The reorganisation of Punjab in 1966 was soon followed by the third general election in 1967 when, for the first time, Akalis came into power in the State and formed a ministry. But the Akali Government fell a few months later, when some of the Akali legislators led by Mr Lachhman Singh Gill left the party and formed a cabinet with the support of the Congress.

Dr Jagjit Singh, the man behind the present Khalistan movement, was Finance Minister in the Gill Ministry. This ministry was also short-lived.

Dr Jagjit Singh fled to England in 1970 and it was there that, for the first time, he raised the slogan of Khalistan—an independent homeland for the Sikhs. Soon he was shuttling between London and Pakistan and between London and the USA and Canada. But he had no support from the Sikhs living either abroad or in India. During the 1971 war between India and Pakistan, he was used by the Pakistani authorities to win support from the Sikh community in India. He made appeals to the Indian Sikhs from Lahore Radio to side with Pakistan in the war. He continued his activities abroad until the end of the Emergency in 1977 but without success.

After the 1977 elections, when the Akali-Janata Government came to power in Punjab, Dr Jagjit Singh came back and stayed in India till the middle of last year, but even Mrs Gandhi's regime did nothing to curb his anti-national activities, though the authorities were fully aware of what he was up to. He had openly resorted to gimmicks like the attempted installation of a radio station at the Golden Temple, Amritsar, last year. Soon thereafter he left the country and reached London.

Earlier, the Akali Party had met at Anandpur Sahib in October 1973 and passed a resolution demanding that an autonomous region should be immediately set up in the North and the primacy of the Sikh interests should be constitutionally recognised therein as a matter of fundamental state policy. This autonomous region, the party said, should include a number of other Punjabi-speaking areas of Haryana, Himachal, Rajasthan and Uttar Pradesh. What is more, the Akalis sought to invest the region with virtually sovereign powers, including the right to frame its own Constitution, though they conceded that three subjects—foreign relations, defence and communications—could remain within the purview of the "Federal Indian Government"

The resolution was ratified by the general house of the Akali Dal at its annual conference in 1978 during the Akali-Janata regime. But the Akali Party, then a partner of the ruling coalition in the State, chose to avert its eyes from what the Akali Dal was doing under its nose. Indeed, Mr Parkash Singh Badal, as Chief Minister of Punjab, egged on by the CPM, even called a meeting of the non-Janata Chief Ministers at Chandigarh in 1978 to demand greater autonomy for the States.

But when the Janata leaders—particularly the then Prime Minister, Mr Morarji Desai—expressed annoyance to Mr Badal over the move, the Akali Party quickly backtracked. Mr Badal abruptly cancelled the proposed meeting of Chief Ministers without a word of explanation. Later he somewhat lamely said that he only wanted more financial powers for the States.

Separatists

The separatist movement, however, acquired flesh and bone in March this year when a Sikh educational Conference was called at Chandigarh by the Chief Khalsa Dewan, a non-political organisation meant primarily to promote Sikh educational institutions. Mr Ganga Singh Dhillon, a Sikh residing in America, was asked to preside over it. From this unlikely forum, Mr Dhillon blandly declared that Sikhs are a separate nation. And, for good measure, he moved a resolution demanding that the Sikhs be admitted to associate membership of the United Nations as they were not a part of the Hindu mainstream and had a separate identity.

No one of any consequence in India had heard of Mr Ganga Singh Dhillon earlier. Those who know him well say that he is close to the US Administration and also to Pakistan's President, Gen Zia. Mr Dhillon describes himself as a businessman, but few are aware of what his business is. He is, however, →

MARTYR IN THE MAKING? Sant Jarnail Singh Bhindranwale offering himself up to the police at Chowk Mehta in Amritsar. The police later released the Sant to pave the way for talks between the Prime Minister and Akali as well as other political leaders in the State to seek a solution. He was earlier arrested in connection with the murder of Lala Jagat Narain, a respected editor and a staunch opponent of the Khalistan movement.

Below: The five Sikhs who hijacked the IA Boeing to Lahore.

TO FUEL THE FEUD—HERE'S THE ILLEGAL TENDER! Khalistan conspirators have printed passports and currency in foreign presses.

indisputably the moving spirit behind the Nankana Sahib Sikh Foundation, which ironically has its headquarters not in Pakistan, but in the USA. He often shuttles between the USA, Pakistan, Canada and UK.

An Indian who recently visited Nankana Sahib in Pakistan says that there is a fully furnished suite reserved permanently for Mr Dhillon near the gurdwara and that he is always treated as a personal guest of President Zia and is received by the latter whenever he visits Pakistan.

Mr Dhillon has now convened the first World Sikh Religion Conference at Nankana Sahib from November 8 to 11 this year to coincide with Guru Nanak's birthday. Dr Jagjit Singh is scheduled to participate. In fact, he has already announced the establishment of the "Khalistan Government in exile" and set up a radio station at Nankana Sahib.

The Resolution

The resolution of the Sikh Gurudwara Prabandhak Committee declaring that the Sikhs are a separate nation was moved by Sant Harchand Singh Longowal, President of the Akali Dal. A fusillade of criticism greeted it because the SGPC's role by tradition and custom is limited to the preaching of Sikh religion and the management of Sikh gurdwaras. That is why perhaps Sant Longowal and other leaders of his group, including Mr Badal, later "clarified" that they were against an independent Khalistan and all they wanted was an autonomous state as demanded by the Akali Party's Anandpur resolution. But that did not mend matters.

The Dal Khalsa organisation came into existence about two years ago. It became very active in March this year and openly raised the slogan of Khalistan. Its activists had nothing to do with the Akali Dal. Nor do they have any tangible link with Sant Jarnail Singh Bhindranwale. Even so, the Sant has strongly supported the hijackers of the IA plane to Lahore. Though the total number of its activists is still small, the Dal Khalsa has without doubt gained considerable strength during the last few months, largely due to the ineffectiveness of the Government. Some of its workers are former Government employees. Who is financing them is still a mystery.

Mr Sukhjinder Singh, a former Akali minister, for instance, has of late come to the fore in the movement launched by Dal Khalsa. He has a police background and until only two months ago, he was the General Secretary of the Akali Dal. A known extremist, he is now openly plugging for Khalistan.

The Government has been receiving reports from abroad for some time that Dr Jagjit Singh and Mr Ganga Singh Dhillon had intensified their activities. It could do nothing to curb Mr Dhillon because he is an American citizen but Dr Jagjit Singh is an Indian citizen and it did impound his passport.

Complacency

In fact, it should have done more to counter the Dal Khalsa's anti-national movement—in cooperation with the Congress (I) and other parties. Instead it chose to sit on its haunches. The Prime Minister was known to be keen that Sikh leaders in her party should "fight the Dal Khalsa's demand at the political level". But the two senior leaders of the State, the Home Minister, Mr Zail Singh, and the State Chief Minister, Mr Darbara Singh, were more involved in personal quarrels. Thus the so-called conspiracy was hatched with impunity.

Mr Gurcharan Singh Tohra, President of the SGPC and a well-known extremist, along with Mr Sukhjinder Singh, took a trip to Singapore. The two returned after a few days but again Mr Tohra left for America, ostensibly for medical treatment. Jathedar Gurdial Singh Ajnoha, head of the Akal Takhat, was already there. They were followed by Mr Rajinder Singh Bhatia, General Secretary of the Akali Dal (L), who is supposed to be looking after the "foreign affairs". Reports those days from America were tell-tale: it was clear that the three Sikh leaders from India had several meetings in that country with Mr Ganga Singh Dhillon, Dr Jagjit Singh and Yogi Bhajan Singh. They had set up a branch of the Akali Dal in the USA and resolutions were passed demanding a Sikh autonomous state on the specious ground that Sikhs were being discriminated against in India by the Hindu majority.

The Government knew that their movement was being financed by a foreign power which it did not

SANT JARNAIL SINGH'S ARREST at Chowk Mehta triggered off fierce riots and police firing in which several persons lost their lives Picture shows a police tent on fire.

wish to name; in fact, Mr Zail Singh has been openly saying so. The Chief Minister, Mr Darbara Singh, also told a press conference at the end of July, after his return from England, that "the biggest power was behind the Khalistan movement". Still the Centre and the State Governments did nothing to smash the conspiracy.

Specious Line

Indeed, Mr Zail Singh claimed that the "movement was confined to newspapers". Mr Darbara Singh complacently took the same line even after the extremists had visibly stepped up their campaign for Khalistan. Mr Sukhjinder Singh, who was meanwhile expelled by the Akali Dal, defiantly told the press that, if need be, he and his followers would not hesitate to get foreign help for the creation of Khalistan. Two members of the Dal Khalsa, armed with the so-called Khalistan Government's passports, crossed the border to Pakistan in full glare of self-contrived publicity.

Speaking on the subject at her press conference on July 10, the Prime Minister, Mrs Gandhi, hedged. "So far, of course," she said, "Khalistan exists only in Canada and perhaps in the USA also, but it does not mean that we should lower our guard or not exercise the utmost vigilance."

All in all, the Government did not wake up to the gravity of the situation even when the activities of the extremists were being extensively reported in the press. Did the intelligence agencies fail to alert it to what was afoot? Or did the inept and feuding politicians in charge pay no heed to their warnings? Perhaps it was a bit of both.

Be that as it may, the protagonists of Khalistan were emboldened to print dollar currency notes, issue postal stamps and distribute passports—all in the name of the "Khalistan Government".

The Speaker of the Lok Sabha, Mr Balram Jhakar, received a letter from Canada containing two such currency notes. He sent the two bills to the Prime Minister with a letter on September 4 saying: "I strongly feel that things have reached a stage when very effective action is required to deal with this type of elements who have no political following here or anywhere else and are out to disturb the peaceful atmosphere in the State. Things have reached so far that currency notes have been issued. I feel it is a serious matter that should receive your personal attention to curb anti-national activities."

All that the Government did in response was to register a few more cases against relatively minor activists of Dal Khalsa. Nor did it move vigorously enough to unearth and suppress the conspiracy in its wider ramifications even after the murder of Lala Jagat Narain on September 9. Even in the middle of the savage Hindu-Sikh riots triggered by the crime the extremists continued their activities from a room in a *sarai* attached to the Golden temple, Amritsar. It was there that the plot to hijack the Indian Airlines plane to Lahore was hatched.

In A Fix

The Akalis are now in a fix. Although some of the important party leaders, like Mr Badal, are totally opposed to the demand for an independent Khalistan, they cannot afford to condemn its protagonists because they are committed to the Anandpur resolution which, in essence, seeks something similar. No Akali leader has the courage to take a stand counter to that resolution. The Akali leaders with extremist leanings (Mr Tohra, for instance) are thus having a field day. ■

THE ILLUSTRATED WEEKLY OF INDIA, OCTOBER 25, 1981 29

ZAIL SINGH

Zail-Darbara Feud While Punjab Bleeds

They have been old rivals in Punjab politics and they make no secret of their intense dislike for each other. The bickerings between them have done great harm to the State.

by G.S. Chawla

REMEMBER what Punjab's Chief Minister, Mr Darbara Singh, told a Bombay weekly a few months back? "My biggest problem," he said, "is the Union Home Minister." And a few weeks back, he told a Calcutta daily that Mr Zail Singh was "engineering" reports against him on the Punjab situation.

The strained relationship between the two Congress (I) leaders of Punjab, Mr Zail Singh and Mr Darbara Singh, is an open scandal. Indeed, political circles trace most of the ills of the State to the unconcealed animosity between them. During her visit to Chandigarh on September 22, Prime Minister Indira Gandhi, asked by newsmen what the situation in Punjab was, on account of the continuing feud between Zail and Darbara, made no attempt to deny the existence of differences between them, though she refuted the allegation that this was the cause of the present situation.

Mr Atal Behari Vajpayee, BJP leader, while speaking on the calling-attention motion on the Jagat Narain murder case in the Lok Sabha, on September 11, had stated that Punjab could not be allowed to burn because of bad blood between Mr Zail Singh and Mr Darbara Singh. On November 18, another M.P. bluntly told Mr Zail Singh in the consultative committee of Parliament attached to the Home Ministry: "The entire trouble in Punjab is due to the fight between you and Darbara Singh."

Actually, Mr Zail Singh and Mr Darbara Singh are old rivals in Punjab politics. Their dislike for each other is intense. Some party leaders in Punjab have repeatedly tried to bring about a compromise between them but the resolve of the two men now and then to work unitedly for the organisation could last no more than a week on each occasion.

Mr Darbara Singh has never hesitated to pick up any stick to beat Mr Zail Singh with. In fact, Mr Vajpayee, while speaking on the Punjab situation in the Lok Sabha, recently disclosed: "Mr Speaker, I was asking Punjab's Chief Minister about who are the people behind the Khalistan movement, about whether it is true that he had met Ganga Singh Dhillon, who had raised the Khalistan demand? And you know what the CM replied? That he had not met Dhillon, but the Union Home Minister, Zail Singh, had."

If only in comparison with Mr Darbara Singh, Mr Zail Singh is shrewder: he expresses his feelings about his political adversary only indirectly and obliquely. He never uses harsh language. Yet, in a subtle way, he is prone to say things against Mr Darbara Singh.

Both have some similarities. In Punjab, it is known that Mr Darbara Singh is weak-willed and the Government is run, as the S.G.P.C. President, Mr G.S. Tohra once told me, by "Khannapuri". Mr Khanna is principal secretary to the Chief Minister and Mr Puri is the Chief Secretary. Likewise, it is widely believed that Mr Zail Singh's Establishment Officer and his Special Assistant, Mr Bindra, wield undue influence over their chief. This apart, both Mr Zail Singh and Mr Darbara Singh tolerate all kinds of hangers-on.

Ever since Darbara Singh became Chief Minister of Punjab, about seventeen months ago, he has been living in the hope that a cabinet reshuffle at the Centre would lead to Mr Zail Singh's ouster—or appointment as Governor of a State. But Mr Zail Singh continues to use his vantage point in Delhi to consolidate his position in Punjab.

In fact, both men have links with the rival Akali factions. Ironically, these links lead them to a common centre of power: the group loyal to Sant Jarnail Singh Bhindranwale. Mr Darbara Singh is said to have cultivated Sant

DARBARA SINGH

Bhindranwale through Mr Sukhjinder Singh, an extremist Akali who is now in jail. Mr Zail Singh did so through Jathedar Santokh Singh of the Delhi Gurdwara Prabandak Committee who is a protege of the Congress (I) and whose election to the DGPC had provided an opportunity to the Longowal group of Akalis to threaten a "Dharm Yudh".

Evidently Mr Darbara Singh has been lenient in dealing with the extremist Akalis so that he could use them against the dominant Akali group of Sant Harchand Singh Longowal and Mr Parkash Singh Badal. Mr Zail Singh, on the other hand, is said to have developed links with the Badal group through Mr Ravi Inder Singh, former speaker of the Punjab Assembly, and a close relation of Mr Badal.

"The entire trouble in Punjab is due to the fight between Zail Singh and Darbara Singh," says Atal Behari Vajpayee.

If Mr Zail Singh can have his way, his endeavour probably will be to put the State temporarily under President's Rule without dissolving the State Assembly. If this happens, a section of the Akalis may be only too keen to end the President's Rule by joining forces with the Congress (I) to form a coalition ministry. This is likely to spell disaster for Mr Darbara Singh and enable Mr Zail Singh to re-emerge as unchallenged leader of the State.

Both Mr Zail Singh and Mr Darbara Singh are beholden to Mrs Gandhi for their cushy berths. Neither dares to do anything which may displease her. Even so, she has been unable or unwilling to end their feud. Perhaps this is her way of ensuring that the two stalwarts should always look to New Delhi for guidance.

Be that as it may, Mrs Gandhi is now reported to be convinced that Mr Darbara Singh has miserably failed in dealing skilfully with sensitive issues like the demand for Khalistan. And she finds that Mr Zail Singh has been equally ineffective at the Centre. Both of them should have by now realised the great injury their rivalry has done to Punjab. It is largely due to the bickering between them that Mrs Gandhi now faces a twofold task in Punjab: she must repair as best as she can the consequent damage to her own party in the State and at the same time come to terms with the Akalis. If she is able to achieve both these goals, it will be in spite of the two Singhs who thoughtlessly persist with their hymns of hate. •

SANT J.S. BHINDRANWALE (left) and SANT HARCHAND SINGH LONGOWAL